**Subu Soto:** The former ...endo champion was the head of Japan's second-largest criminal gang. Now, with the help of a Chinese triad godfather and an American gangster, he was moving into the big time . . .

**Dao:** For Stark, making love to the slender Oriental beauty was like an addiction—but when he started asking questions, he didn't like the answers . . .

**Louis Scalish:** The American mobster had a penchant for young girls and bad food—and his Oriental partners despised him. But Scalish had the key to the puzzle: someone who could build a nuclear bomb . . .

**Koiichi Soto:** Stark's *shihan,* or martial arts teacher, had made Stark into the man he was. When the CIA said that Soto had gone bad, Stark went to Japan—and found a shadow of the man Soto used to be . . .

**Peter Wong:** The carefully controlled Hong Kong police inspector was impervious to corruption—and was stalked by both his fellow police and the underworld. He knew Stark was on a CIA mission, and he had to trust him . . .

**Robert Stark:** Loyalty and love led the ex–CIA man back to the Orient, into a world of deadly turmoil—and a plot to turn a whole island into a capital of crime . . .

**Books by Mark Schorr**

Overkill
Seize the Dragon

Published by POCKET BOOKS

# SEIZE THE DRAGON

## MARK SCHORR

POCKET BOOKS

New York   London   Toronto   Sydney   Tokyo

This book is a work of fiction. Names, characters, places and incidents are either the product of the author's imagination or are used fictitiously. Any resemblance to actual events or locales or persons, living or dead, is entirely coincidental.

An *Original* Publication of POCKET BOOKS

 POCKET BOOKS, a division of Simon & Schuster Inc.
1230 Avenue of the Americas, New York, NY 10020

ISBN: 978-1-451-67236-7

First Pocket Books printing March 1989

10  9  8  7  6  5  4  3  2  1

POCKET and colophon are trademarks of
Simon & Schuster Inc.

Printed in the U.S.A.

*To* Shihan *J. Miller,* Sensei *G. Adams,*
Sensei *S. Imaizumi,*
Sensei *N. Yang, and all the* ukes *and* toris
*who have taught me, on and off the mat*

# SEIZE THE DRAGON

# *Prologue*

Despite the incredibly bleak surroundings the women chattered happily in Cantonese. They were working, they were healthy, and they were in Hong Kong, where a fortune could be made if you had a good job.

More than two hundred of them labored in the four-story wooden building in the Kowloon district. They trudged up rickety stairs to take their places at cutting machines, sewing machines, pressing machines, turning out cheap clothing that even with the cost of transportation would be among the cheapest in the world.

The air was thick with the smells of cooking oil from the food stands in the streets below. It mingled with the ever-present Southeast Asia mildew smells and the scent of burning joss sticks. The little shrines, some barely more than a tin can with a prayer written on it, were in doorways, on shelves, and at the temples throughout the British colony. There were almost as many gods to worship as there were dummy corporations in this city of international trade.

The singsong Cantonese, with nine different tones to change the meaning of words, varied in volume on the different floors. On the fourth floor, where the heavy machinery hissed and banged, there was no point in trying to talk. Women on the second floor, where the sewing machines

1

were, could share the latest gossip while their machines hummed under nimble fingers.

Mai Lee was forty-five and had some of the nimblest fingers in the factory. Her eyes were bad from years of working under dim, bare bulbs. But she wouldn't complain. Wasn't she among the highest paid pieceworkers in the Colony? Didn't she have a son about to become a partner in a clothing shop on Nathan Road? And a daughter whose marriage was being arranged to a wealthy merchant with a store in Tsimshatsui, the tourist enclave. Those two could help their three younger siblings rise from the two-bedroom apartment they all shared. The future was bright indeed.

She gossiped with the woman next to her about a popular soap opera star. The woman, like many of the workers, was a recent émigré from the People's Republic of China. She was still undergoing culture shock. So many things to buy, so many things to see. There seemed to be more cars on one narrow street in Hong Kong than in all of the PRC. The stores were packed with frivolous consumer goods, the clothing colorful and cheery. There were never shortages of delicacies, let alone the basic foodstuffs.

Mai Lee got up to drop off a load in the front bin. The supervisor, one of the few males, noted her contribution on a clipboard and bobbed his head. That he showed any sign was an indication of respect for Mai Lee and her nimble fingers. With most of the women he didn't even grunt, and they had to wonder if they were getting proper credit for the work they had done.

On her way back to her chair Mai Lee sniffed the air. There was a different smell. The old graybeard who ran the nearest *dai pai dong* must be burning his food. His greasy *chow fun* noodles were often too crisp.

No. It was stronger than that. She sniffed deeper. A couple of women around her noticed and thought she was insulting them. But they saw her expression was concern and not conceit. They, too, sniffed.

"*Ch'ow how!*" a girl yelled. She was a northerner, and used the Mandarin for "fire."

The word was picked up in Cantonese, and then English. Almost immediately, no words were intelligible as the screaming began.

2

# SEIZE THE DRAGON

Twenty women tried simultaneously to descend stairs that groaned when holding five. A woman fell down the stairs and was trampled. Others tripped over her body, and themselves were trampled. The stairs collapsed.

Puffs of black smoke came from below. It got hotter. There were bars over the windows, and women pulled furiously at them. In the streets, people looked up, laughing at first, and then horrified as they saw the smoke.

Mai Lee saw dozens packing into the freight elevator, but the door shut before she could get in, which was fortunate for her. The fire spread to the elevator shaft. The car lowered into the blaze. The people inside it were cooked like a paper-wrapped chicken.

Mai Lee raced to a door. It was blocked by large cartons. The room was getting dark from the smoke. The screams rose and fell. She remembered a window in a rear storage room. Stumbling over bodies and toppled tables, she made it to the room. The window was painted over, but she smashed it with a shoe. She was looking out into the back alleyway.

She saw a lone figure in the alley, a young man looking up at the fire, a satisfied expression on his face, a metal jerrican in his hands. He took off when he saw her.

She climbed out the narrow window onto a six-inch-wide ledge. She balanced there, calling for help. But all the action was around the front of the building. The wall she clung to was getting hot. And smoke billowed out of the broken window. Her hands had been cut. She watched her blood trickle down.

The wall was too hot for her to hold. Her blood loss made her dizzy. With a final silent prayer to Kuan Yin, the goddess of mercy, she closed her eyes and stepped forward.

Peter Wong held the flashlight in one hand and the sniffer in the other. Water dripped on his helmet. He inhaled and exhaled. The barest hint of an organic solvent. He squeezed a bulb on the sniffer and air was drawn into the kettle-shaped device. No response on the readout.

He played his light around the basement, clearly where the fire had started. There were hard black carbon patches called alligation because of their rough, ripply texture. He

3

knelt where the pattern was most evident. Taking the half-meter pry bar from his belt, he broke out a chunk of the wood and put it into a clear plastic evidence bag. He marked the date, time, and where in the building he had removed it, then carefully sealed it.

There was no question in Wong's mind that this was arson. The burn pattern around the room, the way it had spread so rapidly, the fact that two fire doors were wedged shut from the outside. But it had to be provable in court. Under British rules of law. So Wong was meticulous.

This was the biggest case he had worked on. At thirty-five, he was one of Royal Hong Kong Police Force's rising stars. He had risen from constable, to sergeant, to station sergeant, and now was an inspector. There were nearly twenty-six thousand members in the department, with responsibility for keeping the peace among six million people of varying cultures, finances, and ethics. Inspector Wong, like most of the junior officers, was Chinese. The top brass was virtually all British. In fact, if he had been a white, he would have started at inspector level.

That was guaranteed to change in nine years, when the British would hand Hong Kong over to the Communist Chinese. Who was worse, the round-eyed *gwai lo* imperialists, or the erratic, dogmatic Communists?

He emerged from the basement and wiped the soot smears from his cheeks with a handkerchief. His British supervisor still believed in spit-and-polish inspections, white gloves, and shoes he could see his reflection in. Of course the supervisor sat behind a clean desk all day.

A half-dozen people lingered at the police barricade. The fire had been extinguished ten hours earlier, but parts still smoldered. The bodies had been taken to the morgue. To several morgues—municipal facilities, hospitals, even private funeral homes. There were seventy-five bodies to be identified. Most were charred beyond recognition. Some were illegal immigrants who had snuck across the border from mainland China. How many unknowns did they have lying at the morgue?

Wong got in his dark blue police sedan, hit the siren, and drove back to headquarters.

* * *

4

"Very good, Peter," his supervisor said the next day, "The lab report confirms your suspicion. Would you care to guess what sort of accelerant was used?"

"Barbecue fire starter."

"Exactly so. There was quite enough in the sample you took for the laboratory to be quite confident. How did you know?"

"It's the best. No smell. The sniffer works on the same principles as the human nose."

"I'm quite proud of you," the commander said.

Wong believed the man didn't try to be unctuous and condescending. It just came out that way.

"There is more good news. We have a witness. A Mai Lee. I'd like you to go to the hospital and interview her. Forthwith."

Mai Lee, groggy from morphine, didn't want to talk to any policeman. Her family tried to keep Wong out. The doctor ordered that she not be disturbed.

"There are seventy-five people dead, another thirty critically injured," Wong said to the surgeon he encountered in the hallway. "If need be, I will get a court order and have her taken out of the hospital."

"You can't do that." The doctor was a big-bottomed, florid-faced Britisher and had the same attitude of smug superiority Wong hated in his boss. But Wong was not helpless with the doctor.

"Maybe not. But I also will have our narcotics squad do an audit of your supplies. I will have our traffic control division ticket illegally parked cars within two blocks of this hospital. I will have every orderly checked for immigration papers. Then I will notify the health department, and have them investigate your facility from top to bottom."

The doctor sputtered. He wasn't used to a white man talking to him like that, let alone a cheeky Chinese. He'd found they usually avoided confrontation, produced lots of polite hissing and grinning, and then wouldn't do what they were supposed to. "Sod."

"Perhaps I will charge you with public obscenity."

"You have fifteen minutes." The doctor decided he'd ask around his club, see who knew someone high up in the police force. Squeeze the Chink's nuts from above. That would show him.

"Thank you so much for your cooperation, Doctor. You can further assist me by getting the family out of the way."

Then Wong was alone in the room with Mai Lee.

Addressing her respectfully as "auntie," he commiserated with her in Cantonese. Both her legs were broken, and if she was lucky, she'd be able to walk with a cane. Nerves in her hand had been cut; she would never be known for her nimble fingers again.

"But you were among the lucky ones," he said, citing the grim statistics. "We need your help to catch whoever did it."

Mai Lee had the traditional distrust of authorities. "I'm not sure anymore."

"Auntie, I know you are as sharp-eyed as the kites that perch on the skyscrapers. How would you feel if the motherless, flea-infested rat who did this were to do it again? Would you want to know that you could have helped us and chose not to?"

They went back and forth a few minutes, but ultimately Wong got the description he wanted. He arranged for a police artist to come in and work under the survivor's direction.

"It went well," Weng Cheng said.

"Yes."

"So, where is my money?" It was nearing four P.M. Closing time.

"I have it."

"Give it to me."

They were in the Aw Boon Haw Gardens, built in 1935 by Tiger Balm mogul Aw Boon Haw. The hillside gardens were populated by grotesque and garish statues from Chinese mythology, made all the more disturbing by their peeling paint and generally shabby appearance.

Weng Cheng was nervous. The courier delivering the money was not the man whom he had been dealing with. Cheng had done his share of dirty work, for a variety of masters, and he knew a fellow predator when he saw one.

6

Cheng felt like a tough barracuda in the presence of a hungry great white shark. He kept one hand near his gun.

This had been his biggest job ever. With the money he'd earned, one hundred thousand Hong Kong dollars, he could get papers to escape to the United States. He didn't want to be in Hong Kong when the Communists took over. They might remember his misdeeds in Guangzhou.

The courier casually looked around. No one in sight. He produced a wad of bills. Cheng's eyes focused on it. The man's other hand whipped out and chopped down on Cheng's gun arm. Three fingers buried themselves in Cheng's throat.

He dragged Cheng behind the pink statues commemorating the Buddhist fable "Two Dragons Fighting for a Pearl." The tale, like all the garden scenes, had a moral. In this case it was don't interfere in matters that don't concern you.

The courier hadn't had a chance to practice on a live body for a while. He took a little extra time. Within one minute he had broken Cheng's clavicle, four ribs, and his right humerus. Cheng sagged to the floor, barely alive. The courier braced Cheng's body between his legs and held Cheng's head in his hand. He twisted hard, and Cheng was no more.

Before leaving, Kwan, the courier-killer, slipped a piece of paper into Cheng's pocket.

Within hours after police began blanketing the city with the artist's rendition of the arsonist's face, a guard making the rounds at Aw Boon Haw Gardens found the body.

A ten-thousand-dollar reward had been offered by the Hong Kong Trade Association, and the guard had already decided which horse at Happy Valley he would bet it on. Was not finding the body a sign from the gods that good fortune had at last come his way?

The next day's newspapers were filled with the story. The day after that there were unconfirmed reports that papers found on the body had linked Cheng to the CIA. The rumors spread nearly as rapidly as the fire had, the main one that the CIA was plotting to destabilize Hong Kong before the Chinese takeover in 1997. There was angry talk of American and British imperialism, Antiwhite sentiment exploded.

# SEIZE THE DRAGON

A gang of youths stopped a minibus filled with tourists on their way to Repulse Bay. They rocked the van until it toppled. As the terrified tourists struggled out of the vehicle, they were beaten and robbed by the crowd.

Someone threw a rock through the window of a jewelry store on Nathan Road, and snatched a dozen watches. The sound of the alarm had the opposite effect to what merchants wanted. Dozens of the city's disaffected, goods-hungry youths began tossing rocks through windows and grabbing all they could.

By the time police got there, several hundred young people were in a frenzy. Someone had a gun, and fired on the police. The police fired back. Three rioters were killed, a dozen injured, twice that many arrested.

Four times the police caught young men trying to set western hotels on fire. Grafitti saying "Get Out, Foreign Devils" was sprayed on the sides of hotels and western-owned businesses.

The number of immigrants trying to flee the colony doubled. Thousands lined up at embassies and consulates although there was no hope of getting a visa. There were miniriots, and more casualties.

A state of martial law was declared and troops in Britain were mobilized.

Then just as suddenly the panic subsided. Tourism had dropped by eighty-five percent, but those brave souls who stayed, or ghouls who liked visiting a war zone, found it peaceful. The scars—broken windows, burned-out stores—remained, but the Chinese, who over the years had endured so much, went about their business as if nothing had happened.

# PART I
## *The Shihan*

# CHAPTER
# 1

For someone who had scared millions of people, Gregory Marlowe was remarkably gentle-looking. Soft brown eyes, hangdog expression, a distracted manner. He sat in the plane, attaché case open on his lap, apparently doodling.

Marlowe was *the* man to see if you wanted an alien, a witch, or a pirate. Or a reasonable facsimile thereof. He designed masks that had appeared in dozens of horror and sci-fi movies, as well as at two amusement parks, and in store displays. Now he had a deal with Zippy Toys, Inc., to mass-market his designs.

Marlowe was so involved with his sketching that he didn't notice the man sitting next to him. But the man kept a constant eye on Marlowe. It wasn't until they were about to begin their descent into New York that the man spoke.

"Mr. Marlowe? My name is Les Halliwell."

"How'd you know my name?"

"I've been hired by Zippy Toys to protect you. We've received word that there will be a kidnap attempt."

The stewardess announced, "All seats to the upright position" and the usual litany about extinguishing smoking materials. Halliwell had waited until their descent. If Marlowe showed fear, it would appear related to the landing. Halliwell wasn't sure if they were already being watched.

"Mr. Marlowe, I had twenty two years with the Secret Service," Les said reassuringly. "I've protected presidents, diplomats, whatever. Just do what I say and this will be your smoothest trip ever to New York."

"How do I know you're who you say you are? How do I know you're not a kidnapper yourself?"

Halliwell handed over a letter from Stu Zanville, the president of Zippy. It asked that Marlowe cooperate fully with Halliwell. "You can compare the signature with papers you might have. Besides, Mr. Zanville will be waiting at LaGuardia."

The landing gear locked in place with a thump that made Marlowe jump. He glanced over at Halliwell, who had a cool professional smile on his face. Marlowe studied his features. Thinning brown hair, mustache, alert, deepset eyes. Marlowe decided to trust him. Cautiously.

"Here's the game plan," Halliwell said. "As we deplane there'll be a door on the jetway. Just walk right through it, down the stairs. My partner will be at the foot of the stairs, disguised as you."

"As me?"

"Yes. We're going to let the kidnappers grab him."

"Why?"

"So they can be scooped up away from the crowded terminal. Also, that way we get them for kidnapping, not just attempted kidnapping."

"It sounds dangerous."

Halliwell made a gesture of dismissal. "Not for you it isn't."

The plane's wheels hit the asphalt and the pilot threw the jet engines into a braking mode.

"She's down," Pedro Quesada said, watching as the makeup artist finished on his boss, Robert Stark.

"Ta-da," the makeup artist said. She was one of the hundreds of consultants and per diem ops the agency used, everything from bomb disposal experts, to meteorologists, to prostitutes, to electronics whizzes.

"Perfect timing," Stark said, standing up and studying himself in the mirror. At six feet, he was a couple of inches taller than Marlowe, and at one seventy-five, he was ten pounds lighter. Standing side by side, they'd never be mistaken for twins, but anyone working from a photo might be fooled.

The trio was in a small room just off the cargo bay, under the gate where the flight was scheduled to arrive. The airline had cooperated fully with Halliwell-Stark Associates. They were an HSA client, and the firm had successfully ended a hijacking in the Middle East. The president of the company was only too glad to help, after being reassured that the trap would be closed on the kidnappers away from the airline's property.

"We're all soldiers in the war against terrorism," the company president had said. Then he'd asked for ten percent knocked off HSA's bill as consideration for his cooperation.

"The plane's taxiing in," Quesada said. He had a walkie-talkie attached by an earplug and was in contact with HSA operatives as well as the control tower and Port Authority police.

Quesada was a stocky, one-armed fifty-year-old with a neatly trimmed mustache and accusatory eyes. He had overdeveloped his remaining arm, giving him a slightly lopsided appearance. Still, when he attached his prosthetic arm, he had a remarkable knack for blending into a crowd. His swarthy appearance had allowed him to play an American Indian, an Indian Indian, an Italian, a Jew, an Arab, a Greek, a Turk, as well as a variety of Hispanics. Although born in Mexico, and fluent in Spanish, his English was accent free.

He adjusted Stark's tie with one hand and studied his boss's new face.

"It's an improvement," he said.

"Maybe I'll keep the new look," Stark joked. He was calm, and not just putting on a mask.

When he'd first entered the Zen monastery in Japan, after his abrupt departure from the CIA, he'd been on the verge of a breakdown. But months of the rigorous monastic life, coupled with demanding martial arts training, had brought him an internal peace that was rarely violated.

He'd grown as much from the jujitsu training as he had from the meditation. One lesson repeated over and over was "don't reach out." When a mock attack was launched, the idea was to wait until the last minute to repel it. The attacker was most committed, and most vulnerable, like a bull charging a red cape. Overreach, and the attacker could compensate and launch a different assault.

The plane roared into the gate. Then much quieter as the engines were killed.

"Ready?" Quesada asked, lifting the walkie-talkie to his lips while looking at his boss.

"Fire in the hole," Stark said.

Marlowe stepped onto the jetway and looked through the glass panel in the service door. He saw Stu Zanville down on the tarmac. Zanville gave a quick wave. Marlowe pushed through the door, Halliwell one step behind him. They were the last to get off the plane.

Marlowe reached the bottom of the metal stairs. Who is that funny-looking guy, he wondered as someone very familiar looking breezed past. Then he realized that was his double.

"Is that what I look like?" Marlowe asked, staring at Stark's retreating figure.

"You're much better looking," Halliwell reassured him. "Now get in the car quickly, please." Halliwell scanned the field as they walked through the open space. Although he knew that two HSA sharpshooters were in position, he was anxious until he got Marlowe into the car.

Zanville, a serious-looking gray-haired man in a thousand-dollar suit, began explaining things to Marlowe. The driver, a plainclothes Port Authority cop, handed Les Halliwell a belly holster and a .357 Magnum, and Les immediately felt better.

Marlowe and Zanville, however, nervously watched him handle it.

"Ahhh," Halliwell sighed involuntarily as the familiar weight pressed against his midsection. He turned to the company president and the artist and said, "How would you gents like a helicopter ride?"

Stark's feet echoed down the jetway. The chauffeur was waiting, holding up a sign that said MARLOWE.

One of the first rules Stark laid down when HSA was hired was no chauffeurs at airports with signs. They increased executive visibility and vulnerability a thousandfold. The only way it was acceptable was if the sign had a phony name, and still that was too attention-getting for Stark's taste.

He breezed up to the uniformed chauffeur.

"This way," the man said, leading Stark from the terminal.

Stark was on the alert, waiting for a figure to step out of the crowd with a gun hidden under a coat. Nothing. But his instincts were humming. What was it?

The chauffeur opened the door and Stark slid into the stretch limo. Stark laid the attaché case, which matched the one Marlowe had been carrying, next to him on the seat.

The limo pulled away from the curb with a slight jerk.

The chauffeur was not quite right. There had been a hint of a sloppy shave, a manner that was more jittery than deferential. The driver was in his late twenties with greasy long blond hair peeking out from under his cap. The cap looked as if it had been sat on, the uniform not pressed. Even iconoclastic rock stars expected a chauffeur who looked sleek and who knew to ask "Any bags?"

They reached the end of the parking lot, paid the fee, and pulled out. The limo slowed and a man jumped in. He shoved a gun in Stark's face. He was about the same age as the driver, with nasty blue eyes and a twitchy upper lip.

"Just do what we say and you won't get hurt," the twitchy gunman said.

"Whatever you say," Stark said. Sometimes it was best to agitate a kidnapper, distract him. Sometimes it was best to try to calm him. Twitchy needed calming, judging by the whiteness of his trigger finger.

Twitchy lowered his gun, out of sight to other drivers, but kept it pressed against Stark's groin.

"Where are we going?" Stark asked softly.

"Shut the fuck up. Just shut the fuck up," Twitchy shouted.

"Take it easy, man," the driver said.

"Just fucking drive, okay."

Amateurs, Stark thought. Professional kidnappers could be trusted to keep you alive. Amateurs made mistakes, bad for themselves and their victims.

"You didn't even frisk him," the driver said.

"I know what I'm doing," Twitchy snapped. But he roughly patted Stark down. He would have missed an ankle holster, Stark thought, but of course there was no way to guess that beforehand.

They rode in silence through heavy traffic, then across the Williamsburg Bridge. Twitchy grew more nervous with each minute, like a miser watching a taxi meter tick away.

"I think you must have the wrong person," Stark said. "I'm just a maskmaker."

Twitchy shoved the gun hard into Stark's groin. "You speak when I tell you to, asshole."

Then they were in Manhattan, pulling into TriBeCa. The area was a mix of warehouses, artists' lofts, and gentrified yuppies' condos. It was after eight P.M., the dark streets practically deserted.

Stark took out a pen.

"What're you doing?" Twitchy demanded.

"I have to jot myself a note."

The pen was a new gadget Les had fobbed on him, a deluxe version of a tear-gas pen which fired six shots of a microfine spray.

Stark wrote a note. "Buy milk and eggs," then squeezed the clip.

No spray.

The gunman looked over at the note. "You're fucking crazy, you know that?"

He grabbed the pen from Stark's hand and threw it out the window. He crumpled the paper up and threw that out too.

In the chopper three thousand feet above them, Les Halliwell couldn't see what was happening. He continued his nonstop spiel to Zanville. The president of Zippy Toys had lost his glum expression, and was caught up in the excitement of the pursuit. Marlowe looked as if he were suffering from airsickness.

"Any minute now he'll use a special incapacitating pen," Halliwell said, taking a duplicate of the one Stark had from his pocket.

"Where are the police?"

"All around. We work hand in hand with the NYPD on

matters like this. Our pilot"—Les gave the chopper pilot a friendly pat on the shoulder—"is one of New York's finest." He leaned over to Zanville and whispered, "Of course, in matters involving organized crime or possible corruption, we can handle it without letting the boys in blue in." He resumed talking in a normal tone. "We pride ourselves on our fine relations with departments across the country. The deal is, we run an op with them watching, they get the credit. Of course, if it fouls up, we get the blame. But we don't foul up."

"It sounds impressive. When will your partner be arresting them?"

"Any minute now, I'm sure. A firm like yours would benefit from our deluxe package. This includes our full intelligence program. We have access to everything from Interpol, to the Rand Corporation, to the *New York Times* data base, to give you the latest in threat assessment. We have risk management specialists who will visit your facilities, tell you what's safe and what's dangerous."

"You provide security guards?"

"More often we recommend firms that do. We keep our overhead down by limiting our full-time personnel. We can steer you to firms that will provide quality security."

"Sounds expensive."

"How much is your life worth? How much is your family's life worth, or that of valued employees like Mr. Marlowe here?"

Marlowe was looking sicker as the pilot circled above the TriBeCa streets.

"Okay," Zanville said. "Give our comptroller a call."

"That's not all you get," Les said, as wound up as a late-night TV huckster. "If there is an incident, we provide twenty-four-hour service three hundred sixty-five days a year. Crisis management, hostage negotiation, liaising with law enforcement. We even have former journalists who'll fend off the media for you."

"Okay, okay."

"Now you have overseas plants in Hong Kong and Taiwan. We protect you there as well. We have superb government contacts around the globe."

Deciding there was no way to turn Halliwell off, Zanville

opted to redirect the conversation. "Tell me about your partner. What's his background?"

"CIA. Clandestine ops. Earned medals so classified, you can't even mention them. They're called jockstrap awards."

"He seems young to have retired from the government."

"He quit."

"Why?"

"Uh, better opportunities," Halliwell said, quickly changing the subject. "Me, I was with the Secret Service for twenty years. Half that time assigned to the protective detail. I could tell you stories about our leaders that would make your hair curl. Like the time—"

"Something's going on down there," Marlowe interrupted. "They've stopped the car."

Halliwell and Zanville pressed their noses against the glass and looked down.

The limo pulled up to a brick warehouse.

"Help me get him inside, then go dump the limo by the river," Twitchy said.

"The East River or the Hudson?" the driver asked.

"The fucking Mississippi," Twitchy said. "The Hudson, moron. Don't forget to wipe all the prints out of it."

Twitchy took out a pair of handcuffs. "Put these on," he told Stark.

"Can I take my medicine first?"

"What medicine?" Twitchy asked.

"It's in my attaché case. I've got asthma."

"They didn't tell us nothing about that," the driver said.

Twitchy hesitated. "Okay. But open the case real slow." He turned to the driver. "Go open that fucking door. We ain't gonna sit here all day."

The driver got out and entered a side door. A few moments later the big steel warehouse door began to rise as he tugged on a chain inside.

Inside the car, Stark gingerly opened the case. "Can you remove the gun from my privates?" he asked Twitchy. "I'm an artist, not a hero."

"Fucking wimp," Twitchy sneered. He shoved the gun in harder, then pulled it back.

Stark took out a medicine jar. "I need water to swallow."

"You're lucky I don't shove the jar down your throat."

Stark's hands quivered. He opened the jar, and spilled pills. Twitchy's eyes followed the falling medicine.

Stark moved suddenly, twisting the attaché case and slamming it down on Twitchy's hand.

Twitchy pulled the trigger.

The attaché case, lined with bullet-resistant Kevlar, bucked violently but absorbed the bullet. Stark squeezed the case tighter, and the edges bit into Twitchy's hand. The gunman yelped and released the weapon.

Twitchy flailed at Stark, but the pain in his trapped hand kept him from getting in an effective blow. Still keeping up pressure on the case with one hand, Stark used his elbow, the hardest striking surface of the body, to jab Twitchy's chin. Twitchy wavered, stunned. Stark grabbed Twitchy's neck between his thumb and index finger, pinned Twitchy against the rear window, and applied pressure. With his carotid artery depressed, Twitchy's brain was soon starving for blood. In fifteen seconds Twitchy was unconscious.

Stark released the pressure and straightened him up. The driver was returning.

"All right, what do you want me to do now?" the driver asked, leaning over Stark to ask Twitchy the question.

Stark grabbed his hair, pulled him halfway into the car, and rolled up the automatic window to pin him in place. The driver waved his hands ineffectively. He tried reaching down for the window button.

"Naughty, naughty," Stark said, smacking his hands with a hard chop. Stark took the gun out of the attaché case and held it an inch from the driver's face. "Just relax. Help is on the way."

Stark slid out the other side. He spotted Pedro Quesada lounging in a doorway halfway up the block. Quesada, who had spent much of his youth as a street-gang member, was adept at hanging out and not looking out of place. Stark gave him a thumbs-up.

Within five minutes, four police cars had closed off the block and the dazed, would-be kidnappers were being advised of their rights.

Pedro had a car waiting. They were scheduled to rendezvous with Les by the heliport. Stark expected that by now his partner had sold Zippy Toys on everything but the Brooklyn Bridge. It gave the whole scenario the feeling of a stage show. But Halliwell kept them in business. They both knew if Stark had his way, he probably wouldn't even charge for their services.

# CHAPTER
# 2

FBI agent Adam Dawson browsed the shop windows on Kam Tin Road, trying to be unobtrusive. His height of six feet four inches was more of a handicap than an asset in the Orient. He couldn't even ride a double decker tram in Hong Kong without bending.

He had been posted to the embassy in Hong Kong for a year now. Not a bad assignment. Dawson was a whiz with paperwork, and ninety percent of his job involved double-checking passport applications against files, telexing reports to Washington or FBI field offices, reading local newspapers, and writing up significant news. He also kept up good relations with local law enforcement during frequent meals out at splendid restaurants. He'd gained fifteen pounds since his transfer to the city. He figured obesity was the biggest danger he faced. That, and suicidal Chinese drivers who made tail jobs a nightmare.

He hated field work, but sometimes it was inevitable. Like now. He was in the New Territories. While he pretended to gaze at overpriced jade knickknacks, in reality he was using the window reflection to keep an eye on the building across the street.

Hi Fashion Clothing Manufacturing was housed in a six-story concrete structure, one of the hundreds of new buildings that seemed to spring up each week in the New Territories. Most were apartment house skyscrapers, skinny twenty-six-story buildings that looked like insect hives from a distance. But with prices in Hong Kong proper ranging from high to astronomical, more and more firms were opening factories in the New Territories, the 588 square kilometers north of the city, geographically attached to mainland China but legally part of Hong Kong.

Dawson watched the building because of the man who had entered it two hours earlier. Louis Scalish. Also known as The Diplomat. Scalish's diplomacy usually involved a baseball bat to the kneecaps. He was a former New Jersey strongarm who had risen in the Genovese crime family to become the underboss. He had moved to Palm Springs, and served as the East Coast mob's West Coast representative, supervising their Las Vegas skim. Scalish also owned three garment-center firms, thus his visit to the Hi Fashion factory.

Dawson wished he had a few assistants. For one man to watch a building was ridiculous. It was too easy for the quarry to slip out a back way.

When he returned to his office six hours later, he was in a foul mood. He was used to air-conditioning and had all but melted from the hot, damp Southeast Asian air. His skin was raw from moisture and rubbing.

What he found on his desk added to his rotten mood. A buddy in the Hong Kong Immigration Department had faxed over travel documents. At about the time Dawson was skipping his lunch hour, Scalish must have been slipping out the rear. He was on his way to the People's Republic of China, on a tour of Guangzhou.

Why? Dawson couldn't imagine Scalish with an Instamatic around his neck, admiring the industriousness of the natives, looking for vestiges of Chairman Mao. But joining a tour group was one of the easiest ways to enter the PRC without much scrutiny.

Stapled to Scalish's papers was a second form, for his fourteen-year-old granddaughter. Carmelita Scalish.

Dawson flipped open the extensive file they had sent him from the SOG, seat of government, the hindquarters in D.C.

There was no granddaughter of that name or age. There was a report on Scalish's sexual preferences.

Dawson felt bad for Carmelita.

Pigs rooted through piles of garbage, speckled geese honked, and a gray water buffalo felt the switch on its back as it marched up and down the rows in the rice paddy.

The guide, who asked to be called Mr. Lau, was a smiling young man in a white shirt and blue pants. He didn't seem to sweat, although the fifteen tourists in his group were dripping moisture like overused air-conditioners.

They stood on a dirt road engraved with bicycle tracks. Bikes with geese imprisoned in wicker baskets on the back wobbled past them. They were at the Da Li Township, formerly the Da Li Production Team, and before that the Da Li Commune. Lau, in English with a singsong lilt, explained the production responsibility system, the problems of raising rice, and the free enterprise-encouraging administrative method at the township.

"In China, nothing is wasted," Mr. Lau said in conclusion, repeating what was to be a theme of the tour. "The pigs help dispose of the garbage. When they are ready, they will be sent to the butcher. When the water buffalo is too old to plow, it, too, will become food."

"What happens if your wife refuses to work?" asked a fat man who had already established himself as the group comedian.

Lau smiled politely while the tourists chuckled. It seemed that in every tour some *gwai lo* would make the same joke.

"What is that brick building over there?" asked a woman whose high heels had sunk into the mud of the road.

"That is the bathroom. You see, it is above a pond. The waste goes right into the pond, and acts as fertilizer."

"In China, nothing is wasted," someone piped up.

"Very true," Mr. Lau said as if it were the tourist's original thought. "You may take pictures if you like. Then back to the bus in ten minutes and we go to the Shiwan Pottery Factory."

At the back of the group, a tall white-haired man watched the rest of the tourists disperse to click away. He impatiently glanced at the diamond-studded gold watch on his wrist.

Standing next to him was a teenage girl, slightly pudgy, with long black hair.

Lau knew them to be Nicholas and Carmelita Machiavelli. He was convinced the name was an alias. Lau had done very well in western history while a student at the People's University in Shanghai. He remembered the name Niccolò Machiavelli as belonging to a cunning Italian adviser from the sixteenth century. He also didn't believe the girl was the man's granddaughter. There was something about the way the man touched her and the way she flinched, like a dog that had been beaten.

Special arrangements had been made for Machiavelli and the girl to escape the tour to meet with an official of the Central Committee. Although Mr. Lau carried credentials from the China Travel Service, he actually worked for the Public Security Bureau, the PRC's equivalent of the FBI. He didn't know what Machiavellis' business was, but he knew it was of vital importance.

In Guangzhou, the city the foreigners had called Canton, the group would be split in two. That way no one would notice when Machiavelli was taken to the meeting. Each group would assume Machiavelli was in the other group. He was definitely a noticeable presence, and several of the unattached women had flirted with him. But Machiavelli had been abrupt and they had moved off.

Lau glanced at Machiavelli. Their eyes met. Lau decided that whatever Machiavelli's business was, it was not good.

Louis Scalish, who had evaded Dawson and was a puzzle to Lau, gazed at his gold watch for the fifth time. He had an appointment with the Communist Chinese foreign minister in an hour. And here he was, standing in five-hundred-dollar shoes in wet mud punctuated by pig shit.

God, it stunk. The whole place looked like what Europe must have during the Middle Ages. These Chinks were hardworking—he'd seen that at his factories—but their country was backward as hell.

Carmelita stood next to him, staring out at the lush greenery.

"Remind you of your home?" Scalish asked her tenderly.

# SEIZE THE DRAGON

The girl, who understood about a hundred words of English, just nodded in response to his gentle tone.

In public, Machiavelli enjoyed playing the role of the doting grandfather. In private, well, he had not yet taken her cherry. He was saving that for a special time. But each bruise on her body marked a different moment of passion.

Usually he got South American girls, used them for a few weeks, then installed them in a whorehouse he owned in Nevada. Many of the girls were kidnapped off the streets, their disappearance blamed on death squads. More often, they were bought from their parents.

Carmelita had been waiting for him in the factory. Duly paid for and shipped from her home in the Philippines. Just the way Scalish liked them, with the baby fat still intact, making that transition from little girl to woman. Breasts fully sprouted, but still moving with a little clunkiness.

Scalish had been seduced by a girl about that age when he was barely eleven. She had been the daughter of a maid in his father's house. His father had slapped him on the back, commended him for being a cockhound while others were still reading comic books. The girl, however, had to be punished, his father explained. Scalish had watched while she and her mother were gang-raped by a dozen men at one of his father's live sex show theaters. Scalish got hard just thinking about it, the struggles and screams gradually subsiding into low sobs as the men grunted and rammed into the mother and daughter.

"Men got to sow their wild oats," his father explained. "It's up to the girl to keep herself pure."

At last the morons on the tour were done taking pictures. Scalish had to be constantly on his guard, making sure that none of them captured him on film. The Feebs would probably know about his China trip, he figured, but there was no point in being like some bozo politicians, and posing for pictures.

Mr. Lau was joined by two other guides. One took half the group to see Liu Rong Si, the Temple of the Six Banyans. The second guide took the remainder to the Guangxiao Si, the Bright Filial Piety Temple.

"We allow anyone to worship who wants to," Mr. Lau

25

had explained, noting that there was an active mosque and Catholic church as well as Buddhist and Taoist temples in Guangzhou. "We will split the group to create less of a disturbance. Most unfortunately, I must leave you for a while. Please enjoy yourselves."

Lau took Scalish and Carmelita aside. They were escorted to the Xi Yuan Restaurant. Carmelita was led off to a side room while Scalish was seated in a larger room, away from the main dining area. He waited.

Carmelita was watched over by two young men while a young woman brought her a bowl of soup.

"Help me," Carmelita said in English to the young woman, who appeared to be almost the same age. She tried the same plea in Spanish and Tagalog.

The waitress looked at her quizzically.

In Tagalog, Carmelita blurted out, "This man is no relative. He hurts me. He is going to dishonor me. He makes me—" She broke into sobs and struggled to compose herself. "I was sold to him by my parents, who were starving. They thought I was going to be his maid."

She got down on her knees and threw her arms around the waitress's thighs. The waitress carefully balanced her tray and rattled off a few words in Chinese to the male guards.

They calmly lifted Carmelita into a chair.

"Eat soup while it is warm," one of the guards said.

Her tears dribbled into the bowl.

The Chinese looked on impassively.

"At last," Scalish said when the foreign minister came, a half hour after Scalish had been led to the room.

The foreign minister's name was Li and he was expected to inherit the top spot within five years. Li had a large birthmark on his pleasant moon-shaped face and an easy smile which meant less than nothing. He had walked with Mao on the Great March, survived various cultural revolutions, "great leaps forward," and revisionist denunciations. Always smiling.

"It is nice to see you again, Mr. Machiavelli," Li said.

"Bullshit, Li. Let's cut the cheese."

There was a translator standing behind Li, a serious-looking woman with a stocky build. She also served as his bodyguard and lover. Li looked at her quizzically. Although his English was good, he had little experience with idioms.

"Could you repeat please?" the woman asked Scalish.

"He's about as happy to see me as I'd be to pick up a case of the clap. Let's skip the polite talk and get down to business."

She translated quickly, with Li nodding.

"There is a saying that it is best to be born in Suzhou, live in Hangzhou, eat in Guangzhou, and die in Liuzhou. Suzhou has the most beautiful women. Hangzhou the best scenery. Liuzhou, the finest wood for coffins. And we are in Guangzhou."

"Yeah, yeah, yeah."

"A meal has been prepared for us. In China it is a crime to waste food," Li said.

"Okay, okay. We eat and talk."

A sixteen-course meal began, with delicacies like stewed fishhead with vegetables, braised dove, shark-fin soup, broiled bear paws, and roast suckling pig.

Li explained the significance of each dish, how it was designed to balance the yin and the yang, the positive and negative elements that make up the universe. Scalish wolfed down the portions. A few times he tried to get to business, but Li avoided the subject. Scalish gulped bottles of Tsingtao beer while Li drank sweet orange soda.

When the last dish was cleared, Scalish leaned forward. "We ate. Now, a few weeks ago me and my partners made you a simple offer. We didn't get any response. So we caused that trouble in Hong Kong. I can understand your position. You didn't know who you were dealing with. Now you do. What's your answer?"

Li sipped from a teacup. "You are a brave man, Mr. Machiavelli. How do you know we will not arrest you? This is not America. Our justice system is very different."

"I've done time."

"Our methods of questioning are much less pleasant."

"I'm a tough nut to crack," Machiavelli said.

Li turned to the translator, who explained.

"No doubt," Li said when he understood. "But we have cracked tough nuts in the past."

"My partners and me have certain contingency plans. If I'm not back in Hong Kong safe and sound on schedule, they'll turn up the heat. You saw what our marshmallow roast at the factory did? How many people dead? How many millions in property damage? How many investors skipped out?"

Again Li's aide fired forth a rapid translation in Mandarin.

"Your partners. Sun Tzu and Musashi. Obviously you have a sense of humor. Choosing the names of three of the great strategists. Or perhaps it is delusions of grandeur?"

"We'll know soon enough. What's your answer?"

"We need more time to consider your offer."

"A guy I knew one time was doing a piece of work. The guy he was dealing with said, 'I need more time.' My buddy tells him, 'Sure, take three months in the hospital on me.' Capish?"

"Ka-peech?" the translator repeated.

"That means 'Do you understand?' " Scalish said.

Li nodded.

"Good, good. We'll give you another week. Then we'll have to show you how serious we are. It's too late for me to go back tonight. You've got a room at the White Swan for me and my granddaughter?"

"It has been arranged."

"We like our privacy. The girl sometimes has nightmares. Cries in the middle of the night. I don't want to disturb anyone."

"Your privacy will be undisturbed."

# CHAPTER
# 3

"Nice job," Halliwell said as they rode up in the elevator after handling the kidnapping.

"Thanks. But no thanks to your superpen," Stark said.

"I'll get a refund from those crooks. But you got to admit, the attaché case worked like a charm."

"It did."

"Speaking of working like a charm, I think I sold Zanville on a deluxe package. I convinced him the toy business was a dangerous world."

"Does he know which rival it was that planned to kidnap Marlowe?"

"I haven't told him yet. I'll give that to him at the contract-signing. There's no way to legally connect those two punks to the other company, is there?"

Stark shook his head.

"Maybe we'll need street justice," Halliwell suggested.

The elevator door opened. They passed through two-inch-thick swinging glass doors that said Halliwell-Stark Associates into the reception area where Bunny held sway.

Bunny was a former three-hundred-pound dope dealer who had gone straight and been hired by Halliwell-Stark. She was still a tough piece of work, but now had a svelte figure that caught every male visitor's eye. She was absorbed in paperwork when the men entered.

"What're you working on?" Halliwell asked, leaning over her shoulder and trying to nibble her ear.

She gently slapped his face. "Last guy who tried that without my permission, his voice still is an octave higher. You dig?"

"I dig," Halliwell said. He cleaned out a few papers that had piled up in his In box, and sulked off to his office.

With great dignity Bunny uncovered the crossword puzzle she had been working on. "That man ain't got but one thing on his mind," Bunny said.

"Making money?" Stark asked with an innocent expression.

"Making trouble. What about you?"

"I avoid trouble wherever possible."

"Then why do you keep Catherine the Great around?"

"She called?"

"Not yet. She must be out shopping."

"Jealousy is unbecoming."

"Me. Jealous? Hmmmph."

As he picked up his papers, she mumbled, "Wonder what's a six-letter word for a male falcon."

"Tercel," Stark said.

"What?"

"A six-letter word for a male falcon."

"Damn. I wish you hadn't told me that."

She filled the word in on her newspaper and was quickly absorbed. Stark headed into his office. He switched to sweats and a T-shirt, and did fifteen minutes of stretching exercises, sit-ups, and push-ups. Then he did fifteen minutes of *katas*, prearranged martial arts movements that looked almost like a dance. He showered in his private bathroom, got back into a suit, and dug into the paperwork on his desk.

The intercom on his desk purred. "Mr. Stark, there's a gentleman here to see you from the Department of Commerce."

"Have him make an appointment."

"He says it's urgent. He's threatening to use the vast resources of the federal government on poor little old us."

"Don't hit him, Bunny."

"You don't allow a girl any fun. What do you want me to do?"

Stark glanced at his watch. "Send him in. I've got a few minutes to spare."

The Commerce official walked in, stiff as a board and about as friendly. Stark could only imagine the hard time Bunny must have given him. The official was in his late thirties, with a jowly arrogance and an expression like an owl with hemorrhoids. He looked old beyond his years, and quite impressed with himself.

"You really ought to discipline your help," the man said without offering to shake hands.

"If you have the time, you can watch me flog her. It's kinky, but fun."

For a second the visitor took the comment seriously, and his confusion was a pleasure for Stark to watch. Then circuits seemed to click over in his brain. He smiled, a beamish salesman's smile, and offered his hand.

"Bill Roberts. I'm not really with Commerce."

Stark shook his hand. "You know my name and who I'm with. Have a seat and tell me your life story. In five minutes or less."

"Your country needs you, Mr. Stark."

"I gave at the office."

"I'm serious. What I'm about to tell you is classified information."

"Maybe you shouldn't tell me then. I'm such a gossip."

Roberts—and Stark was sure that wasn't his name—acted like he hadn't heard. "Have you been following the disturbances in Hong Kong?"

"I read the papers. It appears that things have quieted down."

"Looks can be deceiving," Roberts said as if he were confiding a major secret.

"You don't say."

"We have evidence that hidden forces are trying to destabilize Hong Kong. The Agency is being blamed. We want you to go find out who really is doing it."

"When you say 'the Agency,' are you talking about William Morris?"

"You know who I'm talking about."

31

"The gang from Langley, right?"

"Correct. We can arrange transport for you to a secure facility for a complete briefing."

"Thanks, but no thanks."

"You're refusing?"

"You got it."

"Why?"

"I did my dirty work for Uncle Sam. There are plenty of other fresh-faced spooks who can handle this problem."

"But you know the Orient."

"So do a few thousand other ops. Good-bye."

"This assignment comes right from the DCI's office."

"I hope I don't break his heart."

Roberts stood up. "I'm not supposed to tell you this, but I will anyway. Koiichi Soto is involved."

"Who?" Stark said, feigning ignorance.

"Your former martial arts instructor in Japan."

"Oh, yeah, him. Why does that concern me?"

"Your file says—"

"I don't give a damn what my file says. Good-bye again." Roberts stormed out.

Stark tapped the intercom button. "Bunny, book me on a flight to D.C."

"You gonna take the job that government jerk was offering?"

"Just book the flight."

Koiichi Soto. Stark's *shihan*, the master instructor who had brought him back from the brink. It had been a long time since Stark consciously focused on him. And yet each day he lived according to principles the *shihan* had taught him.

A minute later Stark got back on the intercom. "Sorry I snapped at you. I've got a lot on my mind."

"No sweat. Just wait till I renegotiate my contract. I got you that ticket. And the Russian princess called."

"She's no longer empress?"

"She's a royal pain in the ass, I'll tell you that much," Bunny said.

"Why must you go?" Dr. Sultana Mirnov asked.

"I have to find out more."

32

"Why is it so important? Do you realize how little time we have together? We were supposed to see a movie tonight."

"I'm sorry."

Mirnov, a tall, buxom brunette, locked her piercing green-gray eyes on him as if he were a wayward experiment. She had been a leading Soviet microbiologist until she defected in an act of conscience, and hooked up with Stark.

In America she had taken to capitalism and conspicuous consumption with a vengeance. Her monthly charge card bills were never less than four figures. She loved going to plays and was convinced the only way to see them was from the front row. Mirnov and Stark ate in the city's best restaurants.

Her salary as a researcher for NYU Medical Center couldn't support her tastes. Stark didn't mind covering the bills, since money wasn't that important to him. Watching her go consumer crazy was as much fun as giving a kid a thousand bucks and turning him loose at Toys "R" Us.

But one of the major conflicts in Stark's life came from Sultana's need to acquire goods and Halliwell's desire to acquire cash. Les felt she was taking advantage of Stark, and nicknamed her the "Siberian gold digger."

Sultana folded her arms across her chest. "I know who it is. Your partner. Or that secretary Bunny. She tells you rotten things about me."

"No. She thinks you're very nice."

"You can't lie to me."

"Well, she and Les saw the bills you've racked up. They think I'm turning into a sugar daddy."

"What's that?"

"A man who is a walking piggy bank for a beautiful woman."

"Is that what they think? What about you?"

"What about dinner?"

"I made reservations at Santangelo's."

"It'll take too long. Let's just grab a quick bite somewhere."

"I want to talk about this sugar daddy business."

He took her in his arms and kissed her. A little resistance at first, but she gave in and soon responded.

"Is that what sugar daddies do?" she asked.

"Let it go," Stark said. "How was work?"

"I want to talk with you about that."

"I'm listening."

"I'm thinking of quitting."

"I thought the research on schistosomiasis was going well?"

"It is not that."

"What is it?"

"It's not much money. I want to be independent."

He gave her a peck on the lips. "Don't do it for my sake. Your research is important. How many millions of people in third world countries have schistosomiasis?"

"That is the problem. Third world countries. There's not much money to be made in the research. It's an unpopular disease for study, like river blindness or sleeping sickness. Onchocerciasis, trypanosomiasis."

"So what do you plan on doing?"

"I've had offers. I haven't had a chance to tell you about them. A few of the drug companies."

"What will you be studying?"

"The common cold," she said, embarrassed.

"Oh."

"In Soviet Union we use interferon to treat. I was involved in important research into hundred viruses that cause colds." When Mirnov got upset, her Russian accent became stronger.

"It's your decision."

"Colds cost millions of dollars every year. People absent from jobs. Can't take care of children. Can get worse with complications."

"You don't have to convince me."

"I see in your face contempt."

"Not at all. Maybe you're projecting."

"You Mr. Holier-than-Thou. Why do you have to go away anyway?"

"I have a debt to my instructor, the *shihan*."

"Money?"

"Not money. *Giri*. A sense of duty."

"You are saying I do not have this by going to work for drug company?" She was shouting now. "First you tell me

I spend too much. Then you tell me I have no sense of duty. To hell and back with you."

She marched into her bedroom and slammed the door.

It was a two-bedroom apartment, and although they shared a king-size bed in one room, their clothing was in separate rooms. He went into "his" bedroom and packed an overnight bag. He knew her sudden storms, and it was best to let them blow over rather than directly oppose them.

She came in when he was just about done.

"You're going?" she asked softly.

"I must."

"I still do not understand why."

He took her in his arms. "When I quit the Agency, I was a mess. In the dojo, in the monastery, at first it was miserable. I think they gave me a particularly hard time because I was a *gaijin,* a foreigner. But then I saw why. *Shihan* Soto spent more time with me than anyone else. For some reason he gave me special attention. He never explained why, just the way I never said thank you to him. It was all understood. There was no way I could thank him enough."

"For showing you jujitsu?"

"For showing me everything. It's not like here over there. There's no real need for self-defense in Japan. Street crime is a fraction of a percent above zero. People study martial arts for the same reason they study calligraphy, dance, flower arranging."

"As a hobby?"

"To perfect themselves."

"I do not understand how throwing someone, or cutting flowers, or dancing can help you like that."

"You learn to focus on the perfection of the moment. I can't explain it. Like Lao-tzu said, 'Those who say do not know, those who know do not say.' Some things are best without words."

"Like what?"

"If I labeled them, they'd have words."

As they spoke, she had been pressing harder and harder against him. She nestled her face on his shoulder.

"When we met, it seemed so perfect," she said.

"Those were unusual circumstances."

35

"You were like a knight in shining armor. You still are. But I don't like you going off on quests."

"We knights have to slay a dragon every now and then or our armor rusts up."

She nodded. Then they were kissing and despite the fact that she was no petite damsel, he lifted her easily in his arms.

He tried to push thoughts of the *shihan* from his mind. The past and the future are meaningless.

Her full lips kissed their way down his chest. She undid the buttons on his shirt as his hands gently kneaded her tense shoulders.

His mind continued to flash back to scenes in the dojo, the training hall, and Sultana nipped him on the soft flesh of his inner thigh.

"You want me to stop?" she asked.

He responded by undressing her.

Although they hit the high notes, something was missing. And they both knew it.

# CHAPTER
# 4

The director of the Central Intelligence Agency, following a time-honored tradition, lived in Georgetown. Senior spooks had been haunting the elegant turn-of-the-century buildings since the days of Oh So Social, the CIA's predecessor during World War II.

The director's home was on Prospect Avenue, with a view of the Potomac River and the Washington Canoe Club. Brandon Marshall had inherited the brownstone from his parents. He had also inherited his father's patrician good looks, and memberships in all the right country clubs. From his mother he had gotten his intelligence, which stood him in good stead at Yale, and later as a corporate lawyer.

Under his rule, covert ops had been cut to a minimum and actual intelligence work increased. The CIA had gotten less negative press than under any previous director. The President was quite pleased with his performance. Marshall was even discussed as a possible presidential candidate. But noblesse oblige went only so far, and Marshall would never stoop to the vulgarity of kissing babies or trying to convince the masses he was "a regular guy."

He sat in his study, half glasses perched on his nose, reading reports. He avoided, whenever possible, the synopses and briefing papers prepared for him, and went directly to source material. Nuances were inevitably lost in the condensation process.

His wife and two children were at their summer home in Southampton. The District of Columbia was built on a filled-in swamp, and during summer months it could be as hospitable as the Everglades. His only companions in the house were two Agency security men, his bodyguards. At least one was always awake, prowling the house, checking the alarms. It would be quite a terrorist coup to capture or kill the U.S.'s top spy-master.

Outside in the street, Robert Stark had similar thoughts. He looked up through the open window to Marshall at his desk. Stupid. One sharpshooter with a rifle, or a clod with an RPG, and Marshall would be history. In Stark's opinion every top U.S. official, with the exception of the president, received inadequate protection. Most cabinet-level officials, senior judges, and ranking congressmen had either no bodyguards or only one during business hours. The guards were lackadaisical, there more to ward off loonies than to protect against a determined attack.

With one shot from a silenced automatic, Stark took out the streetlight nearest the brownstone. Then he shimmied up the massive oak directly in front of the building. A branch reached out to within four feet from the window where the director sat. Stark eased out on the limb. The branch sagged and swayed.

There was always an advantage in unpredictability. Stark hoped to put the director on the defensive, intimidate him by showing how vulnerable he was. Rather than confronting the massive bureaucracy, Stark would beard the lion in his den.

Stark braced himself and leapt.

A figure in black flew in through the window, rolled, and stood up, a silenced gun in his hand.

Marshall looked up, his sangfroid intact. "Mr. Stark, I presume."

"Mr. Marshall."

"Please, call me Brandon. I've read your file so many times, I feel like we're old friends."

"I can't say the feeling is mutual."

"Would you care for a brandy?"

Stark shook his head and lowered his gun. "What about your guards?"

"I told them I was expecting you. You could've knocked on the door and been let in. But this is so much more dramatic."

Marshall smiled, took off his glasses, and extended his hand. "I thought you might find a breach in our security," he said. "There will be a tree surgeon here in the A.M." He scribbled a note on a piece of paper.

"You should keep the window closed. It's bulletproof laminate."

"It gets so stuffy in here."

"Coffins are even stuffier."

"You don't hear many corpses complaining about the accommodations. Getting off this morbid tangent, by initially refusing the assignment you also reduce your visibility. If only you and I are aware of your involvement, there's no chance of leakage."

Marshall took a bottle of brandy from an antique sideboard. He poured snifters for Stark and himself.

"Why do you assume I'll say yes?" Stark asked, accepting the glass.

"Would you fly into my chamber just to say no?"

"What's it all about?"

"Your *shihan*, I believe that's the proper Japanese term for master instructor, has been linked to the violence in Hong Kong."

"Linked?"

Marshall dug out papers from an oak roll-top desk, but Stark noticed that he didn't refer to them. They were to refresh his recollection, or perhaps to impress Stark. Paper was never supposed to lie.

"*Shihan* Koiichi Soto has a brother by the name of Subu Soto. Subu had been seen meeting with the arsonist whose handiwork precipitated the Hong Kong disorders. It's just a bit of luck that an MI6 informant saw this, and a sympathetic Brit passed it on to our people."

"That's a pretty weak link."

"Your *shihan* had visited Hong Kong several times and met with a strange assortment of people. He also had been seen with known *yakuza*."

That struck Stark as peculiar. The *shihan* almost never left the dojo, and the farthest he had ever traveled when Stark knew him was Tokyo. He also had nothing but contempt for the *yakuza*. The word itself meant "worthless," but it was understood to refer to the Japanese Mafia.

"Any plausible reason for Subu Soto and the arsonist to have met?"

"None."

"Why are you bringing me in?"

"Because you can get close to Koiichi Soto."

"Why the concern on the Company's part? Isn't it mainly a problem for MI5?"

"We are getting blamed for it. Every time some fourth-rate strong man in a fifth-rate third world country gets indigestion, we get blamed."

"We're only responsible for it one time in how many?"

"Not as often as the press makes it out."

"It still doesn't smell right to me."

Marshall raised the brandy snifter. *"Nas drovya."*

*"Nas drovya."*

The men drank.

"There is another factor. The arsonist, a Weng Cheng, did work for the CIA."

"Wonderful."

"As you are no doubt aware, we draw our contract agents from among the most disreputable sorts. Not many ministers and Boy Scout leaders are experienced in the kind of activities we sometimes find necessary."

"Like beatings, break-ins, and murder. What sort of credit to humanity was this torch?"

"I'm sorry that espionage is not a gentleman's game. I'd be the first to adhere to the Marquess of Queensbury's rules. But until the opposition does, I will be as willing to kick someone in the balls as the next fellow."

"What do you want?"

"Go back to the dojo. See what's up. Clear your instructor's name."

"That's it?"

"That's it," Marshall said.

"You're a cunning bastard."

Marshall frowned.

"If he is involved, and I go sniffing around, I'll flush out something," Stark said.

"You could just leave if you want. You can even skip the acrobatics and go out the front door."

A long pause, then both men smiled tightly. Stark extended his hand and shook Marshall's.

"For now, only you and I will know about my involvement," Stark said. "If I want Agency backup, I'll need a countersign."

Marshall looked over his desk. A picture of his wife holding a horse's reins smiled up at him.

"How about Buffy's Tuffy? My wife is Buffy. Her horse is Tuffy."

"Now it all makes sense."

"When will you be leaving?"

"I return to New York tonight and catch the first flight to Tokyo tomorrow."

"We'll pick up your expenses. And a fair market fee. Will you require any cash immediately?"

"Wait until it's over. Too many people know how to follow the money."

"Very true. Good luck. I'm glad we're on the same team."

"So am I."


Both Les and Sultana took the news badly. Halliwell had a couple of appointments scheduled with clients and possible clients. He knew that there was something about Stark that helped persuade corporate chiefs to sign on the dotted line. Sultana had planned a long weekend in the country for her and Stark, a reconciliation. She pouted, Halliwell sputtered, but by noon Stark was on a JAL flight for Tokyo.

He spent the flight brushing up on his Japanese. He had a knack for languages, and could make himself understood in French, Spanish, Russian, and Mandarin Chinese. After five years in Japan he could speak the language fluently. But aside from conversations in restaurants, and periodic listening to instructional tapes, he hadn't used Japanese in a couple of years.

He was strangely anxious, and had trouble concentrating.

What would the *shihan*'s reaction be to Stark's turning up at his door? Could his *shihan* be involved in the trouble in Hong Kong? And what would Stark do if he were?

# CHAPTER
# 5

The shogun's capital during the thirteenth century, Kamakura nowadays is a resort town and bedroom community for Tokyo. The main attraction is the big Buddha, whose serene face has gazed out at the environs for seven centuries. The second biggest draw is the temples. Kamakura has dozens of Buddhist and Shinto edifices, ranging from the Hachimangu dedicated to the god of war, to Hase Kannon, the goddess of mercy. During festival days, like the samurai archery ceremony in mid-September to honor Hachiman, the town of 150,000 swells, and hundreds of foreigners are seen on the streets. For the most part, however, *gaijin* are still much more of a novelty than in Tokyo.

A couple of children followed Stark as he walked down the street to a *ryokan*. The owner of the Japanese-style inn was reluctant to take Stark. The place looked half empty, but he said they were full.

"I know not to wear my bathroom slippers outside the bathroom," Stark said. "And to clean myself before I get into the hot bath."

During his first months in Japan, Stark initially had felt awkward. He bashed his head on doorways, forgot to remove his shoes before stepping on tatami, didn't know the little politeness rituals that went with eating and drinking.

Gradually he'd learned, and could now slurp noodles or praise a meal with the ease of a native. Almost.

"Your Japanese is good," the innkeeper said, softening.

"I lived here several years ago," Stark said. "At *Shihan* Soto's dojo."

"Is that so. You are a student of his?"

"I was. Hopefully he will allow me to practice there again for a few weeks."

"So you haven't seen him recently?"

"No."

"I see."

"Has he changed much?"

"We all change," the innkeeper said cryptically. "I do have a room. It is not much, but a warrior doesn't need much comfort, right?"

"*Hai, so desu*," Stark responded. Stark pressed for more information about the *shihan*, but the innkeeper deflected each question the way a skilled boxer evades punches.

The room was small but pleasant, with a view of a tiny bonsai garden and a *koi*-filled pond at the rear of the inn. Stark studied the layout, looking for escape routes or ways that an attacker might enter. He headed out.

As he strolled familiar streets he remembered how disjointed he'd felt when he'd first come to the *shihan*. He'd just quit the CIA in a blaze of glory, under threats from his supervisor, after watching one of his assets get pushed in front of a train. Stark had unwittingly set up the meeting that turned out to be an execution. Later, he'd learned what he'd felt all along. The executed man was innocent. Stark had subsequently had a run-in with the assassin, who ended up puréed by a 747.

He was standing in front of the dojo. Like Poe's visitor to the House of Usher, Stark immediately knew something was wrong.

What? He couldn't quite pinpoint it. Emotional? Yes, but there was more. See what you see, not what you think you see. He went over the building in his mind's eye.

Unlike Kyoto, one of the few cities with more temples per capita, Kamakura had not been spared bombing during World War II. But the jujitsu headquarters had been entirely rebuilt, using traditional materials, in the exact same way as the original structure from 1650.

The property was immense by Japanese standards, with nearly an acre, much of it covered by bamboo groves and pine trees. The *shihan* had been approached many times to sell off a parcel, but he had refused. The woods were used for training, he would say, as if that explained it all.

There was a red *tori* gate and a stone path leading to the wood porch that ringed the building. It had a traditional sloped blue tile roof, with red beams projecting from the side. Many a tourist had mistaken it for a temple, and wandered up to the door despite a sign on the gate that said No Visitors in Japanese, English, and Chinese.

Then Stark figured it out. The dojo was run-down. Not run-down compared to normal standards. Compared to the way he last remembered it. The paint would need redoing in a short while. There were a few tufts of grass at the foot of the gate, dried leaves on the stones in front.

Students would spend at least an hour a day grooming the building. Woe unto anyone who didn't do their absolute best. Everyone swept, wiped, buffed, and polished under the *shihan*'s ruthless gaze. The first few weeks Stark had been convinced that he was trapped in a hellish Japanese boot camp. Later he'd realized it was part of the same process, giving up the ego.

He walked down the path feeling weak in the knees. At the door he inhaled and exhaled several times before rapping.

A muscular young man came to the door. He had a broad face, crew-cut black hair, and a scowl as fierce as a Nio temple guardian statue. He wore a white *gi*, the traditional uniform of the martial artist, and a black *hakama,* the skirtlike bottom which was reminiscent of samurai dress. He held up a sign which stated, This is private building. No vistor well come.

"I've come to see the *shihan,*" Stark said in Japanese. "Please tell him that Robert Stark humbly requests a few minutes of his valuable time."

"He doesn't meet anyone."

"Try."

"I will see what I can do." The man shut the door and

returned in less than a minute. Too quickly. "I'm sorry. He's too busy."

"I will wait here."

"He will be busy for the next few days."

Stark knelt in *seiza,* heels underneath his buttocks. "I have time."

The man reached down and tried to lift Stark up. Stark kept his center of gravity low, his weight underside, and was immovable. The man grabbed Stark's collar. Stark took his hand, bent the fingers back a bit, and brushed them away.

The guard grunted and tried grabbing with the other hand. Stark parried with a circular block. Each time the man reached, Stark would gently slap his hands away. The guard's movements grew quicker, harder, but still Stark knocked each one aside.

Stark felt a cramp in his leg. He was not used to sitting in *seiza* and defending himself. In the dojo they had practiced seated techniques for hours. Samurai had to be ready to defend themselves at the lengthy banquets. But Stark had found it impractical to keep up, and now he was paying the price. He was debating standing up, but the blows kept coming. Then one slipped in, rapping the side of his cheek. Stark used it to give him momentum out of the seated position. He rolled and came up ready, hands extended almost as if he were playing a guitar.

"I see you have studied with our master," the guard said.

"Yes, but obviously not as well as you have."

Before the guard could respond, the rice-paper door slid open. "Stark-*san,* is that you?"

Standing in the doorway was Fumiko. She was in her early sixties, Stark guessed, but she had the ageless beauty that many Oriental women possess. She was barely five feet, even with the wooden *geta* on. Stark knew that underneath that soft, pale skin were muscles that a weight lifter would envy.

She stepped delicately out on the porch. "Stark-*san?*" she repeated.

"*Hai,* Fumiko-*san.* It's been too long a time since my eyes have had the pleasure of viewing you." That was the standard polite way of responding. It seemed awkward in this case, since Fumiko was blind. But he knew that being polite was more important to her than anything else.

She answered with a properly polite response. He excused himself for being a nuisance. She apologized for not being prepared for him. He said it was a privilege for her to greet him. She said she was honored by his presence. Back and forth, two minutes of phrases which really said nothing, but showed they both knew proper courtesy. Stark was happy to recite them, since it was Fumiko who had taught him Japanese etiquette.

She was a masseuse who lived at the dojo. Many times when he thought he had strained or sprained something, a few digs and presses from her stubby fingers, and he was refreshed. Fumiko's hands and a steaming hot bath did as much for him as an orthopedic surgeon and a shot of cortisone.

"Please, honor this humble house," she said, waving him in. "Yamamura-*san,* excuse us, please."

The guard, Yamamura, glared at her, but of course she didn't notice.

Stark and Fumiko sat in a small room, a very small room, where she sometimes performed the tea ceremony. She had brewed bitter green tea for the two of them, and presented it in an abbreviated ceremony. Stark remembered much of the ritual—turning the cup three times, finishing it in one gulp. He sensed that she was testing him.

In the background he heard the muted but familiar sounds of the dojo. The thump of fists and feet into canvas bags or against *makiwara* posts; the crack and thwack of bamboo kendo swords; and the *kiai,* the explosive shout that focused the energy of an attack.

Stark briefly summarized what he had been doing in the fifteen years since he'd last been there. She insisted that nothing had changed in her life. He felt bad lying to her about why he was there, but it was more polite than to admit he was there to investigate the *shihan.*

"Do you think he would allow me to work out here for a week? To polish up my skills."

"I will speak with him."

"Can I see him?"

"Perhaps later. He . . ." There was a slight catch in her voice. From Fumiko, who was always the proper cheery Japanese lady, it was an amazing show of emotion. "He does not spend as much time in the dojo as he used to. He reads a great deal. But I will tell him you are here."

"Should I wait?"

"No. Come back tomorrow morning. And bring your *gi*."

# CHAPTER
# 6

The shipments of guns had been coming into Japan unde-
tected for several months. A Smith and Wesson revolver, a
few hundred dollars in the U.S., could sell for ten thousand
dollars in the country with some of the strictest gun control
laws in the world. The bullets would be three hundred dollars
each. To have a quality gun was a sign of great status in the
underworld, as much a symbol as the large American car, or
the tattoos on the *yakuza*'s back.

The Japanese Customs Bureau suspected the weapons
were coming in at Osaka Airport, but despite rigorous
searches of incoming cargo, no guns turned up. The head of
customs at Osaka had lost much face.

So his joy was considerable when a diligent inspector
noticed that a man picking up a cargo of dangerous snakes
imported from Southeast Asia was a known *yakuza*. It was
a cargo that no one was eager to examine very closely.

The snakes had the correct paperwork, indicating that
they were destined for a restaurant specializing in folk
medicine. Throughout the Orient, snakes, especially poisonous ones, were reported to have various prophylactic, aphrodisiac, and regenerative powers.

It took an hour for the herpetologist from the Osaka Zoo
to get to the airport, and two hours for him to safely package

the cobras and mambas in the carsize crate. The *yakuza* cargo handler complained continuously. Just before the final snake was loaded he made a dash for freedom. He was caught by two fleet-footed cops.

Inside the corrugated steel shipping container was a foot-locker with three dozen Colt revolvers and a thousand rounds of ammunition.

Subu Soto sat at one end of the room. Two rows of men were lined up perpendicular to him. The back room of one of the more celebrated restaurants in Osaka, its use had been "donated" by the restaurant owner. The restaurant was widely known for its *kappo,* the hearty, salty cuisine found in the area between Osaka and Kyoto.

All the men, including Soto, were bare to the waist. Their skin bore elegant designs of snarling dragons, coy geishas, samurai warriors locked in combat, stormy seas, and scowling sumo wrestlers.

In his three-piece gray suit, Soto looked like millions of other Japanese businessmen. But with his tattoos bared, there was no questioning his real career. He had spent more than a hundred hours under the needle, the old-style painful wooden needles. The tattooist had been a master and the dueling warriors on Soto's back seemed to battle as he moved his muscles.

Soto was built like a sake barrel. The squat, muscular former kendo champion still moved with grace. He spoke with the deep guttural bark of a samurai, using the abrupt form of Japanese. Now he was silent, watching and waiting.

From the far end, a small glass jar wrapped in a dark silk handkerchief was passed to him. He took it and gazed at the pockmarked man who had initially produced it. He removed the handkerchief, every gesture a slow and deliberate ritual.

Floating inside the jar was the tip of the pockmarked man's pinkie, from the first joint up, blood barely clotted.

Soto nodded. The gift was accepted. The pockmarked man was forgiven. He was the one responsible for the seized shipment of guns at the airport. He had performed *yubit-sume*, the *yakuza* act of contrition. To give up a pinkie in olden days was a major gesture since it had an important role in gripping the sword.

# SEIZE THE DRAGON

Soto was the *oya-bun,* the leader of the second largest *yakuza* group in Japan. Based in Osaka, they dominated gambling, loansharking, pornography, and prostitution in that major seaport. Soto also controlled amphetamine smuggling, the favorite illegal drug in the high-pressure culture.

Among his legitimate businesses, he owned two pistol ranges in Hawaii, where Japanese businessmen went to let off steam and thousands of rounds. Near the ranges he had a couple of *karaoke* bars, where men could sing along with the music, and brothels, where they could let off even more steam.

The *yubitsume* ritual completed, the men each reported on the profit and loss of their various enterprises. Soto grunted occasional questions and received rapid answers punctuated by bows.

Basically his organization was functioning smoothly. The worst problem, a police captain who had been too diligent in cracking down on prostitution, had been solved. The captain had been transferred to traffic duties. The *yakuza,* like organized crime groups throughout the world, had significant contacts at all levels of the police department.

Soto signaled that the business portion of their gathering was through. The groveling owner of the restaurant was summoned and waitresses brought in hot towels and sake.

By the time the food began to be served, many of the men were red-faced and shouting. But not Ryuji, his second-in-command. Ryuji, nearly as broadly built as Soto but ten years younger than the boss's fifty-five, leaned over so he could speak confidentially.

"This is not a matter which I wished to trouble you with before the meeting, and it is unnecessary for the others to hear," Ryuji began.

Was there the hint of an implied threat of revelation in Ryuji's words, Soto wondered.

"I always appreciate your discretion," Soto said.

"It is about your brother, Koiichi-*san,*" Ryuji said.

A waitress had entered with a fresh container of white rice. A *yakuza* tried to goose her, but she slipped away and he fell over. The others laughed and started singing a lewd ballad.

Ryuji had waited, studying Soto's face, but the *oya-bun*

was unreadable. There was only one way Ryuji could advance in the organization, and that was over Soto's body. Seeing his boss, sitting as strong and still as Mount Fuji-san, he had little hope.

"Your brother was visited by a *gaijin* this afternoon," Ryuji continued. "His name is Robert Stark. He studied with your brother many years ago."

"An old student visiting his teacher doesn't alarm me."

"I had one of our people check into Stark's background. He was CIA. Now he has a company which specializes in antiterrorism. He has many contacts with police."

"Didn't Koiichi chase him away?"

"He didn't see him."

"What about Yamamura?"

"That meddlesome old woman took this Stark in before Yamamura could teach him a lesson. She told Stark to come back tomorrow morning."

Soto reached down with his chopsticks and lifted a slippery mushroom from the *dashi* broth. He held the chopsticks to the side of his face, samurai-style. The old warriors had to be concerned that a rival would shove the sticks into their mouth. Looking over at Ryuji, Soto knew that his aide wouldn't have the courage to try. But good habits were important to keep. As well as traditions.

"Have our people at the dojo keep an eye on Stark. I trust my brother will handle things properly. If not, we can always take action."

Soto spotted a cube of lightly breaded tofu floating beneath a blanket of seaweed in the *dashi*. He snapped it up with his chopsticks. He savored the bean curd while his men launched into the final lewd verse.

# CHAPTER
# 7

Sunrise, quite naturally, is a very special moment in the Land of the Rising Sun. The word for it is *asahi,* and that turns up on beer labels, newspapers, stores, and dozens of brand names. The image itself is part of the Japanese flag.

Stark had come to appreciate the sunrise during his stay in Japan, and found a special spot to enjoy it. There was a ridge on the edge of town, surrounded by dense groves of willow, cedar, and pine. He would sit there, watching the sun come up over the Pacific, mentally preparing himself for what he knew would be a grueling workout.

He went back there that morning. Houses had encroached on his special spot. Where he had once sat was now someone's backyard, complete with satellite TV dish. Disgusted, he went into Kamakura and had a big bowl of noodles at a *soba* shop. The soup at least was as good as he remembered it.

With his *gi* and *hakama* packed into a gym bag, he walked down the street toward the dojo. It was seven A.M. and already the salarymen were swarming toward the JNR train station, gaining momentum for the ride into Tokyo.

The dojo looked different. Yesterday he had seen it colored by his memories. Today he saw it as a challenge.

Fumiko welcomed him with a smile. He heard the students

inside chatting before the day's work began. Once it started, with the accelerating beat of a *taiko* drum, there would be no idle talk. Every breath was precious as they were pushed to their limits, and a little beyond.

"Does the *shihan* have time for me to pay my respects this morning?" Stark asked.

"Maybe."

Stark knew that was the typical polite no. "Perhaps this afternoon would be better?"

"Maybe."

"Or after the workout?"

"We will see. You should get dressed, Stark-*san*. You do not want to be late, *ne?*"

"It's true. Thank you, Fumiko."

"For what?"

"For letting the *shihan* know how much it means to me to be able to return here and refresh my studies. I hope that I will have the pleasure of thanking him in person."

"I hope so too. You know where the dressing room is."

There were fourteen students in the training hall, all brown belt and above. To the Japanese, one wasn't a serious student until he had passed through yellow, green, blue, and brown to the black belt. All but three of the students were black belts. The black belts wore the black *hakamas*.

Measured Japanese style, it was a fifteen-tatami room, composed of fifteen of the three-by-six mats that make up the flooring in traditional buildings. That translated to a fifteen-by-twenty-four-foot room. Under the tatami were a few layers of thin padding, but a bad fall still could easily result in serious injury. The walls were clear pine, as was the narrow walkway around the mat. There were paintings of past generations of Sotos and distinguished martial artists who had worked out at the dojo. Jigoro Kano, the creator of judo, Doshin So, father of *Shorinji kempo,* Morihei Ueshiba, the founder of aikido, and Gichin Funakoshi, the karate pioneer, all punched, kicked, threw, and were thrown within the walls.

In one corner was the *tokonoma,* an alcove reserved for precious mementos. On display was a scroll with the saying, "He who knows others is wise, he who knows himself is enlightened," written in calligraphy. The bold pen strokes had been made by a Soto antecedent in the early eighteenth century. Underneath it was a chrysanthemum and pussy willow arrangement in a gray unglazed vase with brown streaks that dated back to the 1600s.

Dressed in his *hakama,* Stark went to the room, bowed toward the painting of Koiichi Soto's grandfather—the founder of the style they wre studying—and then toward the senior students as he stepped onto the mat.

Stark folded his skirt under him and sat *seiza* in line with the other students. Only three others held higher ranks, he discovered as he was assigned a position commensurate with his rating.

The senior student was the guard who had met him at the door. Two top-ranked students would be allowed the privilege of living at the dojo and acting as the *shihan*'s servants. In return they would dominate the other students, make sure the chores were done, and maybe garner a few advanced tidbits if the old man felt willing. The rest of the students would share apartments in town. Many were on leave from their offices. Some held jobs during the day and could work out only at night and on weekends.

As the drumbeats ended and the meditation began, Stark wondered why Koiichi Soto hadn't at least given him a brief greeting. Stark felt like the prodigal son coming home and having the welcome mat pulled out from underneath him.

With half-open eyes Stark focused on the niche with the scroll. His thoughts skipped around—monkey mind. He pondered the sense of timelessness, of permanence, and impermanence, of belonging, that Soto must have.

After fifteen minutes of meditation the students untangled their legs and waded into a half hour of rigorous calisthenics and stretching. The two-hour workout began.

It was harder than Stark remembered, but then again, he'd been much younger. The system was based on an *atemi* strike—a blow to a nerve center, followed by a joint lock— usually on the wrist or elbow, ending with a throw. Optional techniques included choking, strangling, or breaking the limb of the downed person.

The origins of jujitsu could be traced back to A.D. 500 and the Shaolin Temple in China. While the punching-kicking styles of kung fu became better known, monks at the same time were developing *chin na,* the art of seizing and attacking nerve centers.

By A.D. 800, a jujitsu antecedent was written about in the *Nihon Shoki,* the Chronicles of Japan. Starting around 1400, interest in jujitsu entered its golden era, with a number of schools developing. Over the next 450 years, hundreds of different schools and systems would develop. Each had their most secret, advanced techniques, methods which would be passed down from founder to his most promising student.

As Stark worked out he felt himself a part of an ancient tradition. He had been paired with one of the brown belts by the senior student/guard Yamamura. The pairing with a much lower belt was an insult. Stark merely smiled and thanked Yamamura for his kindness.

Stark and his partner practiced the techniques over and over. The brown belt was in his early twenties, and what he lacked in technique he made up in energy. He threw Stark with gusto.

Although Stark made a point out of working out two hours a day, three times a week, the workout in the dojo was more demanding than anything he put himself through. Particularly since Yamamura paid special attention to him. During demonstrations the senior student illustrated techniques by vigorously bouncing Stark off the mat.

Stark took each mauling with good grace, bowing to Yamamura afterward and thanking him. Yamamura deserved respect for his proficiency. He had the ideal balance of speed, strength, and, most important, technique. His punches and kicks were so fast as to be almost invisible. His arm locks were as immobilizing as a straitjacket. His black *hakama* swirled through the air as he gracefully dumped his opponent on the mat. Stark wondered jealously if Yamamura had been chosen by the *shihan* to receive the most advanced secrets of the art.

Lunch was a light meal of noodles in a miso broth, with a few bits of chicken and seaweed floating in it. Then an hour was spent cleaning the dojo and its environs. Stark was given a short brush and sent to the toilet.

Yamamura came in after a few minutes and criticized his work. Stark smiled, apologized, and resumed scrubbing.

Stark wished he knew if this physical and mental abuse

was under the *shihan*'s direction. If so, was it designed as a test or a way to get rid of Stark? Whatever the purpose, the result was the same. Stark felt like he'd been the tatami mat of a family of sumo wrestlers.

The afternoon session got under way with more meditation, then exercises, then another workout. There was *kata*, the pure-form exercises that looked like a dance. Stark did poorly, since no one had critiqued his form in more than a dozen years.

But in the free-style bouts, where one person acted as an attacker and the other could defend with any technique he wanted, Stark excelled. There were admiring ahhs from the crowd as Stark demonstrated some of his own techniques for disarming a suspect.

Before the drum announcing the close of the workout was sounded, there would be a reading from a traditional Japanese work. *The Book of Five Rings* by legendary swordsman Miyamoto Musashi or the letters of the Zen monk Takuan were favored, but sometimes works like "The Tale of the 47 Ronin" would be read.

Japanese doesn't have many curses—the worst is calling someone a stupid fool—but various levels of politeness modifiers can be used to insult. Yamamura used a super polite form, which was in itself a type of insult. He invited Stark to give the reading. Stark tried to politely decline. Although his spoken Japanese was good, his reading Japanese was never much better than poor.

Yamamura insisted that he come up. Stark was given a copy of Takuan's book. He read, stumbling and struggling. Yamamura laughed rudely and a few others joined in.

Then they meditated again, and the drum sounded.

Was the hostility toward him planned or just Japanese xenophobia? Was it Yamamura's grudge, or was the *shihan* behind it?

Stark's first day at the dojo was over. He was not really closer to the *shihan* than he had been in New York, and he felt like hell.

Back at his room at the *ryokan,* he found that someone had searched his bag. Good tradecraft demanded placing objects in a specific order in the bag in order to detect minute alterations. Someone had gone through the bag carefully. There was nothing in there, however, to give away his mission. Stark also checked if he'd been "flaked," had contraband placed inside. But there didn't appear to be anything.

He stripped, showered, and eased himself into a hot tub the size of a fifty-five-gallon drum, and about as comfortable for his big Western body. He limped out of the bathroom thinking that only a massage from Fumiko could ease his misery.

As if she had read his mind, there was a knock at the door. Fumiko asked for permission to enter.

Stark wrapped a towel around himself and slid the door open, beaming. "You would do this humble room an honor by your entering, but won't the innkeeper be mad if I have a beautiful woman alone with me in my room?"

She answered by covering her mouth and giggling like a coquettish teenager.

She directed him to lie on the *futon* and her hands went to work. He groaned involuntarily as she loosened tightened muscles and brought increased circulation to various abused joints. She removed the towel and kneaded high up by his groin. The first few times she'd worked on him, Stark had been embarrassed, especially after he'd gotten a raging hard-on. She hadn't commented, although it accidentally brushed against her several times. After that he'd decided she was like a doctor or nurse, and being embarrassed in front of her was like being ashamed of your carburetor in front of a mechanic.

He alternated between grunting in pain and murmuring thank-yous.

He didn't know when he had fallen asleep, but he woke up naked, with the rising sun coming in through the window. What did Fumiko's visit mean? She wouldn't have come without the *shihan*'s permission. On the one hand, the *shihan* seemed to be driving him away. With the other, he was beckoning.

Stark wasn't as stiff as he expected he'd be. His skin tingled. Fumiko had left a bottle of herbal medicine and a bottle of aspirin on his bedside. There was a note saying, "Please drink," with the dosage for the herbal medicine.

The label showed that it had been brewed by the *shihan*. At advanced levels of the martial arts, the healing arts are emphasized as part of the *okuden*, the restricted secrets. The *shihan* had his own batch of potions, tinctures, and salves. Maybe he'll poison me, Stark mused. My paranoia is getting out of control.

He decided to trust the old man and took a gulp of the herbal medicine. It tasted like old track shoes mixed with rubbing alcohol. Stark nearly gagged. He also took the aspirin.

By the time he reached the dojo, he hardly felt any aches and pains.

The Korean soap girl's breasts had been silicon-bolstered to the size of cantaloupes. She still had too much meat around the hips and squat legs, but her chest—coupled with her enthusiasm—made her the most popular girl at the Kobe Soapland.

They had been called Turkish baths until complaints by the Turkish government led to the name change. In the U.S. they'd be called massage parlors. The girls would lather their naked bodies, then wash the customer's body with friction from their own. What followed depended on the size of the tip.

Subu Soto was indifferent to the soap girl's attentions. His two bodyguards sat impassively off to one side, wondering if they would get a shot at her or one of the dozen other women who worked in the Soapland. But the *oya-bun* seemed distracted, almost unaware that they were there.

The soap girl made flattering remarks as she slithered over Soto—about the size of his muscles, the beauty of his tattoos, his rugged good looks. But Soto remained limp where it mattered most. The girl began to worry. He had been there before and always performed like a beast. If she failed to stimulate the man who controlled the Soapland, she had little hope for her future. She worked frenziedly.

What was troubling Soto was Robert Stark. He had survived one week at the dojo. Subu Soto had sent word to his brother, the *shihan*, to get rid of Stark. Yet the *shihan* hadn't. It was the first sign of disobedience by his older brother. He would have to be taught a lesson.

Subu signaled one of his bodyguards who, absorbed in the soap girl's movements, didn't notice the summons. Then Subu barked, and the bodyguard scurried over. The soap girl retreated, fearful of what she might hear.

"You know where the dojo is in Kamakura?" Soto asked the bodyguard.

"You were kind enough to allow me to train there, *oya-bun*," the bodyguard replied.

"Yes, yes. I want you to go there tonight. Speak to Yamamura. Tell him that if the *gaijin* is not out of there in a couple of days, he is to have an accident."

"How severe an accident?" the bodyguard asked.

"A fatal accident."

The bodyguard nodded, and hurried out.

Soto beckoned the soap girl over. He was as hard as a samurai sword. He took her from the rear, slamming in deep as he squeezed the flesh at her midsection. She made genuine yelps of pain and simulated yelps of pleasure. Her main emotion was relief.

The second bodyguard hoped that with the *oya-bun* in a good mood, he'd get sloppy seconds.

The bottle of herbal medicine was empty, and Stark no longer needed it. That was typical of the *shihan*. Just enough. No waste. Stark wondered what was in the brew. Some sort of amphetamine to get him through the sixteen-hour training days? A dollop of painkiller? A muscle relaxant? Funny if it was just a placebo, but Stark wouldn't put that past the old man. It would just show how powerful the mind was. The focused mind can pierce through stone.

Most of the Zen sayings, aphorisms, and anecdotes Stark had picked up from reading. The *shihan* wasn't big on talk. The word is not the reality. Saying you were a good person was very different from being a good person.

During his eight long days at the dojo Stark had polished his techniques but learned little about what was going on.

The first solid clue that something was amiss had come during a cleanup period.

Stark had his usual assignment—the bathroom. He sneaked out the bathroom window, dizzy from the stench.

As he leaned against the side of the building, he smelled cigarette smoke.

That was absolutely forbidden, one of the *shihan*'s unbreakable rules. Cigarette smoke was as much a part of the Japanese landscape as *torii* gates, but the *shihan* had known long before the U.S. surgeon general that it was as good for the body as car accidents. Smokers would be the model in a lecture on neck holds. The senior student would choke out the smoker in a variety of ways. After a while the smoker would begin throwing up.

But there were two of the black belts smoking in a bamboo grove. Yamamura was with them.

The following day Stark kept a particular eye on the two smokers. They always worked out together. They had a sneery arrogance toward the rest of the students. Their techniques were not as smooth as the other black belts.

Stark arranged to shower at the same time as one of the men. It confirmed his suspicion, why the black belt always wore a white T-shirt. From shoulders to groin he was a mass of tattoos. Blue and green and red and yellow swirled on his back, a finely detailed portrayal of the famous Battle of Wrestlers and Firemen at Shimmei Shrine. It could mean he just liked getting tattooed, but more likely that he was a *yakuza*.

Why would the *shihan*, who made no secret of his contempt for the secret crime society, admit a cigarette-smoking *yakuza*?

It was at the end of the tenth day that the *shihan* first made his appearance. Stark tried not to show his shock.

# CHAPTER
# 8

When Stark had last seen Koiichi Soto, the *shihan* had been in his early fifties. The grandson of the founder, he had been raised in the martial tradition. As an honor to his family, he was actually above any sort of rank. Nevertheless, he had gone out and earned higher level black belts in *kyudo* (archery), *bojutsu* (staff-fighting), *kenjutsu* (sword fighting), and *iaido* (drawing and striking with the sword in one smooth motion). He was a skilled calligrapher, his haiku had been published and sold well, and he was a Zen master. All in all, he was the prototypical well-rounded Japanese of the seventeenth century.

No longer allowed to ride his horse through the streets of Kamakura, he went few places he couldn't walk. He made as little use of twentieth-century conveniences as he could. His major concessions were a microwave oven and a television set with VCR. The TV was for watching the afternoon sumo matches and the samurai movies.

Koiichi had been timeless, and while Stark had expected some aging, he wouldn't have been surprised if the *shihan* didn't look any different from when Stark had left.

Instead, the man who took tiny shuffling steps out onto the mat looked like an embalmed corpse. He had no more than ninety pounds on his five-foot frame. His skin was sallow, his eyes rheumy, and there was a twitch in his hand. He leaned heavily on his cane.

Stark stared, not really believing it was the *shihan*. Everyone bowed low, and Stark followed suit.

"Please get up," the *shihan* said. There was no mistaking the voice, amazingly deep for someone so small. It came from the years of breath training. His barked instructions had been like a riding crop across the flanks of a thoroughbred. Now the powerful voice coming from the sickly body was a grotesque parody.

They sat facing him. Stark caught Yamamura watching the old man, a peculiar look on his face. Wariness? Contempt? Warning?

"Instead of the usual reading, today I will tell a story," Koiichi Soto said. "It is a story about a *daimyo* a long, long time ago. This *daimyo* was a good ruler, or tried to be. He had many fine warriors, much land, a beautiful wife. He had strong sons, healthy daughters, and loyal peasants. The crops grew, the sun shone on them, and there was contentment in the land. But this *daimyo* had a younger brother, a jealous younger brother. Although the *daimyo* tried to help his brother, giving him generous amounts of land, fine horses, and skilled samurai, still the brother nursed his hatred.

"The *daimyo* heard one day that the Mongols would be invading an area of his kingdom. It was where his brother's castle was. The *daimyo* sent word to his brother and an escort to take the brother's family to safety."

The old man paused and breathed deeply several times. The intensity with which he told the tale held his audience spellbound. "But this *daimyo* had been betrayed by a *ninja* spy. Instead of invading by the brother's castle, the enemy struck where the families of the *daimyo* and his brother had been sent. Both families died horrible deaths.

"The brother's hatred grew more foul. He allied himself with criminal elements and prospered by committing vile deeds. The *daimyo*, racked with guilt, was unable to act manly."

Yamamura cleared his throat. The old man glanced at him and continued. "What the people didn't know was that the brother had learned of a secret from the *daimyo*'s past. The *daimyo,* when a young man, had been a *ninja,* and committed treachery against the shogun. The guilt and the blackmail were too much for the *daimyo* to bear. He contemplated seppuku but his responsibility to his subjects didn't allow suicide.

"One day he learned that not all of his sons had been killed by the barbarians. One had survived. He had grown up under adversity, grown up big and strong. He was a skilled fighter. He returned to his father.

"But his father was too ashamed to tell him what was wrong. He waited for the young man to realize. When at last the young man did, the *daimyo* died happily. The son killed his uncle, and went on to become a wise and prosperous *daimyo.*"

There was a long silence. Stark at first wondered if it was a Japanese version of a Shakespearean tale, the way director Akira Kurosawa had adapted *King Lear* and *Macbeth* into distinctly Japanese stories.

Then the message behind the *shihan*'s words struck him like the blow from a Zen master's stick.

The old man stood on creaky legs. Everyone bowed again. He tottered off the mat.

He had not once looked at Stark.

The next day Stark plunged into the workout with renewed vigor. Every technique seemed to flow, his feet barely touching the ground. When he pivoted, it was with the force of a whirlwind, and no one could withstand it.

During the cleanup assignment Yamamura switched him from the toilet to raking leaves in one of the groves. After his nine days in the toilet, the woodsy smell was almost too wonderful to bear. Even the raking went well, the occasional breeze blowing the leaves into piles.

The afternoon workout went superbly. Stark felt as if he were young and in love. Nothing could go wrong.

For the final part of the workout, Yamamura drafted Stark, once again, to demonstrate techniques. But Yamamura was much slower, gentler, using only the necessary amount of force. It was as if the *shihan*'s appearance had been the storm that washed away the tension.

The final technique was a counter against a straight right jab. They walked through it first at half speed. As Stark threw the right-hand punch, Yamamura ducked to his right and brushed it aside with his left. He simulated an elbow strike to the abdomen, an open palm to the chin, twisted Stark's arm in an armlock, then threw him by kicking out a leg.

Stark faced Yamamura. Yamamura bobbed his head, signaling he was ready to repeat the technique at full speed.

Stark threw the punch. Yamamura blocked. Instead of a gentle tap, he slammed his elbow into Stark's midsection with full strength. Stark felt the air rush out, the pain signals jamming his circuits. The blow doubled him forward.

Anticipating the open palm, which could be a neck break at full speed, Stark managed to twist his face at the last minute, the blow merely grazing his cheek.

But Yamamura had his arm. Stark felt it strain, on the verge of dislocation. He knew the upcoming throw would result in at least shoulder separation, and possible broken bones. He moved into a wide, low stance so Yamamura couldn't knock him down.

Yamamura pivoted, a different move, and Stark was across the senior student's back, his feet in the air. An arm snaked around his head, the setup for a neck break. No way to stop it. By allowing Yamamura to get in for the first blow, Stark had been doomed from the start.

Then he was looking up at the ceiling of the dojo. Gasping for air, in agony, helpless. Yamamura braced himself, preparing for the squeeze that would kill Stark.

Suddenly Yamamura yelped and fell. Stark rolled off him. Hunched, struggling for breath, but ready.

The old man's cane was entwined in Yamamura's legs. The *shihan* had thrown it and caught the senior student across pressure points at the back of the knees.

The other students were hushed. The attack on Stark and the *shihan*'s response had been so quick that no one had had a chance to react.

Yamamura stood, warily eyeing Stark. Stark was grateful for the delay. Every second meant more air in his lungs. He was dizzy with pain. The room was shaking. An earthquake? No one else was reacting to it.

"No more!" the *shihan* commanded. Everyone jumped from the power of his voice.

"I'm sorry," Yamamura said, apologizing to the *shihan*. "I was confused over the technique. I acted hastily." He bowed low.

"You are no longer my student," the *shihan* said. "Get out."

Yamamura glared at Stark and marched from the room. The *shihan* looked over at the two sneery black belts. They rose and exited too.

Then the quake got stronger and Stark fell to the mat.

He awoke in a room he had never been in before. It was dark, nearly bare, with a few feminine touches. A comb on a black lacquer dresser, a flower arrangement more delicate than the one in the dojo.

His shoulder throbbed. There was a painful ache with each breath.

"You are feeling better, Stark-*san?*" Fumiko asked.

"Uhhhhhh. I guess so."

"You have a broken rib, but it did not pierce the lung," Fumiko said. "I put your shoulder back the way it was meant to be. There are no tears in the muscle, but it will be sore."

"Where's the *shihan?*"

"In his room."

"How did he know what was happening to me?"

"I suppose his little secret no longer matters," she said. "He has a peephole. He watched you the whole time you were here. He was very pleased with your progress."

"I didn't do so well against Yamamura."

"He regards that as his fault. In the dojo you must trust your seniors. You put yourself in their hands. They must not abuse that trust."

Stark sat up, a bit woozy.

"The *shihan* is meditating now. He asked that we come in to see him in ten minutes. Can you do *hara* breathing?"

Stark inhaled deeply. The pain was no worse than with the shallow breaths. He exhaled slowly, leaning forward a few degrees. He repeated the exercise. Fumiko sat silently.

"It is time," she finally said. As they moved down the hall on bare feet, she said, "The *shihan* has sent the other students home. He wanted only you to see him."

There was a catch in her tone that put Stark on the alert.

66

His unease increased as she reached for the sliding door to the *shihan*'s room. She would never do that without announcing herself. And there was the foul smell of blood.

She slid open the door.

The *shihan* was sitting on a white rug, his steaming entrails spread out before him. His long sword was in a stand next to the door.

Stark gasped and grasped the doorframe. He accidentally put his hand through the screen paper.

"You must act as his second," Fumiko said calmly. She had withdrawn to another world. "Then I will explain."

"Please," the old man said in a soft voice.

Stark took the sword in his hand, unsheathing it in one smooth movement. He stepped forward.

"I can't," Stark said.

"Then he will die slowly," Fumiko said.

Stark looked down. Could the old man be saved? Was there a hospital nearby? Thoughts jumbled over each other. Then for a reason he could not understand he raised the sword above his head. He was a puppet, barely in control of his own muscles. He emitted a loud scream and brought the blade down between the third and the fourth vertebrae.

A perfect slice. The head dropped from the body as if it had been guillotined.

"Ohhhhhhhhh," Stark said, struggling to keep his knees from buckling and his stomach from heaving.

Fumiko took out a cloth and wrapped the head. Before the drapery hid the face, Stark saw his teacher's expression. He was smiling. How long after the head was severed did it live?

She placed the head next to the body and sheathed the short, bloody dagger the *shihan* had used to disembowel himself.

"Come with me," Fumiko said, and she padded out of the room.

He followed her to the main room. It was eerie, deserted.

"You performed the cut well," Fumiko said. "My husband would be proud of you."

"Your husband?"

"We have been married for thirty years."

Stark's system cried out for rest from the bombardment it was taking. Physical abuse. Emotional shock.

"You understand the story he told the class?" she asked.

"Yes."

"He could not come right out and tell you. It would have been improper to burden you like that," she said. "His brother had sworn him to secrecy. An oath on their parents' grave. It could not be violated, no matter how grievous the abuse. There are no such constraints now. Do you have any questions?"

Stark couldn't speak.

"I will explain," she said. "During the Pacific War, your World War Two, Koiichi-*san*, like other patriotic young men, volunteered. They knew of his skills. He served as a teacher in hand-to-hand combat, using vital points for maximum pain. He became suspicious after a while. He thought he was training elite troops. Actually, they were Kempei Tai. Stark-*san*, Stark-*san*?"

"Yes. I hear you," Stark said, swaying. "Kempai Tai. The internal military police. The Japanese gestapo."

She nodded. "He was training the torturers. He had a breakdown, believing that he could hear the screams of the victims."

Stark felt like he was drowning, gasping for air. "I never knew."

"No one did," she said. "At that time the Allies were bombing Tokyo on a regular basis. The fire storms killed hundreds of thousands of people. Koiichi-*san* was warned that it would get worse. He arranged for his family, and the family of this brother, to go where he thought it was safe. He sent them to a farm on the outskirts of Nagasaki."

"Oh, no."

"Yes. It is unimportant, but that is how I met him. I lived near Nagasaki. I was blinded when I looked at the bomb. There are some things best not seen," she said. Her voice had begun to quiver. She hesitated, and composed herself. "Koiichi's brother Subu was always in trouble as a youngster. But the death of their family decided his path. During the years after the war he became a *yakuza* active in the black market. He didn't have anything to do with Koiichi despite Koiichi's attempt at reconciliation.

"Somehow a few years ago he found out about Koiichi's role during the war. Subu called him 'the war criminal.' He used it the way a robber would a knife. Koiichi refused to defend himself. Subu used the *shihan*'s good name to get introductions. He sent hoodlums here with orders that they be given a black belt after little training.

"Koiichi had given up the will to live," she said. "Until you came back. You helped him die a warrior's death. Both he and I will be forever grateful to you." She bowed low, her head touching the mat.

"Please, get up. I owe you both too much to ever repay it," Stark said.

She faced him. There was a tear in her eye. She struggled to keep it from trickling down, but failed. She gave a quick wipe.

"I must keep this floor cleaner. Dust in my eye," she said, blinking her sightless eyes. "My husband always regarded you as special. He had planned to pass on the *okuden* to you if you had stayed. He deeply regretted it when you left, although he understood."

Another shock. Stark never really thought he had been considered worthy of learning the advanced secrets.

A long silence.

"You should rest for a few days," she said. "But I am afraid you cannot stay here. The police will investigate. They might detain you. Many are sympathetic to the *yakuza*."

"I understand."

She produced a piece of paper from the folds of her kimono. "Koiichi wrote out what he knew, what he thought might help you. His brother is involved with two bad men in a conspiracy. I am just a simple woman, and it is best if you read his words yourself."

Stark patted her cheek. He held her chin in his hand. It was as intimate as he had ever gotten with this woman, who had handled every part of his body.

"You are many things, Fumiko, but a simple woman is not one of them."

A tear was welling up in her other eye. She brushed it away.

"Dust, dust, dust," she said.

"Will you be okay?" Stark asked. "Will the police bother you?"

"No. I have many friends. So did the *shihan*. He trained many of the policemen. The better ones. You must go. Try to find someplace to rest for a few days. Then you can pursue Subu and his partners."

"You have my word on it."

"Thank you. One last matter. The *shihan* wanted you to have the sword. It has been in the Soto family for more than seven hundred years. It is a Norimune blade, made in Bizen province in 1284."

"I can't accept such a gift."

"It would hurt me if you did not. However, the police will no doubt confiscate it initially. When their investigation into the seppuku is concluded, I hope you will come back to retrieve it."

"I'll come back. Thank you," Stark said, bowing low.

"We thank you," she said. "Please go. All this talk has stirred up dust here. I must clean before the police arrive."

He left her sitting in the middle of the dojo floor, the faces of the great martial artists of the past looking down on her.

# PART II
## *Machiavelli*

# CHAPTER
# 9

Stark lay back on the bed in the hotel in Kowloon and read the *shihan*'s note. He had waited until he reached Hong Kong so he could be less emotional, and more analytical. It was the kind of act of discipline the *shihan* would have appreciated.

I have acted foolishly, and regret that I have sullied my family name. A man may die but his name lives forever. For years I hoped the Soto name would remain an honorable one. Between my foolishness, and my brother's malevolence, I fear this is not to be.

I was forced to travel to Hong Kong several times to meet with people who knew of me and my reputation. I used that reputation to help my brother in his plan. He has not told me what his plan is, or who his partners are. I know them only by their aliases. There is an American gangster called Machiavelli, and a Chinese gangster called Sun Tzu. My brother chose the name Musashi as his own.

We met with a petty gangster named Weng Cheng on the Star ferry. I was sent away when they talked, like an errant child. My brother has a talent for humiliation. I regret that I was weak and allowed it.

I met with Wu Wu, who produces kung fu movies at his studio in the New Territories. I made arrangements for rental of the stage. The entire deal was to be kept secret and no one was to see what was to be filmed. I myself do not know what it was. The filming took place last week.

One of my brother's accomplices was named Louie. He was active in the clothing industry but also had some sort of vice business.

The *shihan*'s letter didn't make it clear whether Louie was an Anglo surname or a Chinese family name.

I wish I could tell you more. I wish for many things, but all unwise old men do. Most of all, I wish I had had a son like you to carry on the Soto name, and return it to honor. But the radiation that stole my wife's sight took her chance at giving me an heir. I thank you for helping me.

The vision of the *shihan*'s decapitation flashed into Stark's mind like an unwanted photo shoved in front of his face. What had compelled him to swing, guided his hand in that deadly blow?

Stark had to keep moving or the horrible images would numb him. It was time to nail down his Hong Kong cover story. He called the Zippy Toy plant, and made an appointment to visit late that afternoon.

Shaved, showered, and full of aspirin, he prepared his bags so that he could tell if anyone went through them. He checked entrances and exits, and counted the number of doors to a fire stair. The precaution had twice saved his life in smoky corridors.

He rode the Star ferry, still one of the best ways to get an impressive view of the harbor. He hadn't been in Hong Kong in several years. Using landfill, the city had pushed farther into the channel. The famed Peninsula Hotel used to front on the harbor; now it was a block in from it.

The air coming off the harbor was relatively cool. A lucky break. The climate of Hong Kong, like most of Southeast

Asia, varied from humid to unbearable, from hot to staggering, from unpleasant to rotten.

There were no signs of the riots. The broken glass had been replaced, the burnt cars removed, the loiterers and troublemakers hustled away. It was back to business as usual.

He meandered down crowded side streets, where street merchants offered dazzling assortments of clothing, herbal medicines, electronic gadgets, and foodstuffs. Markets were crowded with livestock, a few hours away from a one-way trip down someone's gullet. Their grunts and squeals and squawks provided a counterpoint to the traffic noise.

He visited a few temples, so different from their solemn religious counterparts in the west. The temples were crowded, noisy, entertaining. Bright red beams with gilt trim. Clouds of incense swirled. Worshippers clapped to signal the gods and scare off demons. Beggars lined the steps, thrusting forth withered limbs, scarred faces, tattered clothes. Children with birth defects did particularly well. Was it true that parents mutilated their young to guarantee them a prosperous trade?

He traveled along sloping Hollywood Road, past funeral shops selling everything from hell money (to be burned for an affluent afterlife), to finery for corpses. Farther on were antique shops, with the paint barely dry on their wares.

In this capital of capitalism, each shopkeeper had a hustler litany down pat. "You my first customer of the day," they would claim to a slow-moving browser. "Good luck to me if you buy. Name a price." Moneychangers claimed deals better than the fixed rate. Jewelers sold genuine "Rollex," "Selko," and "Omiga" watches at prices that were too good to be true.

Past the Man Mo Temple, down Ladder Street, along Queen's Road West to Wing Sing, and into the bustling commercial area of downtown Hong Kong Central. The mixture of British and Chinese names gave a sense of the confused identity of the colony.

Part of the reason for Stark's meandering stroll was to get a sense of the city. There were indescribable impressions that could sometimes help, like the atmosphere in a dying Pennsylvania coal town, or in frenzied Tokyo, or sun- and psycho-rich Los Angeles. He would be dealing with people who lived in this environment, and it would help to understand them.

That was the instinctual eastern reason for his tour. His pragmatic western reason was to check for tails. Counter-surveillance was hard in a foreign city, especially with a different race. The facial features an Occidental looked for weren't what an Oriental looked for. To both sides, the foreigners looked alike.

After a two-hour tour which included a stop to eat in a restaurant, several trips into temples, where he slipped out the side door, and a couple of jaunts down alleyways, he was confident he wasn't being followed.

It was like getting a baseline chest X ray. Now if a spot showed up, he'd know that surgery was necessary.

He had an hour to kill before he was due at the Zippy factory in the Mong Kok section of Hong Kong. He decided to stop at McGregor's, a pub near the foot of the tramway to The Peak, a few blocks from both the American embassy and the governor's residence. There were numerous government offices not more than a couple of blocks away, from the general post office, to City Hall, to the consulates or trade commissions of a dozen countries.

McGregor's was a spy bar as well-known throughout Southeast Asia as Lucy's Tiger Den on Pat Pong Road in Bangkok, or the Blue Lake on Tu Do Street in Saigon. An innocent might wander in off the street, but for the most part the drinkers were spooks or ex-spooks. There were only a few rules in McGregor's: no weapons; no tape recorders; no discussions about politics. McGregor, a former British SAS captain who acted as his own bouncer, could spot the bulge of a gun or recorder even in the dim light, and his ejections for violations were forceful.

The bar itself had no clues that it was a spy watering hole. No cute jokes about "hang cloak and dagger here" or bathrooms labeled "Mata Haris" or "James Bonds." Just a solid pub with dark heavy wood paneling, a dartboard on one wall, a wide selection of liquors, and a long, cigarette-burn-pocked bar. And blessed air-conditioning turned up all the way.

# SEIZE THE DRAGON

There were five customers, one sitting alone at the bar itself, the other four paired up in booths. Two in the booths were arguing about a soccer match. The other two were whispering to each other. The loner at the bar was swaying on his stool, a drink away from oblivion.

McGregor nodded to Stark as if he'd never seen him before. Perhaps he remembered Stark, perhaps he didn't. It was one of McGregor's rules to never recognize a face. The man he knew as Mr. Jones today would quite likely be Mr. Smith tomorrow. So there wasn't much point in it.

"What'll you have?" he asked amiably.

"You still make the driest martini east of the Sahara?"

McGregor grinned. It was one of the drinks he prided himself on and the phrase was like a password for old-timers. "That I do, laddie."

McGregor delivered the drink. Stark made it clear he didn't mind company, and McGregor leaned his log-size forearms on the bar. The Scotsman had curly red hair, fair skin, and a face that conveyed that only the suicidal would want to make trouble in his bar.

McGregor offered his opinion about different nationalities and how nobody seemed to drink their own country's liquor anymore.

"Russians come in, they order Jack Daniel's. Brits ask for Kirin. Australians ask for a Stoli. Japanese want cognac."

"What about Americans?"

"Gin and tonics mostly."

"I'll try that next time."

McGregor never asked questions of his customers, like where are you from, how long are you here. He found cover stories boring, and he didn't expect to hear the truth.

"I used to stop by here in the late sixties, early seventies," Stark said.

"Vietnam War. It was hopping then. Used to toss a couple of Green Berets a night into the street. Thinking they could break this place up like some Saigon dive." McGregor made a "tsk-tsk" sound. "Those were the days."

"Quieter now?"

McGregor noded.

"Anyone still hang around from those days?"

McGregor shrugged. "Maybe. I can't really recall."

With most barkeeps, that would be a hint for a bribe. With McGregor it was discretion.

Stark took out his card and wrote his hotel room number on it. "If there's a friendly around who'd like to reminisce, have him give me a jangle."

McGregor studied the card, then tucked it into his apron pocket. "That I'll do."

Stark sipped the martini. "I'll be puckering for a week after this," Stark said.

"Those were the days," McGregor said, lost in his memories.

# CHAPTER
# 10

The Zippy Toy plant in congested Mong Kok, at the north end of Kowloon, was no worse than other Hong Kong factories. Still, it was a health inspector's nightmare. The heavy stench of solvents and plastics hung in the air, burning eyes and making noses run. The noise level was slightly less than underneath a jet engine. Huge sheets of plastic were cut and fed into vacuform presses. After a monstrous hiss, they squeezed together, and twenty Cinderella masks were dimpled in the plastic. Metal bars swung back and forth, pressing and processing, without a safety rail in sight.

"How long has it been since the last injury, Mr. Randall?" Stark shouted to be heard above the din.

"We don't keep track," his guide said, as if that were a stupid question. Clean-cut, middle-aged Milton Randall had the barest hint of a Boston accent, and the arrogant super-ciliousness of a Boston brahmin. "I don't see how that is relevant to your threat assessment inquiry."

After an hour they ended up in Randall's office. It was furnished in ultramodern furniture that was dazzling to the eye and impossible for anyone but a contortionist to enjoy. Hard, clean lines of gleaming chrome, glass, and plastic. Randall's own chair was a comfortable-looking leather wing-back.

The men had clashed repeatedly during the tour, with Randall objecting to numerous questions. Toward the latter part, however, he had realized that Stark would be reporting directly to owner Stu Zanville, and he tried to make peace.

"May I offer you a drink?" Randall asked.

"No, thank you," Stark said. "I've got to be going."

"Don't I get any input into your report?"

"After Stu sees it, I'm sure you'll talk."

"What does that mean?"

"It means this place is a disaster waiting to happen."

"Mr. Stark," Randall said measuredly. "Many times when people come here from America they just don't understand. This is a cost-conscious industry. The American labor force just doesn't know how to give an honest day's work for an honest day's pay. We have shops in Hong Kong to save money, and the people are grateful to work. So maybe we don't have an exercise room or private sauna. They make more than they would in many other places."

"How many fire extinguishers do you have here?"

"Uhm, I know we had some around."

"I saw one. I checked the date. It hasn't been inspected since 1982. Of course life is cheap. But what about all that valuable equipment out there?"

Randall took him seriously. "Don't worry. It's insured."

"When the insurance company sees my report, you won't even be considered for an assigned risk pool."

"You're not going to put that in, are you?"

"That, as well as blocked fire exits, defunct ducts, missing safety rails, pools of oil on the floor, dim lighting, exposed wiring."

"Wait just a minute. I thought you were interested in terrorism prevention."

"Mao made the point, and others before him, that a guerrilla must swim in the sea like a fish. The sea is the people. How many of the people in this shop would spit on your dying body in the street?"

"Well, uh, I still don't see how that's important."

Stark dropped a sheet of paper on Randall's desk. "Here's my list of observations. You take a week to clean up what you can."

"Do you know how much this will cost?"

"If you don't think you can handle it, I'll merely forward the report to New York." He recalled what he could from the personal file they had accumulated on Zanville. HSA always did a detailed personal work-up on a client, to see where they might be vulnerable to attack. "Maybe I'll hand-deliver it. Stu and I will probably be seeing each other for a round of golf at the country club. You know, this could be a major embarrassment. Here his wife is the president of the Give 'Em a Break charity in New York, and he's unwittingly owning a sweatshop in Hong Kong."

"It's not a sweatshop."

Stark raised his eyebrows.

"I'll see what I can do," Randall said.

"I knew you'd understand." Stark shook his hand. "I'll check back in a few days. Meanwhile, I'll reconnoiter in the community. See what the mood is, how Zippy is perceived."

Randall nodded. He had already taken a pocket calculator from his desk and was mumbling as he punched figures into it. "Three extinguishers for every floor, times thirty-five dollars, plus maintenance . . ."

Stark let himself out. He'd given the plant manager a needed kick in the butt, and bought himself time to snoop around the colony. Not a bad outing.

The message light was blinking on his phone when he got back to the hotel.

"Joy Bang from Good Luck Real Estate telephoned," the desk told him. The name and number was unfamiliar. He returned the call.

"Guess who?" a husky female voice answered when he got through.

He'd last heard that voice five years earlier, in a hotel bar in Rio de Janeiro. Pamela Moore.

"Who else could it be but Pam?"

"I'm flattered you remembered. Are you free tonight?"

"Yes."

"That's what I like. A man who doesn't play hard to get. I'll pick you up at seven. Semiformal attire."

"Where are we going?"

"Heard you were snooping around McGregor's. You tell me what you're looking for, I'll tell you where to find it."

"You haven't changed. What's the price?"

"We'll negotiate. Over drinks. Beforehand. *Ciao.*"

She hung up without waiting for his response.

Pam Moore was part of the international set. Not the kind who get their names in the paper, but the sort for whom six months in Kuwait, a year in Brunei, four months in Belgium, is not unusual. She was a brassy blonde who looked great by dim bar light, and showed all of her fifty hard years when she ventured out in the sun. Which was seldom. She knew her assets and her liabilities.

Her first husband had been a globe-trotting Texas oil man who picked her up at eighteen in a truck stop near Abilene. He died of a heart attack, leaving her well taken care of and with a taste for travel. Her second husband was from the Saudi royal family, who all but held her captive. Husband number three was an arms dealer, who rescued her, then offered her to a client as part of a major deal. Husband number four was an Italian auto exec who was gunned down by terrorists. Number five was a real estate speculator. Number six was a playboy heir who had died in an auto racing accident. Along the way she had had several long and short affairs. She never made any effort to conceal them.

Stark had bumped into her several times during his early years in Southeast Asia. She always seemed to have the inside track, and loved to let tidbits trickle out. In Rio one hot, post-Mardi Gras night they ended up in bed together for what turned into three days of reveling. They were largely incompatible, except physically, where they were made for each other. She was a big woman, of big passions, and knew how to express them. Stark was unintimidated by her and her match when it came to imagination and stamina.

He lay back in the bed, savoring pleasant memories. He felt a trifle guilty and called Sultana Mirnov in the U.S. It was a bad connection, but still he could hear the coolness in her voice.

"I did not think you would call," she said.

"I've been very busy."

"I too. I am packing."

"You took the job?"

"I did. I am moving to San Jose."

"California?"

"Yes."

He tried to warm up the conversation, but it was futile. They rung off.

Still sore from his run-in with Yamamura, Stark gulped a couple of aspirin, lay down on the king-size bed, and was quickly asleep.


Pamela Moore wore a black strapless silk evening gown that set off her pale, freckled skin and revealed just enough of her cleavage. Her long honey-colored blond hair hung below her shoulders. What was most striking about her was her height. At six foot one inch, Oriental men would ask to pose with her as if she were the Eiffel Tower.

She looked even better than she had five years before, and Stark told her as much.

"Darling boy," she said, patting his thigh under the table. "It's true. I discovered the most wonderful plastic surgeon. Not just for face work. I've had my tummy tucked, my breasts enlarged just a pinch, buttocks lifted. Dermabrasion here. Liposuction there. What do you think?"

"Great."

"You ought to try it. You're starting to get worry lines." She ran a finger along the side of his face, near his eyes. "But on you it looks distinguished. Ah, the advantage of being a man. You can age gracefully and you can pee standing up."

"You shouldn't have given Adam the apple," Stark said, and she rewarded him with her husky laugh.

"Before we go any further, I want you to know I've become monogamous in my old age," she said. "And I have a steady."

"Who's the lucky man?"

"His name is Mathilda. He's a she."

She waited for his response. He sipped his daiquiri. "Mankind's loss is womankind's gain," he said.

"You are a classy bastard, you know that. If there were more like you around I might just change my mind."

There was a band playing in the background and they launched into a warbly version of "I Left My Heart in San Francisco." Stark and Moore sat like a longtime married couple, with minimal sexual tension, just enjoying each other's company.

"So, what are you looking for?" she asked when the number was over and the applause had died down.

"I'm here doing a risk assessment for a toy company. I wanted to sniff the air, see what sort of predators are around the water hole."

She snorted and took her time lighting a cigarette. Her three packs a day of Gauloises gave her the Lauren Bacall timbre. "I know a cover story when I hear one. Old spies never die, they just make up a new story."

"Really." He had never told her he was CIA, but she knew. Pamela had access to first-rate intelligence. "What about you?"

"Real estate. It's unbelievable here. A place on Nathan Road just went for an international record. Higher than New York, Tokyo, you name it."

"Supply and demand. Lots of people, limited space."

"Exactly, honeychile. But the Chicom takeover in less than a decade makes for real excitement. You know the background?"

"Only that in 1984 Britain agreed to hand over Hong Kong to China, providing they keep the existing form of government for fifty years."

"The Brits had leased the New Territories from China for ninety-nine years in 1898. If they returned them but kept Hong Kong, it would do no one any good. So Deng Xiao Peng worked out the 'one country, two systems' compromise. Looks great on paper, but if they break wind in Beijing, the price of real estate drops here. Cooler heads prevail, and it soars again. This is more exciting than Texas wildcatting."

"What type of property do you handle?"

"Commercial and industrial. Not enough markup in residential," she said. "I could buy and sell you several times over."

"And raise the price each time."

Again her brassy laugh pealed out. "I'll give you a tip. Macao. That's where the smart money's going. A Portuguese colony that's like a tiny pimple on China's bottom. Six square miles. About thirty miles from here. Highest

population density in the world but it's undeveloped economically. Matter of fact, in 1974 Portugal offered it to China
and they said thanks but no thanks."

"But now it's being handed back to China the same time
as Hong Kong."

She nodded. "There's been a rash of speculation over
there. The true bargains are gone but you can still grab a
nice parcel for one fifth of what it would cost here. I'm
putting together a syndicate, if you're interested. A million
a head to buy in."

"I'll think about it."

"Better think quick. Property over there is being snatched
up left and right."

"You're confident the PRC won't change their mind and
swallow their little neighbors?"

"Heck, they ain't gonna kill the goose that lays the golden
eggs. You know how much of their hard currency comes
from Hong Kong? They own banks, trading companies,
hundreds of goodies here. This place has been their favorite
entrepôt. Confucius say, communism sound good, but need
imperialist running dogs to move out of the stone age." She
stroked his thigh. "Sorry. Old habits die hard."

"So will I."

She laughed so vigorously she spilled a few drops of her
drink. "I remember you, Bobby. You hated the spooks as
much as I did. You played the game but never much liked
the people involved. Why'd you go to McGregor's? Not
because a toy manufacturer is having problems with his
Barbie dolls."

"Would you like to visit the factory with me?"

"Robert, don't bullshit me," she said, her husky voice
threatening. "Okay, how about I guess. Somehow, you're
interested in the riots."

The band was playing "Stormy Monday." "They're quite
good," Stark said.

"Better a non sequitur than a lie, I always say."

"What have you heard about the riots?"

She coyly nibbled at her glass. "Oh, you are interested in
them?"

"I ought to take you over my knee," Stark said.

"In the old days I would've liked nothing better," she

said. "For the sake of the old days, I'll tell you what I've heard. The Communists aren't behind the trouble. You know they had those big riots here in 1967. Uncle Mao and his Cultural Revolution cadets were feeling their oats. They were worse over in Macao. Anyway, the cops are trying to sell everyone the Communists started the rioting. From what I hear, it's the opposite."

"Right wing?"

"More right than left. Actually triads. You call them tongs in the States."

"I'm familiar with them. Chinese-organized crime."

"Go to the head of the class."

"What's their interest?"

She shrugged. "They're like vultures, they swoop down when they smell rotting meat. Other folks reckon they're working for you."

"For me?"

"The Agency. I presume that's who sent you here."

"I'm here on my own."

"Sure, and I'm a virgin. Maybe someone at the party can help you out. I'm not as much in the swing of things as I used to be."

"Where is this party?"

"Up on The Peak. Would I take you anywhere else?"

After Bangkok, Hong Kong is one of the worst cities in the world to drive in. Narrow streets, heavy pedestrian traffic, and drivers who take a fatalistic approach to accidents combine to make a car ride in Hong Kong an adventure.

Pamela Moore had responded to the danger by becoming an even more reckless driver than the Chinese. In her Triumph sports car she darted in and out of traffic, tapping her horn, shouting obscenities, swerving to barely miss bicyclists, double-parked trucks, jaywalkers. They made it through the heavy traffic—Hong Kong streets were jammed all but the latest hours of the night—then zoomed up the snaking roads to The Peak.

"Like my driving?" she challenged after Stark hadn't said anything for a while.

"It's more fun than being tortured by Shi'ite fanatics with fresh batteries in their cattle prods."

She laughed loud and hard, the wind whipping the sound behind them. "You crack me up."

"I hope that remark isn't prophetic."

More laughter. "Don't say anything more until we get inside," she said.

He didn't. He just watched the world race by.

Pamela Moore spoke into the intercom, and the black metal gate slid back. Behind the gate, and the high white walls it was set in, was a two-story white house of indeterminate style. Byzantine-Spanish, with a hint of New England Colonial. Pillars in front, tile roof, what could have been a minaret.

As they drove down the curving driveway and parked between a white Rolls-Royce and red Jaguar, Pam explained, "Pierre, who owns this place, is the local Agence France Presse bureau chief. The party will be full of folks who make information their business.

"There'll be a few professors who'll bore you into submission if they corner you. A couple of top cops from the local intelligence division. If they've invited the A list, some people from Jardine-Matheson and the Hong Kong and Shanghai Bank."

"The real powers in Hong Kong," Stark said.

"You betcha. When J-M moved brass to Bermuda in eighty-four, folks here got real upset. The papers called it the 'Bermuda Bombshell.' After J-M and the bank there's the Jockey Club and the governor. All the rest is just window dressing." Pam patted her hair into place, pulled down the hem of her dress, and got a nod of approval from Stark. "I'm sure we'll see the station chiefs from most of the local spook houses."

"Sounds like my kind of crowd."

"It will be. Pierre, he's the host, knows how to put on a bash. By the by, my relationship with Mathilda is somewhat of a secret. If anyone asks, I'd appreciate it if you implied you and I were lovers."

"I can leave a condom hanging out of my pocket."

"Like I said, a classy guy."

The door opened and they were hit by an explosion of sound. Voices overlapping each other, glasses tinkling, jazz playing.

"Pa-me-la," the woman who opened the door said, drawing out the word. "It's been too long. And who's this?" she asked, giving Stark the once-over. She was about Pamela's age, with bright red hair and a hard stare.

"An old lover," Pam said. "I'm developing an interest in recycling."

"You must tell me about it," the woman said, looping one arm through Pam's, the other through Stark's, and guiding them in.

The house looked as if it had been furnished by raiding the Louvre. Done up in early regal splendor, with tapestries on the walls and gilt trim moldings. Beautiful, dark wood furniture with lots of ornate trim and scrollwork. The Hong Kong craftsmen who could make a copy of any object they saw in a photo had been at work. Not that Stark could see much of the furnishings. The house was close to wall-to-wall with people.

The security men were discreet but noticeable, at least to Stark's trained eye. Two men watching the door, two others roaming independently. Mixing in the most perfunctory way. Alert eyes, bulges at the chest. No drinks in their hands, Stark thought approvingly. He had spotted a BEWARE OF DOG sign near the entrance as they came in, and alarm contacts on the window.

Then Pamela took hold of him and began making the rounds, whispering people's backgrounds before they met.

"Here's one of those professors I warned you about," she said under her breath. The man in front of them had a mustache that looked like a small animal.

"Charles darling," she said, nudging aside his mustache to give him a kiss on the cheek. "This is my friend, Robert."

The men shook hands. "I was just telling Cedric here—" Charles turned. Cedric had escaped. "Well, never the matter, I was just telling him about the dreadful state of the American economy. It's clear that this supply-side nonsense won't work. You need to—"

"Oh, there's someone I must introduce Robert to," Pamela said. "Excuse me, Charles."

She swept Stark away and introduced him to a dozen people. All got warm welcomes, and cutting remarks when Pam could whisper.

"An opium addict . . . that one's MI5 . . . he'd fuck a chicken if someone else held it . . . hasn't had an accurate story in ten years . . . stealing from the office charity . . . about to be fired . . . he's KGB . . . was denied tenure . . . ran over a Chinese girl and beat the rap."

"A charming bunch of friends you have," Stark said as they refreshed their drinks.

"Aren't they. They probably say nasty things about me. I tell you, expatriates are the worst. An incestuous pack of frustrated twits. If they went home, they couldn't live like rajs. And they know they'll never fit in here. So they piss and moan and bite each other's backs. Then you have the bureaucrats, who get more and more plenipotentiary the farther they are from the home office. And you've got the corporate colonialists. The last one I introduced you to is Mathilda's supervisor at the bank. First he came on to her. When she told him to buzz off, he hinted that he knew about me and her. This should set him back."

The man was looking in their direction. Stark reached around and squeezed Pam's rump.

"You break it, you buy it," she said. "But thanks."

"A dirty job, but someone's got to do it. You're right, that plastic surgeon does do wonderful work."

"Maybe I'll show you later." She winked, laughed, and set off into the crowd.

Stark wandered, spotting a few more security people, individual bodyguards for guests. Had there always been such prevalent security, or was it a symptom of a new fear among the elite? Like a tailor obsessed with the cuts of men's suits, he appraised each guardian for diligence. He could tell a lot just by the way they moved. Swaggering bullyboys or lightfooted athletes? Did they scan with their heads or just with their eyes? Were they drinking, ogling women, goofing off?

Stark entered and exited a few boring conversations. Some women were talking about *"amah* dramas," the problem of getting good Chinese governesses. There was chatter about tennis matches at the Ladies Recreation Club, high tea, bridge games. A shrill brunette noted that Filipina maids were always stealing. Stark left as a genius commented on how hard it was to get help nowadays.

Among the men there were a few heated discussions about soccer, a tout offering a sure tip on an upcoming race at the Happy Valley track, another offering an equally sure tip on the stock market. Charles had a poor woman cornered and was explaining currency fluctuations in great and gory detail.

Stark sidled by the man Moore had identified as the CIA chief of station. The man from Novosti, the Soviet news service, was trying to teach him how to say "please," "thank you," and "excuse me" in Mandarin Chinese.

"Try again," the Russian said. Squat, thick-lipped, with expressive features, he was on the verge of being drunk and spoke with a deliberate precision.

*"Knee how. Shay-shay.* Damn, I forgot the third," the American said. He was big, clean-cut, looked like a high-school football star grown-up. He was sweating profusely.

*"Doy boo chee,"* the Russian, whose name was Kropotkin, said. "Your pronounciation is terrible. You must remember to get the pitch right."

"Wish they spoke English anyway," said Miller, the CIA man.

"I don't understand how they can send you people abroad without teaching you the language," Kropotkin said, shaking his head. "If you speak three languages, you're trilingual. If you speak two, you're bilingual. Do you know what you are if you speak one?"

Miller shook his head. Beads of sweat flew off Miller, and Kropotkin made a face.

"You're American," the Russian said.

In perfect Russian, Stark said, "Very amusing. And do you know why Lubyanka is the tallest building in Moscow?"

*"Nyet,"* Kropotkin said, spinning to take in the newcomer.

"Because from the basement you can see Siberia."

Kropotkin looked around nervously. Jokes about KGB headquarters were not boffo at the box office back home.

Miller studied the two men curiously, not understanding a word they were saying. He assumed Stark was Russian, but couldn't place his face. Miller had diligently memorized the photos of all the known Soviet personnel in Hong Kong.

"Don't you think it would be more practical to teach Mr. Miller here Cantonese?" Stark asked, switching to English.

"You mean he's not really teaching me Chinese?" Miller asked, surprised that Stark spoke flawless English and that Kropotkin was wasting his time.

"He's teaching you Mandarin. That's good for mainland China government officials and Taiwan. Here, and in most of the south, Cantonese is the tongue of choice."

"You're Pamela's friend?" Kropotkin said, shooting Stark a dirty look.

"Right." They introduced themselves and shook hands. Kropotkin squeezed hard. He had strong, rough, peasant hands.

The Russian told a long, coarse joke, in English, about a man who tried to pick up a woman who rejected him. She told him she was a lesbian. What's a lesbian? They like to suck tit and eat pussy, the woman said. My God, then I'm a lesbian, too, the man said.

Miller looked embarrassed, but Kropotkin was watching Stark. Stark smiled politely. Obviously Kropotkin wanted to segue into a discussion of Pamela, but Stark responded with a joke about Lenin's sexual preferences.

"In my country that could earn you a few years in a labor camp," Kropotkin said.

"I'm glad I'm an American then, and can make as bad a joke as I like."

"You're an American?" Miller asked. "What are you doing here?"

"I'm a consultant. Working for Zippy Toys."

"Wait a minute," Kropotkin said. "I know where I know the name from. Robert Stark. You persecute courageous freedom fighters who assault the capitalist corporate imperialists. You used to work for the CIA. You kidnapped one of our top biologists."

"That's not the way she sees it."

Kropotkin's ears had turned red. "You caused a great deal of trouble. I remember it. You—"

"Mind if I cut in, darling," Pam said, patting Kropotkin's bald head. "There's someone Bob just has to meet."

She pulled Stark away before the Novosti man could say any more.

"The comrade's got a fearsome temper," she said. "I wouldn't want him to hurt you. Besides, how'd you like to see a genuine triad boss?"

"Let me guess. The little guy over near the wall. The one with the human fireplug next to him."

"How'd you guess?"

"There're only five Chinese here and he's the one who looks most like a blood drinker."

"You are a smartie. That's Tai Lo and his bodyguard. Lo's a Chiu Chao. You know what that is?" she asked.

"Ethnic Chinese. Most come originally from around Foochow, but they've spread all over. Have their own dialect. Distrusted by other Chinese, who say they're ruthless, untrustworthy. Some are active in smuggling and organized crime. Do I pass?"

She put a finger to her lips and pressed it on his head. "A gold star."

"By the way, Tai Lo is not his name."

"What? How do you know that?" she asked.

"*Tai Lo* is like *padrone* in Italian. It means godfather."

"Smarty pants," she said. She flounced away.

The godfather was deep in a discussion with the MI5 agent and four or five others whom Stark hadn't been introduced to. The sharp-featured *Tai Lo,* who appeared to be in his late sixties, had a commanding presence. He spoke softly and the others strained to listen. He was talking about Hong Kong's resources.

"Too dependent on Red China," he said, using the term the Communists least appreciate. "I have tried for many years to get Hong Kong officials to develop resources. I have shown the way for a nuclear power plant. The desalination facilities must be upgraded. Do you realize how much water comes from the Communists?"

"What does it matter anyway?" a woman asked. "The Communists will soon have this place lock, stock, and reservoir."

Before the *Tai Lo* could answer, a big Australian reporter who had been lurking at the edge of the group piped up. "Bloody Chinks. I don't see why the whole bludging lot of you can't get along." The Australian was swaying, obviously drunk.

He pushed toward the *Tai Lo*. The *Tai Lo*'s bodyguard lashed out with a short, quick punch. It traveled no more than six inches but doubled the Aussie over as if he'd been kicked by a mule. Then the bodyguard straightened the Australian up and nudged him away. The reporter stumbled off.

Only those in the group had seen the exchange, and they deemed it polite to pretend not to notice. The *Tai Lo* continued to speak. "There are more than five and a half million people in Hong Kong. Six million if you count the illegals. Scattered on two hundred thirty-six small islands with a total land area barely a thousand square kilometers. Much of the land is unusable, resources are scarce. Capitalism has allowed prosperity under such adverse conditions. Hong Kong's success has been a model for Southeast Asia. She must continue to grow and develop or she will die."

"What about the Communists? What do you think they will do?" the MI5 man asked.

The *Tai Lo* screwed up his face and looked as if he would spit in contempt. "That is all everyone talks about."

"What do you think about the riots they had here recently?" Stark asked.

The *Tai Lo* and his bodyguard focused on the new face.

"Unfortunate."

"Do you think there's anything to report that the triads were behind them?"

The *Tai Lo* lowered his eyes a bit, squinting as he studied Stark's face. "I have heard rumors. I for one think triads are only social organizations, to help the people. They were first formed by Buddhist monks. To get rid of the Ching oppressors and bring back the Ming emperor."

"Yes. Just like the Cosa Nostra. It started out like Robin Hood too. From what I hear, the triads are the ITT of heroin distribution."

The bodyguard took a half step forward. *Tai Lo* laid his hand on the younger man's arm.

"Only a fool tweaks a dragon's nose in his cave," the *Tai Lo* said.

"Are you in the fortune cookie business?"

Once again Pamela swooped in, interrupted, and dragged Stark away.

"Honeychile, that's twice I've bailed your buns out. Three strikes and you know what happens."

"I was just probing."

"Famous last words," she said.

There was a change in the noise at the party. A moment of silence as a woman came through the door.

# CHAPTER
## 11

She wore a red cheongsam with gold filigree. It clung to her like a scarlet skin. The gold matched the thick chains hanging around her neck. She had enough jewelry on to make Sammy Davis, Jr. jealous. Yet on her it looked proper, like tribute for a temple goddess. Her lustrous black hair was piled on her head in the traditional style of Balinese dancers. Her sculpted features had the clean hard lines of a jade statuette, her expression a mixture of sensuality and aloofness. She moved slowly through the crowd. Every man grinned goofily when she honored him with a moment's chitchat. Women watched her enviously and held on to their husbands as she passed. She was more than a mere presence, almost a force of nature.

"That's Dao," Pam said, sidling up to Stark. "She's a model."

"Quite a lady."

"Even the gays get a hardon seeing her," Pam said. "I'll bet there's been more lip licking and gut tightening since she walked in than in the past two hours."

"She does seem to get attention."

Then the party returned to its huzzah-huzzah. Lubricated by alcohol, the voices had gotten louder. Mainly English, some French, and occasional German or Japanese. The usual international-set Tower of Babel.

Stark continued to mix and mingle. A couple of times he caught sight of Dao. Their eyes seemed to meet, but he couldn't be sure. Did she play that game with all the men? Was there a change in her Mona Lisa smile?

He'd been drinking more than usual. It helped deaden the pain in his shoulder and arm. Although loose, he was still very much under control. In various conversations he heard:

The British were behind the riots. They were angry about being ousted by the Communist Chinese and were planning their own "scorched earth policy."

The Americans were behind the riots. They were worried about the PRC growing too powerful in the Pacific. They wanted to collect insurance on their Hong Kong properties and get out.

The Russians were behind the riots. They, too, were afraid of the PRC's growing power. Destroying the virtual capital of capitalism would be a valuable propaganda victory.

The Communist Chinese were behind it—or at least factions within the government who were afraid of the influence Hong Kong would have on the rest of China and didn't know how the area would be handled come 1997.

The Japanese were behind the riots. Primarily western businesses were destroyed and only two Japanese companies suffered minor losses. The Japanese were knocking off the competition so they could be number one in Hong Kong.

Local Communists were behind the riots because they wanted to speed up the takeover by the PRC.

Local right wingers were behind the riots because they wanted to ruin things before the Communists came in.

Everyone preached their theory with absolute conviction and scoffed at other theories. The one common denominator was that no one thought the riots were spontaneous. The trouble was too well organized.

Dao's and Stark's eyes met. She was talking with the CIA chief, Miller. She tapped his arm, said something, and the two of them came his way.

"Robert Stark, this is Dao," Miller said. "The lady thinks she might know you from somewhere."

"I'm afraid not. I would never forget a face like hers,"

Stark said. What a sappy line, he thought immediately. But she accepted it with amusement. She offered her hand in a way that was unclear whether she wanted it shaken or kissed. He chose to shake it.

"It's a pleasure," she said.

"All mine," he said. She dismissed Miller, who looked like a heartsick puppy, with a glance. After a few minutes conversation she said she had to move on. It was crowded at the party, but she seemed to brush against him more than was necessary. He watched her wake.

"A beautiful lady, *desu ne?* Mr. Stark?"

Standing next to him was a dapper Japanese gentleman, in his fifties, with gold-rimmed glasses and a designer suit.

"Yes?"

"My name is Fujimoto. I'm with the Japanese embassy." He handed Stark a business card. Fujimoto had a British accent to his impeccable English. "I understand you have just come here from my country?"

"Yes." Stark's neck hairs were standing up, and like a canny witness, he had reduced himself to yes-or-no answers.

"In my country, you visited a dojo in Kamakura run by *Shihan* Soto Koiichi?"

"Yes."

"Do you know he is dead?"

Stark feigned surprise. "No!"

"Yes. He committed seppuku. We would very much appreciate it if you came to our embassy and made a statement."

Once inside the embassy, Stark would be on Japanese territory. "I tell you what. My schedule is tight. But I can draft up a statement and give it to you. I'll have it notarized."

"We would prefer you stop by the embassy."

"I regret that I can't. Not for a few days."

Fujimoto nodded. "I understand," he said, giving the words an additional weight. "It's most strange. His blind wife claims to be the only one who was with him, that she acted as his second. Yet it is clear that someone much stronger, and skilled, made the final blow. Have you any ideas who it might be?"

"There was a guy named Yamamura who seemed close to him."

"Ah, yes, Mr. Yamamura. We are aware of him." Fujimoto gave a curt bow and said his good-byes.

"What was that about?" Pam asked as she drifted over.

"Nothing."

"Nothing? Your body language was saying full alert."

"Do you know him?" Stark asked her as he glanced at Fujimoto's impressively embossed business card.

"Fujimoto. Sure. He's with the trade delegation, but never seems to have any work to do with them. Turns up in the darnedest places. Like at Royal Hong Kong Police headquarters. Some say he's with Naicho."

"The Japanese cabinet minister's intelligence service," Stark muttered.

"Is that the third strike?" she asked.

"It's a whole different ball game," Stark said.

"You going to tell me about it?"

"Maybe later."

Pamela flounced away.

Stark edged toward the pool. He needed fresh air, a chance to get away from the cocktail party babble. Did Japan have an extradition treaty with Hong Kong? Loud, angry words broke into his thoughts.

"Please let go," a woman was saying.

"Too good for me, you little Chinese cunt?"

It was the Australian, and he'd grabbed Dao's arm. They were by the pool and away from most of the other guests. They hadn't noticed Stark.

"Why'd you come out here with me, then?" the Australian demanded, his words slurred.

"You said you had something for me," she said.

"I've got something for you, all right."

Stark stepped into view. "Can I help you?" he asked.

"Bludge off, mate," the big reporter said.

Stark reached over and took the Australian's arm. The reporter swung with his free hand and Stark easily ducked it. With his thumb he dug into the forearm muscle, compressing a nerve. The pain made the Australian's eyes go wide. With his other hand, Stark grabbed the upper arm. He moved his hands like he was cutting down a sword, and the Aussie fell to his knees.

"Let's call it a night, okay?" Stark said.

"Wait'll I get up, you sodding bastard." The reporter pulled himself erect and charged.

Stark moved his hands again, giving little more than a hard tap to the spot the *Tai Lo*'s bodyguard had struck earlier. The Australian gasped and fell back into the pool. Stark waited until he had grabbed the edge and was sputtering before escorting Dao inside.

"There's a man overboard," Stark said to one of the security guards when he and Dao were back inside. "Had too much to drink."

"The Aussie?" the guard asked.

"That's the one."

The guard nodded. "We'll lead him out a side way." He headed outside.

Dao's hand slid off Stark's arm with seeming reluctance.

"You handled that drunk with great ease," she said. "Have you studied a martial art?"

"I've dabbled."

"Really. I had a cousin who was a kick-boxer."

"Most of them don't live much past thirty."

"He died at twenty-eight. Complications from a concussion."

"I'm sorry to hear that. So you're Thai?"

"I'm a mongrel. I've got Thai, Chinese, and French blood. Plus a few traces of a half-dozen other nationalities."

They were at the bar. She got a Singapore Sling, he another daiquiri. "Here's to mutts," he said in a toast.

"And knights in shining armor."

Her words reminded him of Sultana. He felt a twinge, but as Dao continued to beam her half smile at him—as if she knew every thought he had—it overwhelmed memories of the Russian biologist.

He and Dao talked about the party, "not as boring as some," the weather, "miserable," the riots, "unfortunate but inevitable when you have such a large mass of poor people under pressure," common interests, "Beethoven, Japanese cooking, religions." But the primary communication was nonverbal. The way they stood so close, her hips cocked slightly forward. The way they leaned together to whisper when it got too noisy. His hand across her back, guiding her through the crowd. Eyes locked on each other, unswerving.

"Have you seen much of Hong Kong?" she asked.

"Not really."

"I would be happy to show you around. You have only a few days, I presume."

"A few."

"I have plans for tomorrow night, but my afternoon is free," she said.

"Lunch?"

"Unfortunately I cannot," she said. "But at two-thirty, I will meet you at the lower tram station. Okay?"

She made it clear she was rewarding him with her valuable time. She was remarkably forward for an Oriental woman, but Stark imagined not many men had ever said no to her.

When Dao drifted off, Pamela sidled up. "You devil, you. Now every man at the party hates you."

# CHAPTER
## 12

"Sorry to hear about your teacher," Les said when the operator put through the international call.

"It was on the news?"

"Are you kidding? Modern-day samurai chooses old-style death. Film at eleven."

"They name any suspects?"

"His wife was held briefly and released. The stories hinted that the cops aren't pushing too hard, that it was a consensual sort of thing. How's Zippy?"

"Needs work. Their plant manager is still impressed that he grew up near Harvard. I rattled his cage."

"Not too much, I hope; it's a good account. Speaking of good accounts, I got a promising nibble. Textile firm, plants here and where you are now. Also assets in Nevada, California, and New Jersey. When will you be back?"

"Another week. Maybe less."

"They're gonna make a decision in the next couple days. I might do the dog and pony show without you. Any objections?"

"Feel free. I need you to run an ID for me."

"Shoot."

"Dao. Female Oriental. Anywhere from thirty-five to

forty years old. Probably holds a Thai passport. Worked as a model."

"A model, huh? You don't let any grass grow under your feet."

"What's that mean?"

"The last time I spoke with you, you sounded like shit. Now you're vetting a model and sound awfully perky. Get anywhere yet?"

"Les, take a cold shower and check it out for me, okay?"

"Oh, you wild single guys."

The man known as Sun Tzu had arrived early and taken the seat of honor, facing the door. His partners, especially the American, were usually late. They would arrive sweaty and frazzled, complaining about the weather, the traffic. He was the linchpin of the operation, and the others knew it. Like ornery adolescents, however, they dickered and bickered with him.

Sun Tzu took out a cigarette, and one of his bodyguards rushed forward to light it. He didn't much care what the doctors said about his health. All he had to live to see was the completion of his plan. Then whatever happened was *ming*, destiny.

He had been born in Szechuan province in 1918. Although the Ching dynasty had been overthrown in 1911, skirmishes with various warlords and rival factions made them tumultuous years. President Sun Yat-sen resigned and his successor turned out to be an evil dictator. In 1921 Sun Yat-sen returned with a rival government based in Canton. Two years after Sun Yat-sen's death in 1925, his successor, Chiang Kai-shek, working with the Communist leader Mao Tse-tung, reunited the country. Then came the war with Japan and the Communist takeover. There was a Chinese curse that said, "May you live in interesting times." Sun Tzu had lived in very interesting times. By age thirty-one, the year of the Communist revolution, he had seen starvation, killer earthquakes, floods, torture, mass rape, and brutal murders.

The only security in his life came from the triad. He had joined when he was a young man. It offered the only chance for him to escape a life of impoverished drudgery. After all, Sun Yat-sen and Chiang Kai-shek were both triad members who drew upon that organization for money and muscle. Couldn't he one day rise to their heights?

Years later, he could remember the initiation ritual clearly. Drinking the chicken's blood, swearing loyalty to the group with the thirty-six oaths which were backed up by death from "the five thunderbolts" and "myriads of swords."

He had quickly risen to become a "red pole," an enforcer. After a number of his rivals had died, several of them by his hand or machinations, he became a White Paper Fan, a financial adviser. As money mover for the crime syndicate in the mid 1960s, he pioneered new ways of smuggling heroin.

In Bangkok he met with representatives from the Shan United Army to haggle over their crops. The Shan, who were neither united nor an army, were the rulers of the area known as the Golden Triangle, formed by the juncture of Burma, Laos, and Thailand. The area was to heroin what Virginia and North Carolina were to tobacco.

Sun Tzu would establish a price and arrange shipment to Hong Kong. The drug had been transported inside the vagina, stomach, or anus of travelers, in paste form between the layers of cardboard boxes, pressed solid into statuette form, disguised as soy sauce by being dissolved in liquid with a brown coloring, or strapped to the limbs of refugees. It had even been stuffed into hollowed-out corpses. From the busy international port at Hong Kong, the drugs could go anywhere.

He had no remorse. Hadn't the British with their gunboats forced his people to accept opium? He didn't force anyone to do anything. If weaklings wanted to spend precious moments alive in a drugged world, that was their business.

His timing had been perfect. "When the hawk breaks the back of its prey, it is due to timing," the real Sun Tzu had written more than two thousand years earlier. As the drug trade boomed, so did his own fortune.

Sun Tzu was worth more than a billion dollars. His bribes to police officials alone totaled ten million dollars a year. More than twice that went to various anticommunist causes. His hatred of the Communist Chinese was like an ulcer burning in his gut.

Which was why he had come up with the plan involving Machiavelli and Musashi.

He first had dealings with Machiavelli when the Italian had opened a factory in Hong Kong. There had been labor troubles which Machiavelli tried to solve by hiring strong-arms. He had gone through the wrong channels and Sun Tzu had been forced to correct him. A delicate matter, but they were able to reach an understanding at what Machiavelli called "a sitdown." They had recognized common business interests and made a few deals. Sun Tzu could provide top quality heroin—Machiavelli, unlike some Mafioso, had no reservations about handling the drug, had access to illegal distribution networks. They both prospered.

A similar situation had occurred with Musashi. Only he wanted amphetamine, which was a little harder for Sun Tzu to get. He put Musashi in touch with Machiavelli, and the two younger men had conducted a half-dozen deals since then.

They provided small courtesies for each other. For example, when Musashi needed snakes to cover his gun-running operation, Sun Tzu was able to get them through his contacts. He knew many dealers in Southeast Asia, since he owned a *shecanguan,* a snake restaurant, on the second floor of a rundown building on a back street in the Wanchai area.

That was where he waited, watching the door patiently. The three men did not meet often. Each was of great interest to law enforcement. They used their code names in communications and kept details of their plans from even their closest subordinates. Their rendezvous, if discovered, would set Interpol telexes flying. But sometimes it was important to see your partner's face, to try to read what was going on behind the words.

Musashi entered, and then Machiavelli. Machiavelli grabbed a glass of water and gulped it down before saying a word. In many ways the American was like a child, and Sun Tzu was tolerant of his errors in behavior. The Japanese was more polite. He bowed and exchanged pleasantries. Sun Tzu distrusted him, but he knew it was due more to prejudice than to anything Musashi had done. Sun Tzu remembered the rape of Nanking and Japanese brutality during the war.

The two Orientals exchanged perfunctory pleasantries while Machiavelli gazed at the half-dozen large aquariums along the walls. Behind the thick glass were snakes, turtles, and fish.

"Is that a cobra over there?" Machiavelli asked, indicating a hooded snake.

"Yes."

Machiavelli walked to the tank. He tapped on the glass. The cobra's hood flared. Other snakes in the tank writhed and hissed. A snake spat at the glass. Machiavelli jumped back.

"Jesus."

The restaurant was nearly full. Machiavelli was the only non-Oriental. Patrons chuckled at his behavior, but he was too intent on the deadly snake to notice. He backed up to the table.

"That spittle is toxic," Sun Tzu said. "If it had gotten in your eyes, you would be blinded; in your mouth, you would be stunned."

Machiavelli sat, looking back occasionally at the tank full of nightmares.

"Why do you keep those things?"

"To eat."

Machiavelli made a disgusted face. "Yech."

"They give you vigor. Balance your yin and yang. A meal of them is like a medical treatment. They have also been persuasive when a merchant does not understand the sort of protection I can offer him."

"Yeah. Like Joey Gallo kept a lion in the basement on President Street. A few minutes locked down there and even tough guys paid up," Machiavelli said. "You got anything besides Kentucky fried snake here?"

"I've had the chef get you something special."

Sun Tzu signaled, and the waiters who had stayed discreetly at the far side of the restaurant came forward. Sun Tzu ordered. For Sun Tzu and Musashi there was a lavish meal that would have cost an ordinary customer hundreds of dollars. Krait, mamushi, mamba, habu, bushmaster, cottonmouth, were carefully prepared in varying sweet and sour sauces. Some of the poisonous snakes were milked, a fraction of a droplet of their venom adding a tang to special dishes.

For Machiavelli, Sun Tzu had had a Straw Sandal—a triad messenger—fetch two hamburgers, a large order of fries, and a Coke. A pleased Machiavelli didn't realize how the Chinese looked down on him and his primitive palate.

"You have been quiet," Sun Tzu said to Musashi when they had finished their meal.

Musashi smiled to conceal his emotions. It was not his way to burden others with his problems. "The meal was delicious."

"Sure was," Machiavelli said.

"I have heard about your brother," Sun Tzu said to the Japanese. "I am most sorry."

Musashi shrugged.

"Yeah, tough break," Machiavelli said.

"I have learned that your police are interested in a man named Robert Stark," Sun Tzu said.

"Yes. I would be interested in him as well."

"He is in Hong Kong," Sun Tzu said.

"Think it's a coincidence?" Machiavelli asked.

"Do you?" Sun Tzu asked patiently.

"I doubt it," Machiavelli said. "We're safest assuming it isn't."

"Where is he?" Musashi asked, his eyes as flat and focused as the cobra's.

"First, I must have your word that you will follow my suggestion as to how we handle Stark," Sun Tzu said. "I know you will want to confront him personally to find out exactly what transpired at your brother's dojo."

"How can we agree if we don't know what you're going to say?" Machiavelli asked.

"Revenge is a dish best eaten cold," Sun Tzu said. "You can be sure I will act in your best interests."

"I agree to your decision," Musashi said.

"Me too. Though it's Soto's vendetta. I mean Musashi's. I gotta get back to the States anyway," Machiavelli said. "If I'm away too long, my people will get ideas."

"Have you had success with the scientists?" Sun Tzu asked.

106

"I got one on his way over," Machiavelli said. "A real sharp cookie with a bunch of degrees."

Sun Tzu turned to Musashi, who was still brooding over Stark. "The electronic hardware?"

"As soon as you need it, it will be shipped," Musashi said. "You have not said what you will do with Stark?"

"He will be allowed to live. At least for a few more days." Sun Tzu stood. "The Communists are treacherous and untrustworthy. I am sure we will have to scatter a few more bodies on Hong Kong streets before they will comply. And the body of Robert Stark should draw a great deal of attention."

# CHAPTER

## 13

As an international executive protection consultant, Stark had contacts in police departments around the world. He called the Royal Hong Kong Police Department, got through to an inspector he'd dealt with, and asked to speak with the officer handling the Kowloon clothing factory arson investigation.

"He's a Chinese, you know," said the inspector, who was British. "Uppity chap. On the QT, I think they're half hoping he fails on this one. He's not too popular with the brass here. Not even that popular with the rank and file. Sticks to himself, minds his own business."

Stark knew what he meant. The Hong Kong police had been racked by numerous scandals. One sergeant even became known in the press as the "six-hundred-million-dollar man." The corruption was virtually universal among Chinese officers, and merely widespread among the British offices at the top. To be honest was to be a loner.

"Come by HQ and I'll give you an intro," the inspector said. "I doubt if it will get you anywhere, though."

The block-long gray stone Royal Hong Kong Police headquarters had the look of a colonial outpost, as if any moment the gates could be shut and the officers inside forced to defend themselves against hostile natives. The RHKPD headquarters had been built in the early part of the century and had the old world touches of class. Oak wainscotting and matching banisters. Tile floors. Ornate brass light fixtures. And the British spit and polish had kept the building from getting too run-down. But there was no way a visitor would ever mistake it for anything but a cop shop.

Whether a police precinct in Brooklyn, an RCMP office in Toronto, or a squad room in Buenos Aires, law enforcement offices share a common feel. A shabbiness brought about by frequent confrontations between the underclass and those charged with keeping the peace. A sense of violence never far away, of macho camaraderie, and fear.

After a few minutes of pleasantries, Stark's contact had taken him to see Peter Wong. Clearly the inspector didn't expect Stark to get anything, and he was merely shining him on with a sort of professional courtesy.

The inspector made his introductions, then dropped Stark off at Wong's windowless cubicle on the second floor. Wong had a student-size desk that took up half the room. He had a creaky wooden rolling chair for himself and a wooden folding chair for visitors. Stark sat in the folding chair. Wong regarded him emotionlessly.

"I'd like your opinion on the fire," Stark said.

"Perhaps you would be better off speaking to my superiors."

"I've found that the closer to the source I get, the better the information."

"Why do you want to know?"

"My client, Zippy Toys, has requested a risk analysis report. I believe in doing a thorough job."

"They say being a CIA agent is like being a policeman. You never can truly leave the job."

"I take it you think that means I'm still working for the Company?"

Wong toyed with a pen.

"If I am, would that be of concern to you?" Stark asked.

"If I am to be honest with someone, I like them to be honest with me."

Stark leaned forward and put on his best sincere manner. He decided to tell Wong the truth. At least part of it.

"A few years ago someone did me a favor, taught me a

great deal about myself when I needed guidance. Recently he asked me to look into what was happening in Hong Kong. I accepted that responsibility.''

"Perhaps you are referring to Koiichi Soto?''

Stark had deduced that Wong must have checked his past. And the surveillance reports that the CIA chief had mentioned—of Soto in Hong Kong—would probably be common knowledge. It was prudent to admit a secret that the other person knew, to demonstrate apparent honesty and openness.

"Yes,'' Stark said, feigning surprise. "How did you know?''

"What do you intend to do when you find out?''

"It depends on what I learn.''

Like any good cop, Wong was suspicious of strangers. Yet he also trusted his instincts. Stark was not telling him the whole story. He would not tell Stark all he knew. But they could work together.

"Would you care to go for a walk?'' Wong asked.

"Excuse me?''

"I like to get out and stretch my legs periodically.''

They headed out of the building and walked briskly down the streets.

"What do you think of Hong Kong?'' Wong asked.

"Noisy. Crowded. Vital. Exciting. Dirty. Confusing. Reminds me of New York. Only more so.''

The Chinese cop said, "Hmmm.''

Wong was a man with a lot of anger in his system. Stark managed to slip into the conversation that he was part Irish, that his grandfather had fought against the British, and that he had no love for the Crown himself. He let Wong draw the information out and hoped that it sounded true.

"Do you know why we are taking this walk?'' Wong finally asked.

"Two possibilities. Exercise, or you're afraid that your office is bugged.''

"What do you think?''

"I think if you wanted exercise, you'd join a gym.''

They were on the edge of the Zoological and Botanical Garden. Wong indicated a bench. In the background a dozen elderly people were going through the slow movements of t'ai chi ch'uan. A young couple, dressed in new wave clothing and partially hidden by bushes, were necking. The girl wore a Sony Walkman as the boy fondled her breast. There were other couples in various stages of romance.

"Young people touching in public is scandalous to the old people," Wong commented. "But there is so little privacy indoors."

"In America teenagers favor parked cars."

Wong nodded. He took the plunge. "I more than suspect my office is bugged. I found the device in the desk leg. Having such a small place made it easy to search."

"Who do you think put it there?"

"There are many possibilities. Triads. Fellow officers. Communist Chinese. The anticorruption squad."

"Who's your prime suspect?"

"I think they would like to somehow prove me corrupt. Unless they plant false evidence, they will fail."

Stark nodded. "You left the mike in place?"

"Yes."

"Good idea. They'd just find another way to put it in and you might lower your guard. Have you checked the mouthpiece on your phone?"

"No."

"I wouldn't be surprised if you find something there. A desk leg would be fair for room conversations. The best way to bug a phone is in the phone.

"I'll check when I get back. Do you smoke?"

"No."

Wong took out a cigarette and lit up. "A vile habit. I know why they gave me this case. What I hadn't counted on was the results of my investigation leaking to the newspapers before the ink was dry on the report."

"How many people had access to your report?"

"Too many to pinpoint."

"I've heard a lot of theories as to who was behind the fire," Stark said, recounting some of the conversations he had heard the night before. It was important that Stark volunteer information before Wong began to feel that cooperation was a one-way street.

"The man who was killed, Weng Cheng, was a street punk," Wong said as Stark finished his recital. "He did work for a number of people."

"Triad?"

"Surprisingly not." Wong ground out his cigarette under foot. "Actually, your CIA."

"Are you sure? Could it be faked?"

"From other informants I have gotten full details."

"I appreciate that you're still willing to talk to me," Stark said.

"I found it strange that he was not with a triad. Do you understand?"

"Sometimes what is missing from a picture is more important than what is in the picture."

"Exactly. This sort of trouble would normally be done by triad hoodlums. Then there was his manner of death. The way his neck was snapped. It's a technique favored by a certain school of kung fu. The young men from that school are almost all twenty-four-carat triad."

"Interesting."

"Within the department my work has been hampered. Lab samples have disappeared. I've been assigned to other, less important, but time-consuming cases. This is why I am telling you this. Again, this seems to point to the triads, whose tentacles have extended into all levels of the department."

"What would you like me to do?"

"Investigate."

"If I found out who did it?"

Wong stood up. "I must be getting back to my office."

They strolled back at a slower pace. "Your teacher's death must have hurt you."

"It did. But he would be the first to accept its inevitability."

They were nearing the building.

"This kung fu style you mentioned, do they have a school anywhere?"

Wong gave him an address near the Walled City, one of the poorest parts of Hong Kong. "But a white person in that area is conspicuous. I urge you to be careful."

"Thank you for everything," Stark said.

"I may have put you on a course of destruction."

"If so, it's the path I'm destined to follow."

*"Ming."*
*"Ming."*

As soon as Stark reached the door to his hotel room, he knew it had been tossed. The tiny paper he'd left between the door and the doorframe had fallen to the floor. He entered cautiously, ready for attack, but his visitor, or visitors, were gone. They had been professional, leaving few signs of their entry. Stark's shaving kit was at a seventy-five degree angle on the counter instead of the thirty degrees he had left it in. His clothes, which had been deliberately spaced two inches apart in the closet, were now in a different pattern.

He checked the room for contraband. He didn't bother looking for hidden microphones and just assumed the room had become a broadcasting studio. Without the proper gear, debugging would take too long. With gadgets like a spike mike, which could be driven into the wall from an adjacent room, or a laser vibration detector, which could be bounced off his window from a building across the way, it would be virtually impossible to detect.

He suspected the intruder was someone from the party, but that narrowed it down to only half the intelligence agencies in the world.

He peeled off his clothes and began preparing for his meeting with Dao.

As soon as Musashi left the meeting with Sun Tzu, he had contacted his underboss and ordered him to track down Robert Stark.

"I suspect he is in Hong Kong, or the Chinese wouldn't have found out before I did. Find him."

"What do you want done with him?"

"I cannot have the personal satisfaction of killing him, since that would jeopardize my relationship with the Chinese. But if Stark is killed by someone else . . ."

His underboss regarded him quizzically.

Soto picked up a copy of the *Yomiuri Shimbun*. There was a front-page story about the arrest of a Japanese Red Army terrorist. Soto tapped it with his finger. "Surely these people would be proud to take credit for the death of Stark."

# CHAPTER
## 14

A half hour before Stark was due to leave, there was a knock at the door. He hurried to the closet and pulled from the wall the metal bar that clothes would hang from. He previously had worked it loose, so it took less than a second to jerk free. Standing to one side of the door in case shots were fired, he asked, "Who's there?"

"Dao."

He stepped to the peephole. It was she, apparently alone. Only after he had opened the door, let her in, and relocked it did he put the pipe down. She watched him, bemused.

"A fine greeting," she said.

"I didn't expect you," he said. He was bare-chested and barefooted, with a dab of shaving cream still behind one ear. She was wearing a black leather miniskirt, a white silk blouse, and a hint of pale red eye shadow and lipstick. The radio he kept on to make eavesdropping more difficult was blasting "Dizzy Spells."

"I dreamed about you last night," she said.

"Really?"

"I came to see if it would be as good as in the dream."

She moved closer as she spoke. A finger reached out, wiped away the shaving cream. He took her in his arms. Their kiss was long, slow, and deep.

He lifted her petite frame and lowered her into bed. She pulled him down. Her clothing seemed to melt off. He took her small, pointy breasts into his mouth, reveling in her scent and taste. She gave a throaty purr.

"Sing, Sing, Sing" came on, with Gene Krupa pounding his soul out while Benny Goodman led the group through the demonically overwhelming tune.

She took a red Passion Flower condom from her purse. Then Stark was on her and in her and they were on a mutual path to oblivion.

They were both covered with a sheen of sweat. Lying in bed, stretching in the afterglow, Stark asked, "How many years can we stay here like this?"

"As long as you like." She had one arm and one leg wrapped over his body. It felt as if she were stuck to him. She reached down and manipulated him.

"Mmmm," he said. "You're going to kill me with kindness."

Her tongue darted into his ear. He started to roll her over.

"No. Just lay back."

He got harder. And larger. And harder. As she toyed with him. The skin of his erection stretched taut, like a water balloon about to burst. He had never felt such exquisite pleasure at the verge of pain. He wanted to be buried in her softness more than anything else. There was nothing else.

She jumped out of bed and ran to the bathroom. "I think I'll shower."

"Wait a minute. You can't leave me like this."

She laughed and slammed the door to the bathroom. He went over and knocked. The water was running. He stood there, full of throbbing indignity.

"What are you doing?" he asked through the door.

"I'm showering, silly, silly."

"Let me in."

"Why should I?"

"Or I'll huff and I'll puff and I'll kick this door in," he said.

"The door's open."

He stepped inside. The room was clouded with steam.

Her naked body was as sleek as a wet seal's. She seemed indifferent to him.

"Could you wash my back?" she asked.

He began rubbing down her back. He nuzzled her neck and got a mouthful of soap as a reward. He toyed with her breasts, but she slipped out of his hands.

"Naughty boy," she said. "C'mon in. You need to cool off."

He stepped into the shower stall and she washed him down. She paid special attention to his groin, which only added to his longing.

Then she got down on her knees and took him in her mouth. When he came it was like an explosion. He leaned against the wet tile walls, panting as he caught his breath.

With endorphins soothing his system, Hong Kong seemed like a wonderful tableau seen through a gauze filter. Dao started them out at the Wong Tai Sin temple. Following her lead, Stark knelt and lit a joss stick in front of the main altar.

"What did you wish for?" Dao asked.

"I can't repeat it in mixed company."

She covertly patted his arm. In public they did not touch, for that would offend the Chinese.

At the nearby fortune-teller's stall she shook the bamboo container holding a sheaf of numbered sticks until one fell out. Then Stark did the same. They brought the numbered sticks to an old woman sitting nearby who pronounced their fortune by digging out a piece of paper with the same number on it.

For Dao the future involved an exciting man who would show her a world she could not imagine. There was much great joy in her future.

To Stark she said, "You have had a tragedy recently. It weighs heavily on you. But a good woman can help you forget. Rest assured, there will be an end to sorrow."

They tipped her and moved into the temple.

"That was a mixed fortune you got," Dao said. "If you would like to get another fortune, we can try one of the others." All around the temple were seers. Some had mynah birds who fetched random fortunes from tiny drawers. Others divined the future from bits of meat. The air was thick with smoke from their joss sticks.

"Can you change your fortune by buying a new one?"

"You can get another interpretation. In the east we know truth is relative."

"Sounds more like solving a problem by throwing money at it. That's western."

She covertly patted his arm again. The secretiveness of the gesture added to its thrill. Her touch was electric. She reduced him to a primal beast who had only rutting on his mind.

"What was that you did back there in the hotel room?" he asked. "I never felt so sensitive down there in my life."

"I can't give away my secrets."

"Let me guess. You pressed on the vein that drains blood from the penis."

She screwed up her face in disgust. "How unromantic. I prefer to think that I did acupressure. I reduced your yin to allow your yang to grow. You understand the yin and yang?"

"Japanese call it *in-yo*. Female and male. Dark and light. Night and day. The opposites that come together to form the whole. The Tao."

She gave him another covert squeeze and they continued their tour.

Wong Tai Sin's main building was the usual rainbow of colors, with red pillars, golden roof, blue friezes, yellow lattice work, and multicolored carvings. She pointed out the side altar, dedicated to the monkey god.

"He is a rascal who was thrown out by the Taoists after creating trouble in both heaven and hell," she said. "The Buddhists made him a god." They walked to the adjacent Hall of Three Saints, dedicated to Buddhism, Taoism, and Confucianism.

"Unlike in the west, our religions coexist peacefully," she said.

"Except that the Confucianists think the Taoists are lazy do-nothing mystics. The Taoists think the Confucianists are neurotics trying to make unnatural changes in the world. And the various Buddhist sects quibble with one another about the proper way to achieve enlightenment."

"You have studied our religions?"

"They're not really religions."

"What would you call them?" she asked, annoyed.

"Belief systems, ways to live, philosophies. Perhaps there isn't a proper word for it. Some things cannot be named. As Lao-tzu said, 'Those who say do not know, those who know do not say.' I'm sorry. I'm becoming pedantic."

"It is a pleasure to meet someone who knows about our beliefs."

"Yes, but my cup should be empty."

She regarded him quizzically.

"There's a story about a samurai who visited a Zen master seeking enlightenment. But the samurai kept talking, didn't let the master get a word in edgewise. Finally they sat down for tea. The master filled the cup but kept pouring. When it had flowed down the table, the samurai said, 'Stop. I'm too full.' The Zen master said, 'Then you must empty your cup before I can fill it.' "

She savored the anecdote. "I am glad I met you."

"The feeling's mutual."

They wandered all over Hong Kong, by taxi, train, double-decker tram. They nibbled food at sidewalk stalls and shopped at the hundreds of stands. Dao, after ferocious negotiating with a merchant in Contonese, bought Stark a T-shirt which said, "My karma just ran over your dogma."

They stopped at the Jade Market. Under dozens of picnic umbrellas a few hundred vendors sold everything from tiny rings of precious jadeite to nephrite statues that were supposedly valued at thousands of dollars. It was wall-to-wall customers and merchants. While haggling, the merchant wrote their price on a scrap of paper and handed a pen to the customer. The customer scratched the number out and wrote in a response. This way rivals couldn't hear prices.

Dao admired a string of pearl-shaped jade, green with gold highlights. The battle with the merchant began, concluding when he said, "You're stealing my lunch money." Dao allowed Stark to drape the necklace around her neck.

As they left the market, Stark got a feeling of uneasiness. Instincts were firing on a level he couldn't identify. Something in the pattern of faces, or the movements of bystanders, made him wary.

**118**

They spoke of their childhoods. He told her about being an army brat whose father had risen to the rank of captain. The elder Stark had been assigned to bases in California, West Germany, and Japan.

"I suppose that's how I first became interested in the Orient," Stark said. "What about you? What's your life story, in a nutshell?"

"My real name is Dao Lin, as far as I know. I was brought up in a Catholic orphanage in Thonburi. Abandoned on a doorstep when I was a few weeks old."

She told about her hard childhood, of neglect and beatings. The fear of being abandoned again. There was something about her story which didn't quite ring true. It sounded like a well-practiced sales pitch. Perhaps it was just her cavalier tone, feigned indifference. Or maybe it was Stark's overall uneasiness from the feeling of being followed.

They visited temples dedicated to Tin Hau, the seafarer's goddess; Kwan Yum, the Buddhist goddess of mercy; Kwan Ti, the Taoist god of war; and Shing Wong, the god of good city administration.

"Every neighborhood should have a Shing Wong," she said. "He also protects against epidemics, famine, and invasion."

"A good deity to have on your side. They all are."

"You believe in only one God?" she asked.

"I believe there are many paths to follow. All religions have value to them. Like the notion of selflessness, acting for the good of humanity. What do you believe?"

"Growing up in Thailand, Buddhism is the religion. To desecrate an image of the Buddha can earn a stiff jail term. Of course the nuns tried to beat Christianity into me. I suppose I am more confused than anything else. Is something the matter?"

"No."

It was hard in crowded Hong Kong for him to separate object and field, followers from fellow strollers. He dawdled, then abruptly reversed direction. He led her down alleyways and cut through buildings.

"What's going on?" Dao finally demanded.

"I thought we were being followed. I guess I'm wrong."

*     *     *

Tanaka, the pockmarked *yakuza* who had had the misfortune with the guns, watched Stark's reflection in the window of the eyeglass shop. His partner was the moon-faced Saito. Both men had been detectives in Osaka until they were caught in a payoff scandal and encouraged to resign. They were skilled at surveillance.

This was the most important duty they had ever been honored with. They had been chosen, Tanaka knew, in part because their features looked the most Chinese. They were able to pass easily through the crowds. As long as they didn't open their mouths, they were safe. Their mission did not involve any talking.

"You are behaving most strangely," she said. "Are you thinking of another woman?"

"No. I keep feeling we're being followed."

"It might be police."

"Why?"

"They may be following me. I'm sorry if I embarrass you."

"Why do you think you're being followed?"

"You know I deal in antiques."

"Yes."

"Sometimes the country they come from does not approve of their being sold. There are restrictions. I sell to legitimate people. Museums. Collectors. But there are too many rules to keep track of."

"I see," Stark said. "It's no matter."

"You really don't care?"

"I can't say I don't care, but it's a gray area. I know countries like Burma and Cambodia are tough on smuggling antiquities but do little to protect them. It's a tough call whether they're better off tucked away in someone's private collection or eroding in the jungle."

She hugged him.

"Which doesn't mean I won't try to reform you," Stark said. "But that will be later."

"I hope we have many laters together."

Tanaka's instructions were quite clear. Get Stark somewhere alone. Shoot him. Then leave the note on the body.

# SEIZE THE DRAGON

The note stated, "Imperialist filth Robert Stark has been executed by order of the Japanese Red Army. All enemies of the revolution will meet the same fate."

The hardest part would be getting Stark alone. Hong Kong was as crowded as Tokyo. But Tanaka was patient.

"I should drop you at your hotel," Stark said. "You said you had an appointment this evening."

"I'll cancel it. I'd rather be with you."

"It's best not. If we do have a tail, they may be after me."

"Why would they?"

"I've made many enemies."

"Yes. Like the drunken pig who works for Rupert Murdoch who you cooled off last night. Or the KGB man who pretends to work for Novosti. Or the *Tai Lo*."

"How did you hear?"

"Hong Kong is really a small place," she said. "Circles within circles. I would guess half the colony knows what happened at the party. At least among the whites. As a new face, you would be gossiped about even if you were a wallflower."

"Are you hungry?" Stark asked.

"Ravenous."

He signaled for a cab.

Tanaka and Saito hailed a cab and directed the driver to follow the taxi bearing Stark and Dao. They rode through the tunnel linking the north end of Hong Kong Island with Aberdeen. Called "Little Hong Kong" by the Chinese, the community of Aberdeen was once a typhoon shelter and land base for pirates. For a while it was a major shipbuilding center. In recent years the three major floating restaurants in Shum Wan Harbor, with innumerable smaller seafood eateries, were the main attraction.

The *yakuza* followed, watching as Stark and the woman walked to the waterfront. The wharf was lined with walla wallas, the small boats with canvas roofs that ferry customers out to the restaurants. The elderly females who piloted the crafts shouted to get attention, waving arms made wiry by hours spent poling on the harbor. Dao haggled and eventually settled on a price with one woman. Stark helped Dao step into the boat. Her short leather skirt rode high on her leg and earned a disapproving glance from the elderly pilot.

The two *yakuza* hurried to the walla walla at the far edge of the line. The woman quoted them a price. They agreed without bargaining. With greedy glee she started the small motor on her boat.

It was a moonless night, the strings of lights illuminating the floating restaurants standing out gaudily in the gloom. A fog was rolling in, softening the multicolored lights. In the distance, barely visible lights twinkled from apartment houses on the shore.

On the water a motley mix of working boats—tugs and junks, sampans and barges—made their way through the dark. The darkness and fog hid the pieces of floating garbage and the worn surfaces of the boats, creating a mysterious, romantic, and somewhat threatening mood.

The walla wallas made their way toward the restaurants. There was a light chop in the water, and the ride was bumpy.

"Should we do it?" Saito asked.

"What about the woman with him?" Tanaka responded.

"She looks like a whore. For him to be killed with her will add to his dishonor."

The elderly woman piloting the boat eyed them, not understanding their Japanese, but sensing the seriousness of their words.

"We could wait a while longer," Tanaka said.

"What if we do not get another chance? What if he takes her back to the hotel? There will be more witnesses then."

Tanaka finally nodded.

"It is time to lighten the load," Saito said. He drew his silenced .32 automatic and shot the surprised pilot through the head. He dumped her body overboard.

They began to gain on Stark's skiff.

As they had pulled away from the dock, Stark had carefully watched the other boats. He had seen the two *yakuza* climb aboard, and the boat set out after them. He hadn't been able to clearly see them kill the old woman but he had surmised what happened after hearing the splash.

"Dao, I'm afraid I was right."

"What?"

"We are being followed. And if they're cops, they've got unusual methods of law enforcement."

# CHAPTER
# 15

The mist shrouded other boats from view. Many cruised without running lights or with only a weak lantern on the bow. Sound traveled well through the moist air, and Stark could hear the noises of families living on boats, workmen grunting at their labors, old engines clanging and sputtering. The old woman went slowly, perhaps fearful of a collision in the fog, though she seemed to have a radarlike knack for avoiding objects.

"Find out if she can go any faster," Stark said to Dao.

Dao inquired in Cantonese and the woman answered.

"She says no," Dao relayed. "She says you westerners are always in a hurry. If she had more money, she could get a better motor, she says. It burns more gas to go faster, and strains her engine."

"If that's a hustle for a bigger tip, tell her we'll pay it."

Dao spoke in Cantonese. The woman extended a gnarled, arthritic hand. Stark passed her money. The woman flicked a knob on the motor and they went faster.

But not enough.

Stark heard the *spllllllit*, then a ping as the bullet struck the motor. He recognized the sound of a silenced weapon and guessed what had happened. The engine sputtered and died.

"Get down," Stark said, shoving Dao to the floor and reaching to do the same for the old woman.

She pushed his hand away and fiddled with her engine. She cursed, then found the bullet hole. Another *splllit*. Then five more in rapid succession. Two shots caught her in the chest, one piercing her aorta. A plume of blood gushed out. Stark tried to catch her, but she fell overboard.

The *yakuza* came closer.

Stark grabbed the old woman before she could drift away. But as he pulled her head out of the water he saw her eyes were lifeless. He let the body slide back down. There was blood on his hands from the old woman. He smeared a few streaks on Dao's forehead and neck. He did the same for himself.

"Whatever happens, don't move," Stark whispered to Dao. Then he sprawled across the boat with one hand resting on the walla-walla pilot's short oar. He could hear the gunmen talking. In Japanese. The voices had an Osaka accent, with a slightly stronger pronunciation of the *u* at the end of Japanese verbs.

"Do you think they're dead?" Stark heard one man ask.

"Must be."

"What if he has a gun?"

"He would've used it by now."

"Let's check."

"Don't forget the note"

Stark could hear Dao's breathing. He hoped she didn't panic and cry out. All he had on his side was surprise.

"What about the woman?" a voice asked in Japanese.

"We'll see."

There was a gentle thump as the *yakuza*'s skiff banged into the walla walla with Stark and Dao.

A face peered over the gunwale.

"Can you see anything?" the pockmarked *yakuza* asked.

"I see him. He has got blood all over him. The woman too."

Moonface clambered into the boat. He wore surgical gloves and held a piece of paper.

"Make sure he is dead," Pockmarks said.

Moonface stood over Stark, his finger tight on the trigger of the .32 in his hand. When the *gaijin* was positively dead,

125

he would have to throw the murder weapon into the ha
He hated giving up the silenced .32. A Beretta. He w
he had a picture of himself with it.

"Come on. Move it," Pockmarks yelled from the
boat. "We'll get visitors soon."

Stark swung the oar with all his strength, the paddl
catching Moonface in the throat. He gagged and cough

"Saito, what's happening?" Tanaka hissed.

Stark reached up and grabbed Saito by the testicle
yanked. Saito fell, one hand clutching his throat, the
his groin. Stark heaved him overboard.

"Tanaka! Help!" Saito croaked, his voice a weak
from the blow to the throat.

"Saito? Where are you?"

Saito was trying to swim, speak, and clutch his
simultaneously.

"I fell overboard," Stark said in Japanese, mimi
Saito's harsh voice.

"Where are you?"

"To the left."

"Don't listen. It's a trick," Saito gasped.

"What was that?"

Tanaka was scanning the water as Stark, holdin
paddle like a samurai sword, leapt into his boat. T
twisted to bring the gun into play. Stark's paddle caug
wrist. He yelped and dropped the weapon.

Tanaka threw a light jab at Stark's face, a distra
move. Stark blocked it and anticipated a follow-up. It
with an attempted hook to the ribs. Stark blocked wi
elbow.

The boat rocked as the men scuffled. Kicking was ii
sible and keeping balance difficult.

Tanaka whipped a short-bladed knife from his pocke
he charged, Stark sidestepped, grabbing Tanaka's colla
arm, and turning at the hips. Stark swept out Tanaka
with the left foot.

Tanaka hit the water like a whale doing a bellyflop.

He swam to the boat and clung to the gunwale.
leaned over and laid the paddle across Tanaka's han
noticed that the pinkie had been snipped off on one ha

"What is the note you were supposed to leave?"

asked in guttural Japanese. He applied a little pressure to the paddle. "The note. I'll break your arm and leave you here to drown."

"From the Japanese Red Army. That's who sent us."

"Bull. You are a *yakuza* punk. Who is your *oya-bun?*"

There was a sudden splashing sound in the water nearby. Stark let up on Tanaka's hand and scanned where he had last seen Saito.

The Hong Kong government tries to keep the more than twenty species of sharks native to the waters away from the coast. But people throw garbage in the water and the waste is as inviting as chum.

Killing the old woman who'd piloted Stark's sampan had doomed the *yakuza*. Her leaking blood stimulated the scent glands of a few cruising sharks more than a mile away. They raced toward the blood.

The first one to hit the old lady was a leopard shark. She was dead, and didn't notice a leg being ripped out of the socket and the resulting feeding frenzy. Saito was not so lucky. He was still alive when the hammerhead hit him and took off an arm. He had a chance to see the horrid face, eyes out on the sides of the protruding fleshy body as it swam off with a piece of him. Then the others closed in.

Tanaka turned to see the splash of water, the blood, the fins. The *yakuzu* thrashed, trying to climb aboard. It was the worst thing he could do. The violent, jerky movements were nearly as exciting to the sharks as blood. A hammerhead swallowed his foot.

Stark grabbed Tanaka's arm and tried to pull him aboard. But Stark couldn't win a tug-of-war with a ten-foot thousand-pound fish at the other end. Then other sharks discovered the fresh meat. Tanaka screamed as a tiger shark bit his side.

Another shark hungrily crashed into Tanaka. Stark nearly toppled into the water. Using both hands, he caught his balance at the railing. His face almost touched the bloody water. He could smell the foul breath of a leopard shark as it snapped within inches of his face.

He pulled himself upright.

The boat rocked violently as the sharks smashed into it and each other, rending the three corpses in the water.

Dao was sitting up in the other boat, staring, wide-eyed.

The two boats were drifting apart. Dao's boat was lying lower in the water.

"Are you okay?" Stark called out.

"Yes."

"I'll see if I can find a line to bring us together. Just lie on the floor of the boat."

"Robert." Her voice was quivery.

"Yes?"

"There's a leak in this boat."

# CHAPTER
## 16

"I'm really glad you could come to Las Vegas, Les. You don't mind if I call you Les, do you?"

"Not at all. The same goes for my calling you Lou, right?"

"Right." Lou lifted a glass of Moët champagne and clinked it against Les's. Drinks had been poured by a scantily clad redhead who kept brushing against Les like a cat with a scratching post.

The men lounged on a mammoth, plush sofa in the Golden Luck Casino's penthouse suite. Normally the room was offered free to high rollers who could be counted on to drop at least one hundred thousand dollars during a weekend visit to Las Vegas. It had lavish furnishings—lots of gold trim and silver sequins, gaudy chandeliers, airbrushed autographed photos of stars who had stayed there. Everything to set a nouveau riche businessman's or backwoods cattle baron's heart a-flutter.

"Les and Lou. Sounds like an act I booked into the show room one time," Lou said.

"Well, I'm sure our act will be a hit," Halliwell predicted.

"Me too. I don't think you can ever spend too much money on security. Electronics, backed by skilled humans. You know, I was thinking of starting a company once, to handle casinos in Atlantic City."

"Perhaps we could work something out."

"Sounds possible."

The pair had been drinking for three hours and still hadn't settled on a price for security coverage. Les Halliwell knew his host was a mobster and that Stark wouldn't approve of the deal. But it would be hard for his moralistic partner to say no to a fait accompli.

Lou was offering to pay premium rates, and he was asking them only to protect legitimate businesses he owned. So what if Lou were a bit of a crook. Hadn't Rockefeller, Carnegie, and the other pillars of American industry played rough in their time? And now their names were on libraries, charities, and universities. Still, Les felt uncomfortable. Which is exactly what his adversary wanted.

Louis Scalish had learned the value of moving slowly to wear down an opponent during his time as Machiavelli.

He had decided that he was better able to take care of Stark than Sun Tzu. But there was no point in confronting a master counterterrorist head-on. Scalish would get at Stark through his family, friends, loved ones, associates. Everyone ultimately was vulnerable.

An hour later, and Scalish and Halliwell were watching a floor show downstairs. Bare-breasted women ran across the stage while music blasted. They changed costumes quickly in the wings, putting on high headresses with feathers. Then they ran back and forth across the stage again. After a couple of Rockette-type numbers, there was a comedian-magician, then a hokey drama.

The grand finale offered lots more running back and forth, fireworks, and fancy stage sets.

"Now, that's entertainment," Scalish said. "Right?"

"Nice."

In truth, all Les could think about was the redhead's hand, which rested on his thigh. His wife and kids were a blur. He only had eyes for cleavage, buttocks, and long legs.

Back at the deluxe suite, they were joined by a pretty teenage Hispanic girl who fluttered around Scalish the way the redhead tended Halliwell. As they sank into the huge soft sofa, Les tried to get the conversation on track and get a commitment from Scalish.

"How can we get down to business if your partner ain't around?" Scalish said. "We're talking a multi-million-dollar contract. Several buildings, including my home. You wouldn't want me to risk the life of my sainted wife and kids with some unknown guy." The fact that Scalish had his hand up the Hispanic girl's short dress while he spoke didn't quite jibe with his words. But Halliwell, fogged by alcohol and lust, couldn't figure out why.

"My partner's on assignment in Hong Kong right now," Halliwell said. The redhead's hand was tracing little patterns. He hadn't had blue balls like this since he was in high school.

"What's your partner doing?"

"I can't tell you," Halliwell said. "Company policy."

Scalish got up and pulled the Hispanic girl roughly to her feet. "Okay," Scalish said, hurt in his voice. He marched out, practically dragging the girl.

"Wait, maybe . . ." But the door was already shut.

The redhead embraced Les. "Don't worry. He'll be back."

"You think so?"

"I know so," she said.

"How long?"

"Probably about an hour."

"Maybe I should—" His words were cut off as she pressed her lips against his. She ground her hips into him.

Scalish watched through a peephole. He had the young Hispanic girl, Carmelita, on her knees in front of him. He held on to her hair, twisting, while she took his thrusts into her mouth.

He was already bored with her and let her know it. He'd performed every act upon her body he could dream up, sometimes joined by a couple of men, or women. He had degraded her beyond anything she could have imagined before that terrible day when she was sold to him.

She had lasted longer than the others. There was something inside of her, something he hadn't been able to sully. Maybe a few months in his whorehouse would teach her a lesson. Make her the discount special, for lonely truckers, cowboys, rough and ready.

\* \* \*

131

Dao's boat bobbed like a cork in a hurricane. Sharks rammed into it, tasting it. The water around her was slick with blood, the sharks thrashed in a delirious rapture. A shark would itself get bitten, then turned on by its fellows. The blood in the water spread, and newcomers would join the grisly orgy. The human bodies were long gone.

Yells for help in English and Cantonese had been a wasted effort. The fog reduced traffic and made pinpointing sound impossible. The few boat people who had ventured near had seen the fins slicing through the water and quickly piloted their small craft away.

The only rope in Stark's boat was barely six feet long. Dao, also, had only a short line. There was no way to tow her to safety without getting close.

Stark maneuvered his boat so it was a few feet from Dao's. He couldn't get any nearer without being swamped by the sharks.

"Rip off clothing and plug the holes," Stark yelled to her.

Dao tore the sleeves from her dress and plugged two holes. But there was already six inches of water in the boat, and it lay low in the water. Thrashing sharks splashed water in as they violently rocked the boat.

During a lull Stark pulled up next to Dao and lashed the boats together. It was too dangerous for her to jump to him. The tumult in the water could send her flying off to one side.

The frenzy started anew.

Stark took the silenced gun and sighted through the water. About ten yards off to starboard a couple of fresh sharks were zooming toward the frenzied mass. Stark fired the rest of the bullets. The newcomers began leaking blood into the water. They went from being diners to dinners. The eddies and swirls shifted farther from the boats. The feeding sharks pounced on the wounded newcomers.

Stark, balanced precariously, reached out. Dao took his hand. He pulled her into his boat. They hugged. She was trembling, her lip gnawed bloody from terror.

The wounded sharks injured others as they were attacked. The surface of the water was a writhing mass of silvery fins and bloody body parts.

Stark guided Dao to sit, cut them free from the sinking walla walla, then started up his engine.

The putt-putt of the motor taking them away from the scene was a heavenly melody.

Les sat in the hot tub, the naked redhead next to him. Scalish was in a chair facing them. Les had just finished a lengthy plug for his business. The heat combined with the champagne to create a contented sluggishness.

"Your partner, what kind of guy is he?"

"Great! First rate. The best," Halliwell said.

"He got a wife, kids?"

"Why do you ask?"

"I think family men are more responsible," Scalish explained. "These single guys take risks to show off for broads."

Halliwell thought about his own wife and children and felt guilty. But in the finest tradition of "the show must go on," he persevered with his sales pitch.

"My partner is very cautious, very careful," Halliwell said as the redhead refilled his champagne glass.

"I don't know," Scalish said. "He's single, he's probably so busy hunting pussy every night that he don't think straight."

"No. He's got a steady girlfriend," Halliwell said. "A Russian doctor he saved. They're very serious, probably going to be married soon." I sure hope not, Halliwell thought to himself. "Her name's Sultana Mirnov. She was a very famous microbiologist. Real smart."

"So this Russian doctor he saved, this Mirnov, she's in the States now?" Scalish asked casually.

"Yeah. She just threw a temper tantrum, got a job in San Jose."

"No shit."

After a few more minutes conversation, Scalish suggested they call it a night. Les agreed. Scalish left. Les got out of the hot tub and slipped on a robe. He sat on the couch while the redhead mixed a drink for him. They sipped together while looking out at the lights of Las Vegas.

"I probably shouldn't'a told him all that stuff," Les said, his words growing more and more slurred. "Company policy. Boy, my partner would be pissed."

"Don't worry. You can trust Louie with your life."

"I got that feeling," Les said.

Then the barbiturate she'd slipped into his drink kicked over, and he was snoring. She dumped him on the sofa and sauntered out.

Carmelita was with Scalish in his office.

"Come here," he said.

She approached him. He slapped her so hard she fell to the floor. "Cunt. You're getting boring. The same old pathetic faces all the time. Now, get outta here. I got business to take care of."

She stepped out of the room but pressed her ear against the door. She heard him punch in a long distance phone number.

"That's right. I want you to grab this Mirnov broad. I don't have her address, schmuck. I couldn't make him that suspicious. Hire a P.I., check the new phone listings. She works for a biotech company. Grab her."

Stark and Dao lay in bed in a hotel room holding each other tightly.

"I suppose I owe you an explanation," Dao said, breaking the silence.

"For what?"

"Those men weren't police. They were *yakuza*."

"Yes."

"One time, I was partners with someone on an art deal. It turned out she was working for them. The statues we were handling were hollow and filled with stolen jewelry. I didn't know this. She cheated them and they blamed both of us. The *yakuza* have harassed me ever since. I couldn't go to the authorities because of my own legal problems." She shivered. "But they have never tried killing me before, only threats to get their money back."

"I don't think it was you they were after."

"Why would they be after you?"

"It's a long story. I'll tell you, but not now. The problem is to get you to safety."

She held him tighter. "I am safe with you. We are yin and yang." She rolled onto him, crying softly. "We were so close to dying."

"We always are."

"But that was horrible."

"Can't argue with you there."

"How can you be so calm?"

"The only way to live life is to accept death."

"You believe that?"

"Fear can be crippling. If I have to die, I want it to be for something I believe in. Like saving a damsel in distress."

She kissed him.

"That's why the samurai idealized the cherry blossom," he said. "Bloom and fall. It's not how you live, but how you die."

"You are special."

"Of course part of me says, 'What the hell am I doing here' when it looks like I'm going to be fish food. But dying can't be much worse than high school was."

She screwed up her features.

"That was a joke," he said. "Not a good one, but a joke nevertheless."

"You Americans make a joke of everything."

"Not quite everything," he said, and they kissed again. Her movements against him grew more rhythmic. He knew what was coming. A thank-God-I'm-alive romp. He gave himself over to it. The pleasure might never come again.

At 2 A.M. he got up. Dao's breathing remained even.

*Don't leave the room for any reason. I'll be back,* he wrote to her. He slipped out of the room and checked that there were no hostiles in the area.

Stark stopped at an all-night drugstore on Nathan Road in Tsimshatsui, the major tourist area. Jars of Noxema were adjacent to jars of powdered deer antler, Tylenol on the same shelf as ginseng root.

Stark bought tanning lotion, tape, and an eyebrow pencil. He returned to the room he had first rented, again, only after checking the vicinity. He climbed out of a hall window and made his way along a ledge to his window. He looked, decided it was safe, and climbed in.

Stark applied generous amounts of tanning lotion to his face and hands. He slipped into an all-black outfit. The only weapon he had was a modified Swiss Army knife. Instead of a toothpick, it concealed a two-piece pick set.

The tanning lotion had dried and turned his skin a yellowish-orangish tint. He used the tape to pull up the corner of his eyes, and the eyebrow pencil to reshape his eyebrows. In bright light, or within a few feet, it would fool no one. But from a distance, moving, in the dark, it could confuse an eyewitness.

He headed for the kung fu studio Wong had mentioned.

The phone awoke Sun Tzu from a light sleep. "Yes?"

"The *gwai lo* has gone out."

"Where?"

"I don't know."

Sun Tzu made a clucking noise of disapproval. "Any ideas?"

"No. I am sorry, Father."

More disapproving noises, then Sun Tzu hung up abruptly.

Kwan picked up the phone before the first ring had finished. He was instantly awake, sitting up at the side of the bed.

"Speak," he said into the phone.

"The *gwai lo* is roaming around," Sun Tzu said.

"What would you like me to do?" Recognizing Sun Tzu's voice, Kwan's tone had become deferential. Kwan was a ferocious enforcer. There were few men Kwan was afraid of. Sun Tzu was one of them.

"Go to your studio. Make sure it is secure. My nightingales tell me the police have suspicions about you. Stark may have heard their whispers."

"I will leave immediately."

"Wait at the school. If the *gwai lo* shows up elsewhere, I will call you and tell you where to go."

"What should I do with him?"

"Give him a thorough beating. Teach him it is impolite to make trouble in Hong Kong. Let him go elsewhere."

"It will be an honor."

"Be careful. He is skilled as a fighter," Sun Tzu said.

Kwan snorted. He had won tournaments in kick-boxing, full-contact karate, and no-holds-barred kung fu. He said a polite good-bye and hung up.

As Kwan dressed, he contemplated what a great pleasure it would be showing Stark how little he knew.

# CHAPTER
## 17

Les Halliwell awoke feeling rotten. Real rotten. More rotten than he'd felt in a long time. Someone was banging a sledgehammer into his temples. His tongue had grown hair and swollen to fill his mouth. The softest noise was like a thunderclap. He rolled off the sofa and the fall to the floor felt like a drop from a three-story building. This is the worst hangover ever, he thought.

The night before was a blur. He remembered a redhead, spending hours talking to Scalish. About what?

The phone rang and he cried out in pain. It was the New York office. Bunny tried to talk about business, but all he could do was grunt and moan.

"Let Pedro handle it," he said.

"He's in L.A. with his family."

"Uhhhh."

"Speaking of family, your wife wants you to call."

"Uhhhh. Tell her I'm on assignment. I'm not up to speaking to her."

"What about the Koontz account? We've got to let them know today if we can beat the other estimate."

"I'll call you back. Better yet, you decide."

"Thanks a million. Do I get a raise to go with my increased responsibility?"

"Anything you want."

"You really are sick, ain't you? I'll delay what I can."

She hung up and he staggered to a mirrored wall. The face that looked back at him was as miserable as he felt. He dressed. It took much longer than usual since he misbuttoned his shirt and had trouble lacing up his shoes.

There were two gentle knocks at the door, but each blow reverberated inside his skull.

"Coming, dammit."

He stumbled to the doorway, rapping his shins against a glass table and adding to his misery. Rubbing his sore leg, he hobbled to the door and pulled it open.

The teenage girl who had been with Scalish stood there.

"What do you want?" he asked.

She put a finger to her lips and passed him a note. "My name Carmelita. There is bug in you room," she had written in awkward, childish letters. The note had taken her hours to compose. "You have drug and talk about a lady doctor. Scalish get her."

"Damn, damn, damn, damn," Les said. He clutched his head, trying to squeeze the pain out.

She crooked her finger and he followed her out into the hall.

Carmelita looked both ways, then held out a vial with a white powder in it.

"What's that?"

"*Cocaína*," she whispered.

"I can't."

"Make you feel good," she said.

He reached for it, then pulled his hand back. Halliwell avoided taking any medicine, let alone an illegal drug being offered by a teenager in the lion's den.

I can't feel worse, he finally decided, taking the vial and scarfing a small spoonful up his nose. A cold numbing sensation spread from his nose to the back of his mouth. Within moments he felt ready to take on Louie Scalish, and every mafioso in Las Vegas.

"You're an angel of mercy," Halliwell said to Carmelita.

"I get you out of here," she volunteered. She led him down a fire stairway and out of the hotel. He questioned her about Scalish, but the language barrier made detailed communication impossible. Before they parted, he said, "Carmelita, what can I do for you?"

She shook her head.

He reached into his wallet and took out all the cash he had, a few hundred dollars. "Here. Get away. Or maybe I can take you to the authorities. How old are you?"

"No! No government," she said, recoiling. She couldn't express her belief, not unjustified, that Scalish had enough illegal clout to get her back from the authorities. "It is too late for me. I am no good anymore."

"That's bull."

"I am a whore."

"You're just a kid. I'll take you to someone who can help."

"The pig would find me. Make it worse." She spoke heavily accented English. Every "i" was pronounced like "eee."

"I'll protect you." He realized immediately how ridiculous the offer must have sounded from a hung-over guy whom she had to help.

She shook her head and took a few steps away from him. "There is one thing you can do."

"Name it."

"Each night I pray to Blessed Virgin for him to die. She ignores my prayers. It is not something a good girl asks. But it is all I want."

"I can't say anything about killing him, but my first order of business is making his life miserable."

"Kill him," Carmelita said, and hurried away.

Teenage girls could be melodramatic in their loves and hates, but the power of her desire for vengeance was like a palpable force.

At the first pay phone he could find he called Bunny in New York. "Do you have a number for Sultana?" he asked.

"I don't think she's got a home phone yet. Giving us an update ain't high on her list of priorities, I suspect."

"Call her at work. I just heard the hostiles are after her."

"I thought we kept her and Robert's relationship under wraps. How'd they find out who she is, where she is?"

"Don't ask questions. Just get on it. How long before you can get a team out there to baby-sit her?"

"Using local talent, the San Jose P.D., or New York people?"

"People we trust."

"A few hours. Quickest way would be to get Pedro up from L.A."

"This is an emergency. Do it," Les barked before hanging up.

Bunny muttered as she slammed the phone down. But she was quick to pick it up again and call San Jose. Dr. Mirnov was not yet at work. It was nine A.M., and usually Mirnov would already be at her lab bench. The receptionist who handled the call was surprised. She promised to have Sultana call in as soon as she arrived.

The streets were quiet. Cooler, less sticky. No traffic honk and rumble, no clatter of carts, no shouted Cantonese. Stark's footsteps echoed off the high-rise slum walls. The sound of a few TVs playing floated from open windows.

Passersby ignored Stark. It was the time for dragging oneself home from bars, slipping out of mistresses' apartments, or committing burglaries.

The kung fu dojo was located on the top floor of an eleven-story building. The elevator was shut down for the night. Stark climbed the stairs, all senses humming.

The only light came from distantly spaced low-wattage bulbs that hung from bare cords. There was a figure curled up in a stairwell. Stark pressed against the grimy wall. A slight snoring sound. Stark advanced. The figure shifted. Stark's left hand was about a foot in front of him, fingertips up. His right a few inches behind that, in a fist. He could block, make a hammer fist, and punch with equal ease.

The figure, clad in tattered, stained clothing, curled tighter into a ball. Next to the homeless man was a trash bag packed with belongings. Stark continued up the steps. On the tenth floor landing he paused. He let his pulse and respiration slow to normal. He checked that the heavy metal fire door had no alarms, then eased through.

The floor directory showed there was the usual assortment of companies with "International" or "Trading" in their name. Ten small suites. The dojo was about halfway down the short hall.

# SEIZE THE DRAGON

The dojo was protected from the outside world by a flimsy wooden door. No alarm. Not much inside to steal. It took Stark thirty seconds with a credit card—he didn't need his pick set—to open the snap lock.

The sour scent of sweat assailed his nostrils as he stepped in and shut the door behind him. The school was a large room, with a thin mat on the floor, a couple of heavy sand punching bags hanging in one corner, a cubicle on the other side. On the grimy walls were two posters of Bruce Lee and a few spots stained with what looked like blood.

Dominating the room was a sixteen-by-twenty color photo of a scowling man with a Fu Manchu mustache. SIFU WESLEY KWAN was written in big letters underneath, followed by a list of credentials, including black belts in four different styles of kung fu and *wu shu*.

Kwan was stripped bare to the waist and had one hand tense in an eagle-claw grip. The other held a pair of *nunchaku*. Nunchucks were a couple of foot-long wood or metal sticks linked by rope or chain. Developed from an Okinawan threshing tool, they were deadly weapons capable of shattering bone as if it were brittle taffy.

Stark pulled up a corner of the mat. He played his Mini Mag light back and forth. This could be the kung fu school's version of hiding valuables under the carpeting.

Nothing. He looked behind the Bruce Lee posters and again was unrewarded.

There was a squeak outside. He froze. Quiet again.

He padded into the office cubicle. He checked the neatly organized desk drawer and found pens, pencils, paper clips, tape. He pulled the drawers out and looked in the empty space. He lifted the blotter, checked the cushioning on the seat, and in the small space between the file cabinet and the wall.

The two-drawer file cabinet was locked. A promising sign. It yielded after about thirty seconds with his pick set. One drawer was filled with files for each student. Aside from the basic bio information and a photo, he could only guess what the other Chinese writing signified. He guessed part was an insurance waiver and the student's rank certificate. It looked like there were the results of a written test and an oath on parchment. Stark thumbed through the photos. They were a thuggish-looking crew.

In the second drawer were the business records. Stark thumbed through the papers. The ones in English were routine, no unusual supplies ordered, no unusual income shown. He came to the lengthy phone bill.

He ran a finger down a sheet. A few to Japan. He could tell by the exchange they were to Tokyo and Osaka. Some to Macao.

He would take the bill from the month before. Chances were it was paid already, and only one missing might not be noticed. He'd jot down any repeat numbers from the latest bill. He folded the bill and put it in his pocket.

Something deep in his lizard brain stayed alert. By now he had programmed in the normal creaks and groans of the building and traffic noises. There was a squeak that was different.

He spun to the side just as the aluminum *nunchaku* stick swooshed through the air. It split the thick oak desktop.

Stark rolled again, pushing the desk chair at his attacker. The stick smashed down, heavily denting the side of the metal file cabinet. Stark shined the halogen light of his flashlight in his attacker's face. It stunned him for a fraction of a second, long enough for Stark to lunge for the man's legs.

But the attacker jumped aside and prepared to swing his sticks again. Stark did a forward roll out of the cramped office.

They were on the mat, facing each other. The nunchucks made a whistling-whooshing sound as the man swirled them. A few shafts of light from the window allowed Stark to see his attacker's face. It was the man whose image was on the wall, *Sifu* Kwan. He stood loose but with feet firmly planted. Well-balanced, uncommitted to any direction, ready to attack in a variety of ways.

Stark backed up around the mat. "Maybe we can work something out."

The *sifu* swirled his sticks and advanced. A shot to the head from them would most likely kill or reduce Stark to a lifetime of drooling on his shoes.

"I'm just looking for a few bucks. I thought this was the International Trading Company."

Whoosh-whoosh-whoosh.

Kwan moved suddenly. Stark ducked under the blow and launched a low kick. Kwan blocked it with a downward chop just above the knee, a blow that numbed Stark's leg. Stark limped back a few feet.

Kwan attacked again. Stark managed to get a sandbag between him and the studio owner. The nunchaku crashed against the bag. Stark pushed the bag forward. The stick smashed around the other side. Crack. The heavy canvas on the sandbag tore. Sand poured out as if it were a broken hourglass.

"I'll pay for damages," Stark offered. "What say we call it a night?"

Again the stick lashed out. The bag rocked and creaked on the chains. It was growing skinnier by the second.

"Bruce Lee would never attack an unarmed man with nunchucks," Stark said.

"Fuck Bruce Lee," Kwan responded.

Seeing the intruder in his dojo had enraged Kwan. He had forgotten Sun Tzu's instructions to give Stark just a beating. He would be satisfied by nothing less than the *gwai lo*'s death.

Kwan let out his breath in a long, slow hiss, like a bored snake about to strike after toying with his victim.

# CHAPTER
# 18

Dr. Sultana Mirnov looked at the indentation on the bed next to her and thought about the big mistake she had made.

It had started as a night out with her new co-workers. Two other women, three men. Lots of laughs, lots of drinks. Dinner at a restaurant, back to one woman's home for more drinks. Sultana had been paired, unwillingly, with a man her age who worked in another division of the company.

The company, Personal Industries Technology—jokingly referred to by its workers as "The Pits"—had two major divisions in San Jose, both with a biological orientation. Mirnov worked in their over-the-counter medicine unit, which was responsible for two cold medicines, an allergy capsule, a sore-throat lozenge, a backache-relief medicine, a pill to keep you awake, another to ease you to sleep. Basically the company mixed aspirin or acetaminophen with caffeine or several antihistamines in various proportions.

She was involved in state-of-the-art research on interferon, the protein that interfered with the reproduction of viruses and had been used to treat various infections and tumors. Results were as yet inconclusive. Her unit was doing recombinant DNA research. They had the latest equipment and a flexible budget. The chairman of PIT had decided that they were going to be on the cutting edge of biotechnology.

They had absorbed a couple of small biotech firms, like an amoeba engulfing a paramecium.

Mirnov's "date" had been the founder of his own biotechnology firm. When his company was bought by PIT, he was hired as a consultant. An entrepreneur, his major interest was his business, followed closely by himself. He was divorced, no kids, a rabid jogger, football fan, militant non-smoker, Republican. She doubted if he knew much more about her than her name. She doubted if he even cared about that. He had talked nonstop about himself, pausing only to ask if she wanted another drink.

So how had he found his way into her bed?

That was Robert Stark's fault. He had given her such a cold send-off. The creep. She was going to show him. But instead of feeling smug, she felt soiled.

She rolled up the sheets and pillowcases and stuffed them into the hamper. She picked up the condom wrapper from the floor. He was competent in bed, but interested only in himself. She knew she had made a bad choice in going out with him and a worse decision when they had gotten intimate.

By now half the people at work probably thought of her as the Russian slut. Her date would no doubt boast, another achievement. She cursed herself. Which was why she wasn't going to go into work. She had disconnected the phone the night before and didn't bother to plug it in. Let them be mad at her.

Mirnov didn't value what she was doing. She had been much more fulfilled at UCLA, working on viruses that threatened people's lives. So what if $50 million a year was lost in productivity due to colds. How did that compare to saving the lives of children suffering from hepatitis B? But she couldn't go back to public-sector research. She wouldn't give Stark the satisfaction of an "I told you so."

Wrapped in her robe, she padded around, tidying up. There was no note from her "date," only a dirty plate on the table. He had helped himself to breakfast before leaving. He had tried to wake her up for another romp, but she had feigned being in a deep sleep.

She had been so desperate to make new friends, to get

146

over Stark, that she'd been easy prey. She was working on a heady anger when the doorbell rang.

She yanked the door open. "Yes?"

It was Pedro.

"Is Robert okay?" was her first reaction.

"Yes. May I come in, please?"

"Of course."

He was always polite. Not just because she was Stark's lady. He genuinely liked her. Of those in Stark's inner circle, he could most understand the hardships of emigrating to the United States, learning a new language, and even harder, a new culture.

She could see the tension in him. "Robert is really okay?"

"Yes. It's you we're worried about. Apparently Les got information that someone's after you."

"Who?"

"I'm not sure."

"Why?"

"Don't know."

"When?"

He shrugged.

"What do you want me to do?"

"I'll take you to a safe house."

"For how long?"

"I don't know."

She had wanted an excuse to give up her job. But her anger at Stark welled up. "What is this? I must run my life to suit Mr. Robert Stark. Drop everything when he wants. No." She pulled her robe tight and folded her arms across her chest. "I will not quit my job because of vague threat."

"We wouldn't be bothering you if we didn't think it was serious," he said patiently.

"I will not ruin my life because of Mr. Stark!"

"Maybe we can arrange for you to stay at a motel. I'll sleep on a couch and accompany you to work. You can continue your life without any difference until we pin down who is behind the threat."

"No difference? Except I must look over my shoulder every minute," she snapped.

"I will protect you."

"The whole Secret Service can't protect your President. You alone can protect me?"

"I am not alone."

"Is Robert here?" She felt her expectations rise. Maybe they could patch it up. Had he seen her "date" leaving that morning?

"Not Mr. Stark."

There was a knock at the door. Pedro instantly had his .44 Magnum, a Dirty Harry gun, out and at his side. He nodded to Mirnov.

"Who is it?" she asked.

"Police. Open up."

She peeped through the hole. "It is policeman." She began to open the door. Pedro stepped out and blocked it with his foot. He peeped through. A uniformed cop stood on the threshold.

"Let's see ID," Pedro said.

The cop reached down.

At the same moment Pedro heard glass breaking on the other side of the house. He turned his head. The cop at the door drew his gun.

"Pedro!" Mirnov screamed. She threw herself against the door, slamming it shut as the cop's gun discharged.

Pedro spun and aimed his .44 at the other door just as a second cop came running in from the rear, gun drawn.

"Put the gun down," Pedro said.

"You put your gun down," the cop said. "You're under arrest."

"We'll talk about it later. The bullet from this gun will go right through your bulletproof vest, amigo."

"Backup will be here any minute," the cop said. "We had a report of a suspicious person in the area."

"Pedro, maybe you should ..." Mirnov began.

"No," Pedro said. "Call Chief Ohara. He's in charge of the department," Pedro told her.

"Go ahead and do that, lady," the cop said.

She saw Pedro shift and look over the cop's shoulder. "Backup is here," Pedro said. "Put your gun down."

"That's the oldest trick in the book," the cop responded.

"*Maricon*," a new voice said.

The cop spun. Two gang members with short-barreled shotguns stood in the doorway.

Simultaneously there were three short knocks at the front door and Pedro opened it. The other cop, his handcuffs on his own wrists, was led in by two more gang members.

The gang members belonged to Pony Boys, the east Los Angeles gang Pedro had led as a young man. Pedro had risen to be the president, and then quit. He was the first president to not retire due to death or prison. He occasionally used the more trustworthy members as a strong-arm force. They were fearless. The biggest problem was keeping them from shooting first and asking questions later.

One of them shoved the cop from the front door. The policeman stumbled to the floor.

"Fucking pig," the gang member said.

"He's not a cop," Pedro said. "At least not in San Jose. He didn't know the real police chief's name."

"Not Ohara?" Mirnov asked.

"McNamara. I read a book he wrote."

"A police textbook?"

"A mystery," Quesada said. "He's a good writer."

"Fucking fake pig," the gang member said, and kicked a phony officer in the ribs.

"Easy," Pedro said. The backup squad had handcuffed the cop from the rear and rolled him next to his brother "officer."

One of the gang members went through the kidnappers' pockets and came up with drivers' licenses. Pedro caught a couple of the homeboys eyeing Sultana's long legs and the robe which clung to her curves.

"Don't even think about touching a chair she sat on," he growled in Spanish.

"Are you comfortable?" Pedro asked as the plane took off. "I can get you a pillow if you like."

"No, thank you. Saving my life is enough."

"You saved mine. I will always be grateful."

Mirnov was amazed how smoothly Pedro could go from being a thug to a gentleman. "Pedro, where is Robert?"

"I'm not supposed to tell anyone." He winked. "In Hong Kong."

"Did he know what was happening to me?"

"I don't think so." Pedro read the message beneath her words. "I'm sure he would've come if he could have. But he's involved in something very important and it would have taken much too long for him to get here."

"I suppose," she said. But deep down she wished that it was Stark who had rescued her.

Pedro regretted that they had been unable to squeeze much out of the fake cops. They were small-time thugs hired to snatch Mirnov and ship her, drugged, in a vented box to a Las Vegas address. They had been hired by phone, given a down payment by a courier, and never met their employer.

Rather than deal with lengthy explanations to local authorities, Pedro had left them handcuffed and gagged on the floor of Mirnov's apartment. By the time they got out, Sultana would be tucked away.

Sultana patted Pedro's arm and whispered her thanks. But wasn't it Stark's fault that she was in this mess? Bound for a safe house in another city, forced to leave her new job. Yet she hated the job. And she knew it wasn't intentional that she had been put in jeopardy. If Stark had just appeared at that moment, she knew she would forgive him instantly.

# CHAPTER
# 19

Stark's style of combat—evading and deflecting attacks—only added to the *sifu*'s anger. He was used to hard-style fighting, exchanging blows and blocks. Attacking Stark was frustrating, like battling water.

The sandbag was down to half its initial size. Kwan roared and charged.

Stark shoved the bag at Kwan, momentarily delaying him, and ran to the corner where a *bokken*, a wooden training sword, leaned upright. Stark managed to grab it before Kwan reached him. He swung low, forcing Kwan to keep back, and not allowing him to knock the weapon from Stark's hands.

Then Stark lifted and held it in the kendo "on guard" position, tip pointed at the opponent's face, hilt down near Stark's abdomen.

Kwan sent the nunchucks whirling around the wooden sword, capturing it. But Stark used the weapon like a pugil stick, letting Kwan control the top, and ramming the hilt into the *sifu*'s groin.

Kwan let out a gasp. He threw a punch which Stark easily parried. With one hand on Kwan's wrist, and the other on his elbow, Stark pushed in opposite directions. Kwan yelped

151

again as his elbow was dislocated. Stark slammed him into the wall, stunning him.

Stark had to get out before he was forced to kill Kwan, or Kwan killed him.

Stark ran up to the roof, hoping Kwan would run downstairs if he continued his pursuit. The heavy metal fire door screeched as Stark pushed it open. The sky was aglow with the reflection of the lights of Hong Kong. Stark spun his head, trying to decide which rooftops would lead him to safety.

The fire door complained again and Kwan stormed through. The *sifu* had guessed Stark's strategy. *Nunchaku* whirling, he charged.

Stark ran to the edge of the roof. There was a six-foot jump to the next building. Not much of a distance, but if he slipped, he'd plunge seventeen stories. Stark leapt and landed with a roll. He barely had time to get up before Kwan seemed to fly through the air. The *sifu* touched down lightly right next to him. Stark backed into the sharp point of a TV antenna. Kwan swung, knocking the antenna down. Stark grabbed the pole and used it as a weapon. He caught the *sifu*'s thigh with a point, then smashed the pole against his head.

Kwan dropped his nunchucks, which Stark promptly kicked off the roof.

"Are you ready to forgive and forget?" Stark asked, palms open in a conciliatory gesture.

Kwan responded by launching a progression of spinning kicks. Stark backpedaled.

Kwan closed in, hands in the eagle claw, ready to rip throat, eyes, groin, or any soft tissue. Stark kept his hands up, slapping aside the blows, trying to remain loose. Kwan switched to leg techniques, his kicks high and fast. If he attacked lower, Stark thought, there'd be no chance to defend against them. But the *sifu*'s flamboyance was hurting him. Still, Stark was hard pressed to stay out of his reach.

Kwan backed him to the edge of the roof.

As the struggle continued, Stark slipped into the semi-blissful state he'd often found himself in at the dojo. His opponent was his partner in a peculiar dance. He let Kwan lead. The *sifu* was wearing himself out as the battle raged on for what seemed like days. Actually barely five minutes had passed. But Kwan was expending his energy in ferocious displays of speed and power.

Stark sensed the kung fu master's rhythm. *Munen muso,* mind of no mind, running on finely honed instincts. He anticipated a kick and caught the leg. With his other arm he slammed an elbow down into Kwan's meaty quadricep. Stark followed it with a backfist to Kwan's face, the hand kept loose for maximum speed until the millisecond before it made contact.

Stark felt Kwan's nose crush under his blow. Kwan snorted the blood that leaked from his nose and appeared to gain renewed strength.

He launched a flurry of punches and chops, landing a couple on Stark's chest.

Stark dropped suddenly, one arm at Kwan's crotch, the other at his neck, and lifted him in the air in *kata guruma.* One arm held Kwan at the groin, the other was braced under his chin. He was going to throw Kwan to the tar-paper floor. But the *sifu* twisted and fell backward. Right off the roof.

Stark looked over the edge to be sure that Kwan hadn't grabbed a ledge. Kwan had fallen the entire seventeen stories.

Some of the garbage collectors, elderly men and women with big wicker baskets, were already beginning to make their rounds. They had heard the splat and came to investigate. Stark ducked back over the edge quickly as they gazed up.

Two roofs over, as he searched for an open door, he stumbled upon a family living in a corrugated-tin-roofed shanty. They must have heard the skirmish, perhaps even watched it from a distance. Stark's eyes met the man's. He ducked back into his box. Inside, a child was crying.

Stark had to move carefully. Wires were strung across roofs to act as antennae; clotheslines could be a deadly garrote in the weak light.

Three roofs later Stark found an open door and was able to make his way down to the street. He was two blocks from where Kwan had fallen. He heard a distant siren coming closer.

\*    \*    \*

"What happened to you?" Dao asked as he peeled off his torn shirt.

"Nothing much."

She came close. Her hand pressed against his chest and he winced. She stroked his body, finding spots where Kwan had hit. Several he hadn't even known about.

"Nothing?" she asked.

"I met someone I shouldn't have," he said. "I'm going to take a hot bath, then we'll talk."

She turned the brass spigot in the pink marble tub and started the bath. She helped him ease down into the tub, and gently massaged his shoulder muscles. Then she slipped out of her dress and climbed into the tub with him.

"Dao, I need a rest," he said.

"Rest. I will do all the work."

He was already responding to her caresses. When she took him into her and slowly moved back and forth, he felt as happily helpless as a cork bobbing in the tide.

"You may not believe this," she said. "But no man has ever made me feel like this."

"No woman has ever had this effect on me. I don't know if I like it." He ran his hand across her bare thigh. "I could spend the rest of my life in bed with you."

"A nice idea," she said.

They were lying in the king-size bed, still enjoying the post-coital haze. She spoke softly, her mouth right by his ear. Every so often she nipped his lobe.

"I understand if you do not want to tell me what is going on," she said. "You are a man. That is your right. But I can help. I know many, many people."

"Too dangerous."

"As your lover, I am involved already," she said. "I don't want secrets to come between us. But I don't want your not telling me to come between us either. It's selfish on my part. The more work I help you do, the more time we can spend in bed." She clamped onto his earlobe and gently gnashed her teeth.

"You keep that up, you'll give me an ear like a Thai Buddha," he said. "I've got to get to work. What about you?"

She stretched languidly. From her toes to her brow, it seemed like each muscle was pulled to its limits. "My business can run itself. I will call my assistant later to check for pressing matters. Until then I can enjoy you. How long will you be in Hong Kong."

"It depends how long the job takes."

"Then maybe I won't help you, so you must stay here longer. Maybe forever."

He stood up, bent over, and kissed her. "Do they publish a criss-cross directory here?"

"A what?"

"A reverse directory. Phone numbers are listed by address. So if I looked up a number, I can find the address."

"I don't think they have such a thing," she said. "However, I have a cousin in the telephone company."

"Can you ask this cousin to check a few numbers for me?"

"What do I get for it?" she asked mischievously.

"What would you like?"

"I'll think of something." Her tongue danced across her lips. "Something demanding."

Stark got the phone bill he had taken from the kung fu studio.

"Can you check out these numbers in Macao?" Stark asked.

"I'll try," she said.

"Okay." He went through the list, putting a pen mark next to the calls he wanted checked. Any numbers that appeared more than once had to be investigated.

She called her cousin and they had a rapid conversation in Cantonese.

As they spoke, Stark eyed her naked body. Sex with her was like an addictive drug.

She could call the numbers they couldn't trace. A woman's voice would be less threatening. Her fluency in Cantonese was another asset. She shifted the phone and her hair fell across her breast. The movement sparked more lascivious thoughts. Stark went to the bathroom and threw cold water on his face.

Dao was reading numbers off the sheet when he returned. She hung up.

"She can't help with the Macao numbers but on the others she will let me know right away," Dao said.

"Great service."

"One of the advantages of the extended Chinese family," she said. "It is how we've been able to conquer Asia. I can deal with a cousin in Bangkok, a nephew in Taiwan, a sister in Malaysia. We are all cells in one body."

Her medical analogy made him think of Sultana, and he had a brief pang of regret. "What about mainland China?"

She wrinkled her face. "There too. But I don't like it. In the countryside it's like the stone age. In the cities like medieval Europe. I dread when they take over Hong Kong," she said with a shiver. "They will ruin it, sap people's initiative, put huge bureaucracies in place."

"You sound pretty vehement."

"I am. They are not good. Evil. They want to control the world."

"Doesn't every government? Except maybe Monaco."

"When the government said only one child, peasants were forced to kill little girl babies. When they banned dogs in Beijing, they clubbed pets to death," she said. "They are backward, insensitive, incompetent." She shook her head. "But enough of that."

Stark was wearing only pale blue bikini briefs. She reached over and grabbed the waistband. "I know how I want my payment. You must bring me to satisfaction, but you can't use this"—she patted his bulge—"or this"—she touched her fingers to his lips—"or these," she said, stroking his fingers.

The phone rang. Stark picked it up and a woman's voice asked for Dao. Stark handed the phone over. Dao took notes on a scrap of hotel paper as the woman on the other end spoke. Dao hung up and giggled.

"My cousin said you have a sexy voice," Dao said. "I said when I am done I will send you to her."

"When you are done with me, there will be nothing left."

"I will never be done with you."

He gave her a peck on the lips and asked for the paper.

Three of the calls were to a martial arts supply firm. Two calls were to a woman's apartment on Hong Kong Island. Three calls were to a film studio in the New Territories. The name jogged a chord in Stark's memory. The studio had been mentioned in the *shihan*'s posthumous note.

"These last three calls are to the Hi Fashion clothing factory," Dao said.

"I'd like to find out what sort of clothing they make."

"Why?" she asked.

"If it's martial arts outfits, I'll put it at the bottom of my list. If it's anything else, I'll keep it up high. Could you call them and pretend to be a buyer for a department store? Also, see if you can get the name of the owner."

"This is fun," she said, and made the call. She sat cross-legged on the bed, her sex boldly visible. He walked to the window so he didn't just sit and stare.

This is as bad as being a teenager again, he thought, when the sight of a woman's bra line could give him an erection.

Sultana would frequently creep into his thoughts, but their relationship was more cerebral. Time with Sultana was like an absorbing chess game. With Dao it was more like a good workout at the dojo. Primal, touching those parts of the brain where words were unnecessary and hormones ruled.

Dao hung up the phone and said, "They sell women's and children's clothing. Top quality, if the salesman I spoke to was telling the truth. He didn't want to tell me the owner's name, but I persuaded him. Louis Scalish."

Could that be "Louie," the clothing man from the *shihan*'s list?

He leaned over and gave her a kiss on the forehead. "Let's go out for a bite," he said. "Then I need you to make a few more phone calls for me."

"Will you tell me what this is about?"

"Yes."

"Okay. I must get ready."

As soon as the bathroom door was shut, he called Les Halliwell in New York. Mid-morning in Hong Kong was evening in New York.

"Did you check out that person I asked you to?" Stark asked, speaking softly.

"Sure. Different sources have different birthplaces for her, but most seem to indicate Bangkok around 1950. She turned up on the Hong Kong modeling scene when she was sixteen and was the hot number for about eight years. I got a couple of pictures of her and they practically burned up the fax machine."

"Okay, okay. No more details about her life? Her parents? Married?"

"There were a couple of articles on her but they were full of contradictory bullshit. She's supposed to be fluent in Chinese, both Mandarin and Cantonese, as well as French, Thai, and English. Are you boffing her, you devil you?"

"Les, this call is costing a buck a minute."

"You're right. Well, the down side is she's no longer modeling. Her business is supposed to be antiques. The antiques sometimes have been smuggled out of countries or their ownership has been questionable. She's never been charged but she's been investigated a couple of times."

"Great. Now, have you ever heard of a guy named Louis Scalish?"

Even through the international connection, Stark could hear the gulp. "How'd you find out so fast? I mean, I was going to tell you."

Stark decided to let his partner believe he was omniscient. "Why don't you just take it from the top?"

"I went to sell this guy a security contract. I told you about him, right? You know, the factories in Jersey and businesses in Las Vegas and California."

"You mentioned it."

"That was Scalish. How the hell did you know?"

"Tell me exactly what happened."

Stark listened as Halliwell recited his Las Vegas misadventure. Stark interrupted frequently during the part about Sultana.

"So she's okay?"

"Yes. Safe and sound," Halliwell said.

"Where is she? No, don't say it."

"I've got her under protection. Pedro is with her twenty-four hours a day, with a two-man team keeping a perimeter watch. It's a rural location."

"She's going to get restless. Better give her something to do or she'll go wandering. Have you decided on countermeasures against Scalish?"

"He's mobbed up the kazoo. It's going to be tough. Underboss for the DeLeone family. He handles the Las

Vegas skim for DeLeone and watches over the interests for two other groups. He's got access to *mucho dinero* and *mucho* juice.''

"Let's cut off that access."

"How?"

As Stark explained, Les began to chuckle.

"That'll show that son of a bitch," Halliwell said.

Stark was finishing the call when Dao came out of the bathroom. She strutted over, went down on her knees in front of him, pulled his penis out of his briefs, and put it in her mouth.

"Les, can you hang on a second?" Stark asked.

"I guess. You say this costs a buck a minute?"

Stark covered the mouthpiece. "Dao, stop it."

She didn't. He tried to push her away, but she remained glued to him like a baby suckling at a teat.

He uncovered the mouthpiece. "Anything else?"

"That's about it," Les said. "I've got a few analysts trying to pierce Scalish's corporate veil. The guy's got more going on than a three-card monte dealer with an extra set of arms."

"Mmm. Well, okay. Gotta go."

"Everything okay?"

"Fine. Mnnn. Gotta go."

Stark hung up and Dao stopped.

"Les? Is that short for Leslie?" she asked.

"That's short for Lester. My partner."

"I don't believe that."

"What's gotten into you?"

"When a lady leaves the room and her lover gets right on the phone, what's she to think? That he's calling a girl-friend."

"You're jealous? I can't believe you've ever been jealous of any woman."

"Let's go. I'm hungry." His blue briefs bulged. She patted his erection as if it were a pet dog. "I'll take care of that later. For now, it'll remind you not to trifle with my affections."

"I'm hungry too," he said. He made a mock growl and threw her down on the bed. Their lovemaking was fierce.

# CHAPTER
## 20

By the time they left the bed it was lunch hour. Dao took him to a restaurant that had a daily *dim sum* special. Waitresses rolled metal carts laden with dishes. Shark's fin and pork in thin dough, turnip cake fried with shrimp and pork, steamed duck feet, sticky rice with chicken wrapped in lotus leaf, shrimp in thin dough, sweet rice cake, custard, steamed pork buns, and dozens of others.

Dao ordered and explained each dish. Stark devoured them with pleasure. After forty-five minutes there were eight small, empty plates on the table. The waitress totaled the bill by counting the plates.

"How about we go back to the hotel for dessert?" Dao suggested naughtily after Stark had paid.

"I have to recharge. Anyway there're records I have to check."

"I'll come with you," she said.

"Maybe you should just direct me."

"What are you looking for?"

"Real estate and tax records. See if I can tie a couple of companies together. It's dull work."

"All this for Zippy Toys?" she asked skeptically.

"Another client."

"I see."

"You don't need to tag along," he said.

"You don't want to be with me?"

"If you're around, I can't concentrate on anything else."

She accepted his answer with a smile. "I will check on my assistant. But first I'll make sure you get what you want. Chinese bureaucrats love to pretend they don't speak English when they don't want to do something. Either you'll have to bribe them or threaten them."

The records office mixed colonial grandeur with the barest hint of government-building shabbiness. Ornate pillars, oak banisters and trim, and impressive light fixtures, but many bulbs were out and the black and white tile floor needed polishing.

Painted on a smoked glass door were the words LAND OFFICE, A DIVISION OF THE REGISTRAR GENERAL'S DEPARTMENT. Inside smelled faintly of mildew and old paper. A poster-size color photo of the Queen looked down on high stacks, with ladders on wheels, long tables, and plush chairs for reviewing files. A hushed tone prevailed.

"Let me go to the counter by myself," Dao said. "We'll get better service."

He drifted in after she entered. The clerks had the inevitable I'm-bored-but-don't-bother-me expression of clerks all over the world. Until the male clerks spotted Dao. A senior clerk, a Britisher with round spectacles, swooped down. He knocked the dandruff from the shoulders of his dark suit before offering to help her.

"We're averaging more than three hundred thousand instruments registered each year," he said like a swain trying to impress his lady love with his batting average. "Last year alone we handled better than one point two million inquiries from the public."

"You must work very hard," she said.

"Indeed we do," he said, warming to the subject. "A memorial here contains the essential particulars of the instrument which are then placed on a register card relating to the particular piece of land. Register cards are also kept regarding individual premises such as residential flats, shops, and commercial and industrial premises." He prattled on, proudly pointing out the various stacks and noting that they were in the process of computerizing. "If you come back in a year, you won't recognize this place." He launched into an impassioned speech about the Inland Revenue Ordinance.

"I need to see a few specific files," she said, widening her eyes and looking helpless. "Could you help me?"

"It would be a pleasure."

She gave him the list Stark had prepared. He adjusted his glasses and set off. She sat at one of the tables in the reviewing area. Like a diligent retriever, he bounded to her in a few minutes.

When Stark came over, the clerk glared and harumphed. "You can have only three files at a time," he said, taking back the pile.

"I'll take the top three," Stark said. "Please leave the others by the counter."

The clerk harumphed again and marched off.

Dao reached under the table and brushed Stark's thigh. "I'll meet you back at the hotel in a couple of hours."

"Make that about four hours."

She pouted, but nodded.

Every man in the room watched as she left, even the sulking British clerk.

After a half hour checking records Stark went to a pay phone and called the film studio that the *shihan* had mentioned in his posthumous note.

Stark was left in the purgatory of "hold." He gazed at the large Hong Kong emblem on the wall. Chinese dragon and British lion faced off, their claws and talons dug into a tiny green island. Between them was a shield showing two junks, a crown, and a crenellated wall. Atop the shield was a smaller lion, giving a pearl to the big one.

"Mr. Wu Wu is busy," the secretary said in crisp English when she finally came back on the line. "Give me your number and when he gets a chance, he will call back."

"Tell Wu Wu that it concerns the death of *Shihan* Soto."

"He is in a meeting."

"Tell him. Tell him someone who was there when Soto died wishes to speak with him."

She put him back into purgatory. A couple of minutes

passed before she returned to the line. "Be here in an hour. He can give you five minutes then."

It took him forty minutes to get to Wu Wu's studio in the New Territories. He took a circuitous route, getting in and out of cabs a couple of times. There didn't seem to be any surveillants.

The building spanned two blocks and was designed to look like a low-slung Chinese fortress from the Ming dynasty. A few tourists were out in front, taking pictures. Unlike other castles, this one had a sign which said WU WU PRODUCTIONS—QUALITY MARTIAL ARTS EXTRAVAGANZA CINEMA.

Stark had actually seen a few Wu Wu films. Quality was not the word that came to mind. They were the usual tales of revenge. For the first hour the hero suffered abuse, his property destroyed, his family massacred. In the final half hour he would kick the pulp out of everyone. Hatchets would bounce off his head, arrows would be deflected with lightning-quick punches that made exaggerated snapping sounds. The plots were ridiculous, the acting bad, the martial arts techniques silly. Then why had Stark rented more than a half dozen before outgrowing them? Maybe there was something to their primitive simplicity.

A uniformed security guard intercepted Stark as he stepped through the high gate.

"The lot is closed," the guard said gruffly. The repressed hostility he emanated reminded Stark of Hong Kong cop Peter Wong.

"I have an appointment to see Wu Wu." The guard was skeptical, but spoke into a walkie-talkie. When he addressed Stark again it was with new respect and politeness. The hostility had been covered with a veneer of politeness.

"Right this way, sir," the guard said, clicking his heels in best military fashion.

They passed through the back lot. Two large buildings which looked like airplane hangars were labeled SOUND STAGE ONE and SOUND STAGE TWO. They had signs saying DO NOT ENTER WHEN LIGHT IS BLINKING. The red lights above the doors were blinking.

They walked down a street made up of apartment-house facades, then down another one which looked like the main street in Dodge City, circa 1860. A right turn, a few more yards, and they were in the emperor's palace. They passed through that set into a large waiting room done up like a Ming dynasty reception area.

The stunning receptionist was dressed like a Manchu concubine. Although she had the same heart-shaped face and chiseled features as Dao, the raw sensuality was missing. Like comparing a delicious meal with the plastic meals in store windows in Japan.

"Mr. Stark? Mr. Wu will be with you in a moment. Please be seated."

Stark inspected the chair, the table, the furnishings. From the little Dao had taught him about Oriental antiques, he was able to tell they were fakes. The workmanship was good but the attention to detail—finishing touches, joint work, carvings—was just not the same as Ming craftsmen had done.

After a few minutes the receptionist was signaled that Mr. Wu was available. As Stark entered, Wu Wu's secretary was leaving. She was another gorgeous plastic dish.

Wu Wu was a plump, dapper man. Stark had expected that with such grandiose surroundings, Wu Wu might believe himself to be the last of the Manchus. But from the first moment he spoke, Stark could tell that he was a showman who used the trappings simply to bring in the rubes. Wu Wu knew exactly what he was and was quite pleased with it.

Wu Wu welcomed him and invited him to a screening of his latest film, *The Ninja Princess and the Warlord*. The secretary brought tea, ending the opening round of pleasantries.

"The *shihan* had actually mentioned you," Wu Wu said. "He thought highly of you." Mr. Wu's British-accented English was as impeccable as his tailoring.

"He was a great teacher."

"He was."

"Did you know him through the martial arts community?"

Wu Wu chuckled. "No. He hated the movies I did. Said it cheapened the martial arts, made youngsters study solely so they could beat people up. I told him movies about the spiritual glory of kicking and punching wouldn't do well." Wu Wu chuckled some more. "I was sad when I heard that he had died. Though I am sure he was pleased with the way he went."

"May I ask how you knew him then?"

"During the war I was taken prisoner. I was going to be tortured. He arranged for me to escape." He nodded at Stark's surprised expression. "From what I gather, he had done such deeds several times. Quite a man. As loyal as anyone to the emperor and Japan, but with a strong aversion to cruelty. Not what you'd expect from a modern-day samurai?"

"I thought I knew him and yet I'm constantly finding out new things about him," Stark said. "Can you tell me why he came to you?"

Wu Wu hesitated, then said, "He wanted to rent the sound stage to shoot a film." Wu Wu looked at his wristwatch. "I have another appointment."

"Please, a couple more questions. He asked me to look into something before he committed seppuku. What was the movie they filmed?"

"I wasn't here. It was done at night."

"He didn't tell you?" Stark asked.

"He didn't tell you?" Wu Wu responded.

"You have no idea what was filmed?"

Wu Wu hesitated. A long time passed. Stark noticed a clock ticking in the background and the faint noise of actors yelling.

Wu Wu switched on the intercom. The ancient trappings were mixed with modern hardware. "Tell them I'll be a few minutes late. Get them started on the budget for *Bloody Fists of Vengeance of the Unforgiven Dragon*." Wu Wu sighed and turned to Stark. "I tell you this because you can appreciate my feelings. I find it upsetting and I haven't been able to speak of it to anyone. They filmed a pornographic movie."

"Are you sure?"

"One of my guards recognized several of the actors and actresses. If you can call them that." Wu Wu stood stiffly, a frown on his face. "I'm a good Catholic. I never would have allowed it, even for the *shihan*."

"I would like to check into it."

"You don't believe me?"

"I do. Perhaps there's an explanation."

"I can explain. The *shihan*'s brother. He is a *yakuza*."

**165**

"May I speak to the guard?"

"I will arrange it. If you find out an answer that will soothe me, please let me know. If not, it has been a pleasure meeting you, Mr. Stark."

The guard was another lean, mean, young Chinese man. But he was nervous talking about what he had seen. Apparently Wu Wu had grilled him as to why he was familiar with porno movie stars. The king of chop-socky violence approved only of making war, not love.

"I peeked through a hole in the wall," the guard finally admitted. "Just to make sure they weren't abusing the sound stage equipment."

"Of course," Stark said.

"Do you have contacts to get someone into America?" the guard asked in a hushed voice.

"Excuse me?"

"I've got ten thousand dollars saved. In gold. I would be happy to pay it."

"I'm sorry I can't help," Stark said. "Getting back to the film . . ."

"It doesn't have to be right away. As long as I am out of here long before 1997."

"Can't help you," Stark said. "What about the film?"

The guard folded his arms in front of his chest and pressed his lips shut.

"Perhaps I can make a donation to your escape money," Stark said. He took a U.S. twenty-dollar bill out of his wallet. The guard snatched it.

"They had the room done up like a luxury hotel," the guard said. "A man was fucking two women. Then a boy. Then . . ." The guard laughed nervously. "A goat."

"A goat?"

The guard made a sound like a billy goat, then laughed again. "Then they all combined in a big bed."

"What else can you tell me?"

The guard refolded his arms.

Another twenty came and went.

"The strangest thing was the lead actor. He was an older man. Actually, when I first saw him, he didn't look that old.

But under the lighting, with makeup, they'd made him look older. He looked like someone famous."

"Who?"

The guard refolded his arms.

Stark handed over another twenty.

"The Communist Chinese Premier, Zhao Ziyang."

"Did you find anything in the records?" Dao asked when he returned to their hotel room.

"Nothing definitive. A few individual and corporate names I'm going to phone back to New York and run through our computer. How is your business?"

"A deal fell through. A new deal was made. All I could think about was you." She stepped up to him. "You must leave Hong Kong."

"What?"

"I heard through a friend of a nephew. At the party where we met, you had bad words with a triad leader?"

"We exchanged bon mots."

"There isn't a contract out on you. Otherwise, you would be dead already. But word has spread that you treated him with disrespect. There are many young punks who would happily murder you just to earn his smile."

"Thanks for the warning. Lots of people have put me on hit lists. If I avoided every place I was unwanted, I'd have no place to go." He kissed her.

"I am not kidding."

"Okay. I have to check out things in Macao anyway."

"No. To go there is worse. Because of the gambling, many hoodlums spend their weekends there. It's infested with criminals. It's smaller than Hong Kong and you'll be noticed immediately."

The phone trilled softly. It was the cop Peter Wong.

"How'd you find out where I was?" Stark asked.

"It's not hard," was all Wong would say. "I called with two items of news. One, the kung fu master I mentioned. He had an unfortunate accident."

"What happened?"

"He was working out on a rooftop in the middle of the night and misstepped. We are calling it death by misadventure."

167

"It's a dangerous world."

"It is. There were Vietnamese aliens on the roof who claim they saw a devil fighting with him. But we are discounting that."

"Interesting."

"The other news is a warning. I have heard rumblings among young triad members. Your death would bring great honor."

"So I've heard."

"How did you hear?"

"I have my sources," Stark said, winking at Dao. She stuck out her tongue.

"It wasn't hard for me to find you. It will not be hard for them to do the same."

"I appreciate your calling."

"Think nothing of it."

"Is this a warning to get out of town?"

"The decision is yours."

# CHAPTER
## 21

Louis Scalish was in a great mood as he finished arrangements for a girl to replace Carmelita. This one was fourteen, guaranteed virgin, from a small town in Nicaragua. Her mother and a brother had been killed by Sandinistas. Her father, a brother, and a sister had been killed by Contras. She was placed in a foster home. Her foster parents were selling her and Scalish was getting a good price. He studied the Polaroid of her. Nice. Still baby fat on her bones, innocence and fear in her eyes.

He was in the penthouse office at the Golden Luck Casino. It had been decorated with the finest in nouveau-riche chic. As gaudy and cluttered as a Victorian drawing room. There was a big oil portrait of Scalish on one wall; another displayed photos of Scalish with famous entertainers and politicians.

The scheme involving Sun Tzu and Musashi was crazy, he believed, but it was going well. He had shelled out a million bucks, and made a few arrangements, but never been optimistic. It was the side deals with the two Orientals that kept him involved.

Now it seemed as if they might just pull it off. He'd been amazed that the Red Chinese hadn't just tossed him out on his keister. Sure they were stalling but that was Oriental

S.O.P. From his garment business he knew that they would delay and delay to wear you down. Chinese water torture.

He was reviewing a profit and loss statement from one of the casinos when he got the first inkling of a disaster.

"Mr. S., this is Max." The raspy voice came out of the hot line tied to a few key locations in the casino. Max, a twenty-year Las Vegas survivor, was the supervisor of the pit bosses. He could spot a card counter or a marked deck at ten yards.

"What's up?"

"We're short-staffed. Half the workers came down with a stomach bug."

"A sickout?"

"Nah, it's legit. Looks like anyone who ate breakfast in the staff kitchen got sick."

"You call in per diems?"

"I did. But a few casinos got the same problem. There's a shortage."

"Shut down some tables, close off a couple of the private rooms. Keep the casino running. Get maintenance people dressed fancy and put them out."

"I'll do my best. Uh—" Max hesitated.

"What is it?"

"The casinos with troubles, they're all the ones you, uh, watch over."

"Only them?"

"Only them."

Scalish slammed down the phone, pulled on his tux, and headed downstairs.

Half the blackjack tables were without dealers. Ashtrays overflowed, paper and plastic cups littered the floor, and discarded keno cards were everywhere. Only two cocktail waitresses were circling, and neither was a regular. They both looked awkward in microskirts, and tottered on high heels. They screwed up orders and spilled drinks.

Scalish was prowling the aisle near the roulette wheels when Max hurried to him. "I just heard from Desert Sheikh. Someone dumped rats in the middle of the casino. There was a panic and the joint cleared out. In the confusion, wise guys scooped up every pile of cash or chips that weren't nailed down. We lost a few hundred thousand."

"What the fuck's going on?" Scalish stood for a moment, listening like a jungle scout tracking an elephant herd. "You know, for a place that's half empty, there's a lot of noise here."

The slots. They were designed to whoop and cheer whenever a player hit. They were whooping and cheering continuously.

A couple of middle-aged men were working the one-armed bandits. The scene wasn't right. Slots were favored by older women. They'd come with shopping bags, white gloves and little Wash 'n Dries, and pull the handles until their right arms were bigger than their left. Men went for craps, poker, blackjack.

Max and Scalish ran toward the slots men. They spotted the electromagnets in the players' hands. Max drew his gun.

The players threw down spherical objects. There was an explosion and billowing clouds of smoke.

"Fire!" someone screamed.

The stampede began. Max and Scalish charged into the smoke cloud and came out swinging at each other. The thieves had disappeared.

When the smoke had cleared, the staff found that the open tables had been stripped of money and chips. Scalish glared at the mirrored ball in the ceiling that hid the eye-in-the-sky security cameras.

"What are those dickheads doing up there?" Scalish muttered. Scalish and Max stormed to the mezzanine. The heavy door to the security catwalk had been sealed with Crazy Glue. It took half an hour to break it open.

Four security men were tied and gagged. Scalish ripped the gag off the supervisor. The man cried out in pain.

"What happened?" Scalish demanded.

"A couple of the per diems. They had guns."

"Guns?" an outraged Scalish asked.

"It's been so hectic, we didn't get a chance to really check their backgrounds," the supervisor said.

Scalish kicked the supervisor in frustration.

Workers relayed word of various crimes against the casinos. Two hundred thousand dollars in counterfeit currency had been unloaded at one. The spillage of a foul-smelling liquid had forced the closure of another. Half the slot machines at a third had been gummed up.

"Someone's gonna die," Scalish said.

Back in his office the phone kept jangling with bad news. He gave his secretary-bodyguard orders to hold all calls. The bodyguard was kept busy jotting down tales of woe. When he glanced into Scalish's office, his employer had his head between his hands.

"What did I do to deserve this?" Scalish asked.

"I don't know, Mr. S.," the bodyguard said. "There's a Robert Stark on the phone. Partner of that guy Halliwell you had here the other day. He knows about our problems and says he can help.

Scalish grabbed the phone. "What do you mean, problems?"

"I'm in the information business, Louie. Good intelligence is the backbone of good security."

"You're dead meat, you know that?"

"Don't make threats against the one person who can bail your ass out," Stark said. "Your broken-nosed friends aren't going to take this kindly. How much are you down by? A couple million?"

"I'm gonna personally rip your dick out and stuff it down your throat."

"Louie, Louie, Louie. You come in to the office, make a full confession about what's going on in Hong Kong, and we keep you from the Johnny Roselli treatment. Remember Johnny? His limbs broken, stuffed in a steel drum floating in Biscayne Bay. Not a pretty way to die."

"I'll take your eyeballs out with my own hands," Scalish screamed. "I'll make you die by inches."

"Think about it, Louie. Things will get worse before they get better. Have a nice day."

Stark hung up. Scalish got right on the phone to a contractor in New York. "Vinnie, I need a piece of work done. A fucker named Stark. He—"

"Louie, I can't talk now," Vinnie said, hanging up before Scalish could say any more.

The same thing happened when he called two other *capos* who arranged strong-arm work and hits. How could his world collapse so quickly?

His bodyguard was in the doorway. "Mr. DeLeone in New York is on the phone."

"What the fuck is going on?" DeLeone demanded without any form of greeting.

"Huh?"

"I'm getting reports. Bad reports."

"Everything's gone kablooie. I can't understand it."

"How much have we lost?"

"Uh, I'm not sure. Not that much."

"I heard millions."

"From who?"

"I got long ears. I also looked over your paperwork. You've been coming up short."

It was the money Scalish was skimming to put into Sun Tzu's operation. He had been doing it without DeLeone's approval. If it succeeded, there was no point in sharing the gravy with the old man. If it failed, no point in taking the blame. "The economy's been bad," Scalish claimed. Fortunately the old man couldn't see the sweat on his brow.

"Atlantic City's doing better than ever," DeLeone said.

"It's different here."

"We need fresh blood. I'm sending people out. Work with them."

"Wait. This is just a minor setback."

He was talking to a dial tone.

He knew what would happen. DeLeone had been keeping an eye on him, looking for an excuse to get rid of him. The old man figured on living forever and was only too happy to knock off the most promising contender for his throne.

Scalish called for his secretary-bodyguard. No answer. He stepped into his bodyguard's anteroom. The man was gone.

Scalish hurried down to the garage. He thought about using his red Cadillac, then decided it was too visible. He hot-wired a BMW. It took him five minutes. When he was a kid, he'd been able to do it in no more than two. He had gotten soft. That was his problem. Too soft, too nice a guy.

He raced out to the brothel a half hour north of the city. Whorehouses were legal in Nevada, just not in Las Vegas proper. Typical government crapola, he thought, wondering how much grease had been smeared to get that deal in place.

Scalish was convinced the whole state had been a spread-legged whore since Bugsy Siegel discovered a way to turn a two-bit desert town into a mecca for gamblers.

He took the turnoff for the brothel and nearly slammed into a truck parked on the edge of the road. That's the way life was, he thought. One minute cruising in a luxury car, the next minute wrapped around a light pole.

The brothel was four mobile homes joined at the center. Where the mobile homes met was a small office. There were no johns' cars in the parking lot. The place was the quietest he had ever seen it.

"What's going on?" he demanded of the receptionist, a burned out whore with hennaed hair.

"The girls are sick," the receptionist said.

He didn't have time to argue. DeLeone might try to use local talent to off him. Scalish knew the heavy hitters, but there could always be a new face. He raced to a room that appeared initially to be no more than a linen closet. He pushed aside a large box of paper towels and the safe was exposed. He was spinning the combination lock when Carmelita slunk in.

"Get out of here," he said, concerned that she would see the combination. Then he realized that he was making his final withdrawal and he softened. She would be good to bring along. It might be a while before he could hook up with a reliable source of fresh meat. "No, you can stay. How do you like it here?"

"Not much."

The safe opened and he loaded the valuables into a large aluminum Haliburton case. Five million in diamonds and cash. "You like to come away with me?" he asked, waving a sheaf of hundred-dollar bills. "We'll have good times."

"Sure."

He snapped the case shut and took her hand. "Let's go."

As he stepped into the hall, a blow caught him at the backs of the knees. He fell to the floor. A second blow caught him on the head, and he was in darkness.

He awoke in a dimly lit room. Gradually it came into focus. Pliers, branding irons, whips, needles—an impressive collection of paraphernalia for S & M tricks. A sign on the wall said, THIS TORTURE CHAMBER SOUNDPROOFED FOR YOUR CONVENIENCE. SCREAM AS LOUD AS YOU WANT.

He was trapped in an old-fashioned stock, his neck and arms pinned down between heavy pieces of wood. He bucked and struggled. The wood was padded to avoid chafing the skin or giving splinters. The pain inflicted was designed to be controlled.

Five women from the brothel stepped out of the gloomy shadows. He recognized them, the ones he had bought in Third World countries and broken in personally.

"We can make a deal," he said, trying to keep his voice from quivering. "I've got a lot of money."

Carmelita began pumping a pair of bellows over a charcoal brazier. Another hooker held, with heavy protective mittens, a long metal dildo. She laid it on the hot coals. It began to glow red.

"You can't do this," he said, losing control of his voice. He called out their names and pleaded.

One of the women unbuckled his belt. Another lifted a pair of pliers. A third held long needles.

He screamed for help as they moved in.

The women, and Scalish's five million, were gone when the body was discovered four hours later.

The first cops on the scene, a pair of fifteen-year veterans, threw up. A few weeks later both put in for retirement based on psychological stress. It was granted without question.

# PART III
## Musashi

# CHAPTER
## 22

The tailor shop was located on the first floor of the Ocean Terminal, the shopping mall that stretched into Hong Kong harbor from a prime spot next to the Star ferry. Several hundred upscale stores catering to the tourist trade offered the usual gewgaws and clothing for diverse human shapes.

The tailor shop, although small, boasted three ways in or out. One way was through an adjacent clothing store; another was a fire door straight to the outside deck; the third was the conventional entrance. With the high level of mall traffic and its central location, Sun Tzu had found it convenient for meetings.

"Honored Godfather, your friend is in the back room," the tailor said to Sun Tzu. They shared a vehement hatred of the Communist Chinese and the triad leader had sent the tailor thousands of dollars worth of business.

The tailor was about Sun Tzu's age but talked to him deferentially. The tailor knew that Sun Tzu had arranged the deaths of dozens. Sun Tzu brushed aside a beaded curtain and stepped into a second room. The tailor's wife, working at a sewing machine, didn't look up. She knew the value of minding her own business.

Sun Tzu stopped to greet the tailor's son and daughter. The girl was thirteen, the boy eleven. When not going to school, they worked long hours at the shop. It pleased Sun Tzu to see filial piety. He praised the children. They followed their mother's lead and avoided his eyes. Such respect was proper.

Sun Tzu turned to the mother. "Have you considered your daughter's marriage?"

"Not yet."

"When you do, speak with me. I know many fine young men," he said.

"Thank you," the mother said without enthusiasm.

Sun Tzu considered himself to be very civilized, unlike the barbarians he was obliged to associate with. Machiavelli was a lower form of life, a round-eyed pervert ruled by his gonads. But the American mobster had access to scientists and military hardware.

Musashi was a few notches up on the evolutionary scale. Which was why the Japanese was arrogant, believing he was the equal of a child of the Middle Kingdom. But Musashi had resources in Asia and contacts for Japanese high technology goods.

So Sun Tzu dealt with them. He reminded himself how fortunate he was to have been born Chinese. The rest of the world feasted off our droppings, he thought. Hadn't we begun work on the Great Wall when they still struggled with mud huts? Weren't we using chopsticks for generations when they still ate with their hands? Hadn't we introduced them to rice, tea, porcelain, paper, the umbrella, the mariner's compass, waterproof compartments in ships, paper money, kites, gunpowder, the mechnical clock, and hundreds of other inventions? What did they give us? Opium. Which they forced upon us at gunpoint.

Sun Tzu found it amusingly ironic that he was a leading international heroin smuggler. Payback for the Opium Wars, when Britain and the other imperialists cracked China open like a fruit and ripped out its sweet heart. Leaving it to be scavenged by the parasitic Communists. He grieved for every day the Communists ruled his homeland.

He had deliberately delayed in the anteroom, to keep Musashi waiting. The Japanese was constantly asserting himself, and Sun Tzu had to remind him who was in charge.

Sun Tzu gave the tailor's family final best wishes and slid aside the door into the back room.

Musashi was seated, feet planted shoulder width apart, solid as a mountain. He bowed curtly when Sun Tzu entered. Sun Tzu bobbed his head back. Musashi waited for Sun Tzu to speak.

"There was an incident in Hong Kong. Two *yakuza* attempted to attack Robert Stark." He spoke English, which was the second language for both of them.

"What happened?" Musashi asked, as if he didn't know.

"Stark proved himself superior."

"Hmmm."

"The *yakuza* were from your group."

"They must have sensed my displeasure and sought to curry favor by handling Stark themselves. Since they are dead, there is no need to punish them."

"I hope you will be better able to control your underlings in the future."

"I hope that you will take prompt enough action that Stark's future does not stretch on indefinitely."

"Machiavelli is dead," Sun Tzu said, abruptly changing the topic.

"How?" Musashi responded.

"I have heard that he encountered bad luck and his superior lost confidence in him. Then his whores killed him."

"Does that change our plans?"

"His role was completed," Sun Tzu said. "When we are finished we will have to let the Mafia participate but they will have a smaller piece. I understand he did not keep his superior informed."

"Very bad."

"It is always bad when underlings act without their leader's approval," Sun Tzu said as a barely veiled dig. "Machiavelli's action was bad for them. Very good for us."

"What happens now?"

"The Communist Chinese have taken too long to respond to our generous offer," Sun Tzu said. He launched into a lengthy tirade against the Communists, blasting them for ineptitude, corruption, bureaucracy, sapping individual initiative, and seeking to spread their doctrine worldwide.

Musashi listened patiently. He had seen such displays before. Sun Tzu at last concluded, "Under them, China is like a junk with a torn sail that can only move slowly through the water. We need to provide a gust of wind. They need another demonstration."

"Do you need my help?"

"No."

"Okay. I have business to attend to in Hawaii," Musashi said.

"You have not recovered from the seizure of the guns?"

Musashi made a noncommittal grunt.

"It would be best if you could encourage the scientist to finish the device. We may be more hurried than we had planned," Sun Tzu said. "I'll leave now. I didn't see police following me, but it's safer if you wait, then exit through the side door. You can walk down the fire stairs and out the side entrance. If you prefer to stay longer, our host can make a pot of tea. He is also an excellent tailor and will give you a fair price on a custom suit."

Sun Tzu didn't mention that he got a ten percent referral fee for every client he brought to the tailor. Even though Sun Tzu was worth a billion, the idea of making an under-the-table buck was too appealing. Just like the urge to haggle, which made him bargain with merchants although he could afford to buy their entire stock thousands of times over.

As the JAL stewardess brought him a hot towel, Musashi thought with disgust of his time in Hong Kong. The city was more crowded than Tokyo, noisier, and much dirtier. Even the *eta* live better than the Hong Kong poor, he thought, and they were the descendants of butchers and tanners, the untouchables in Japanese Buddhist society.

The American had been a disgusting human being. Subu Soto had his vice interests and he didn't hesitate to take his pleasure, but Machiavelli had been revolting. He couldn't even eat with chopsticks.

The Chinese thought himself superior and many times had commented on the length of Chinese civilization. True, but where had it gone? Much of China was still living in hovels, spitting phlegm and breeding ignorance. Japan, despite its closure until 1853 and the beating it took during World War II, boasted one of the highest standards of living, long life expectancies, and state-of-the-art conveniences. Economically the Japanese had conquered the world. There was no question in his mind that his were the most civilized of all peoples.

Which was why he didn't like going to Hawaii. He had the same attitude as most colonists do. Hawaii was a barbarous place, but exploitable.

During the 1970 Osaka World Exposition, Hawaii had made an effort to lure Japanese investors. Soto had been one of the thousands of businessmen who took the plunge. Hawaii offered wide open spaces, a lush climate, real estate which was cheap by Japanese standards, and a chance to get away from the constraints of home and cut loose. One of his more profitable legal ventures was a gun range in Honolulu, where respectable Japanese businessmen could let off a few thousand rounds in weapons ranging from a .22 to a .44 Magnum. He used the gun ranges—he had three—as a cover for buying the weapons he shipped back to Japan.

The fact that Hawaii was one quarter Japanese partially redeemed it in his mind. There were small signs of civilization—the popularity of Matsumoto's shaved ice stand, the sumo wrestlers working out in the park in the early morning, the Japanese *departo* stores in the malls, the Byodo-in temple, which reproduced the Uji temple in Japan.

But whenever he was away from Japan, he felt weaker.

He let the stewardess tuck a pillow under his head and drifted off into sweet dreams.

As soon as Stark had sent Dao on her way, he called ANA and booked a seat on the next available flight to Tokyo. He had lied and told her he was going to Hawaii.

Why didn't he trust her? Perhaps it was crosscultural confusion, her manner when she professed emotions he didn't believe were sincere. He had noticed inconsistencies in anecdotes she told, but anyone could make mistakes. He wondered why such a successful career woman seemed awfully disinterested in her business. Maybe it was just ex-spook paranoia on his part. Whatever the reason, he preferred to mislead her.

From a pay phone in the imperial lobby of the Peninsula, he called CIA Director Brandon Marshal in Langley.

"I need an Agency cobbler where I am," Stark said. "Do you understand?"

"I presume you're not inquiring about a shoe repairman."

"Check with ops and they'll fill you in," Stark said. "I need it right away."

"Can you hold?"

"I'll call back."

Stark walked to the Regent, which was a tiny notch down on the posh scale from the Peninsula.

He rang up Marshall again.

"I learn something new every day," the CIA director said. Someone had obviously told him a cobbler was CIA slang for a document forger. "Go to Fang Printers in Kowloon. Ask for Mr. Fang and say you're a friend of Marion."

"How trustworthy is he?"

"He's not a staffer but he's been vetted and vouched for."

"Exclusively ours?"

"Yes."

"Okay." Stark hung up. With all the residents trying to flee Hong Kong, a man who could make passable passports would quickly be a millionaire. A good unethical forger, unless he was on staff, would work for everyone and anyone. He might be willing to sell who was traveling under which name if he was too independent.

Stark decided to hedge his bets. He called Pam Moore and made the same request he had made of the CIA director.

"Still working for that toy company?" she asked skeptically.

"A key employee wants to get out of the Colony."

"Uh-huh. Tops is a Vietnamese in the New Territories. Mr. Binh. Use my name. That way he'll send me a referral fee."

"After gouging me suitably."

"Of course, honeybunch. Plus, you owe me. Isn't capitalism grand?"

Stark got a Canadian passport from Fang and an American passport from Binh. His visits to the cobblers were remarkably similar. Both forgers were small-framed with thick spectacles and ink-stained hands. Fang and Binh haggled enthusiastically, claimed to be the best at their trade, and offered Stark a "special deal."

In the photo for the Canadian passport Stark wore horn-rim glasses and pressed his lips together. For the American passport he slicked his hair back and jutted his jaw. Small differences, but they increased his odds of being unrecognized.

Stark insisted on personally shredding the Polaroid backing from the photos. Both flattered his professionalism and tried to sell him additional papers. They offered business cards in various names and occupations, press credentials, credit cards.

Stark refused, paid his money, and hurried to the Japanese consulate. He got a visa for the U.S. passport. His Canadian passport did not need a visa as long as he stayed in Japan for less than ninety days.

He barely made his plane at Kai Tak airport.

# CHAPTER
## 23

"Passengers suffering fevers, rash, or diarrhea are requested to report to the quarantine office," a pleasant female voice repeated through the loudspeaker in Japanese and English.

As Stark approached the chest-high counter where the immigration officers waited, he decided to test Fang's Canadian passport. He slipped on the horn-rim glasses and puckered up. He held his trench coat folded across one arm. If Fang had convinced the CIA he worked only for them, who knew what other scams the forger was involved in.

Stark handed over the passport. The unsmiling blue-uniformed officer looked at it, and at Stark's face, and turned to check the computer terminal on his desk.

"Gosh darn, I left my wallet on the plane," Stark said loudly. "I'll be right back, eh?"

He hurried away before the immigration inspector could respond. Stark had timed it well and was able to double back into a mass of people and quickly lose himself.

He got on another line, covertly using spit to slick down his hair. He slipped the glasses in his pocket and put on the trench coat. He was two counters away from the inspector he had first approached and could still get there if need be.

The first inspector was on the phone, agitated. Two more immigration men, hands on the pistols in their Sam Browne belts, raced up to the inspector. Stark couldn't hear what they were saying but the inspector was clutching the Canadian passport.

Either Fang had blown it in the forgery—and Stark, who inspected the goods carefully, had been impressed with the quality—or someone had tipped off authorities. Thank you very much, CIA.

Stark eased through passport control with his forged American papers from Binh.

Traveling with only a garment bag and attaché case, he didn't have to wait for baggage. Which was a good thing, since more than a dozen armed immigration special-inquiry officers were fanning out in the terminal.

He passed through customs quickly and jumped in a cab at the curb. From his room at the luxurious Asakusa View Hotel, Stark called the Tokyo phone number that had appeared on the bill.

"Hello, Fuji Fish," a gravelly man's voice answered in Japanese.

"Is this Fuji Fish?" Stark asked in his best impression of a quavery old Japanese man's voice.

"That's what I said," Gravel Voice responded.

"Is this the Fuji Fish in Shinjuku?"

"No."

"Roppongi?"

"No. This is Fuji Fish at the Tsukiji Fish Market. What do you want?"

"Oh, I must have the wrong number. Excuse me."

Gravel Voice slammed down the phone.

The Tsukiji Fish Market covered a full acre, the largest and busiest fish market in a country with an insatiable appetite for anything from the sea. Motorized hand carts, fork lifts, bicycles with huge baskets, refrigerated trucks, motorcycles, pickup trucks, and vans bearing the names of prominent restaurants raced around the lot. It looked like a demolition derby about to happen and yet miraculously there were no collisions.

Stark walked boldly into one of the sooty gray, three-story, warehouselike structures. He scrunched his head into his shoulders, trying not to tower above the people scurrying around him.

A white hard hat and long blue workman's jacket lay on a cart. He put the hat on his head and slipped into the jacket. A couple of sizes too small, it smelled of fish. A seam ripped as he moved his arms. But he was better camouflaged as he moved down the block-long aisle. He adjusted the hard hat so it rode low on his head, covering as much of his face as possible. He lifted a clipboard off a nail and pretended to take notes as he strolled.

The Tsukiji workers were sixth- and seventh-generation fisher folk. Everyone knew one another, as well as all their relatives, neighbors, and friends. A stranger was painfully conspicuous. But Stark, walking with confidence in the public areas, looking official, drew little attention to himself. He was unhurried but didn't linger, casually surveying a fraction of the tens of thousands of cartons.

The fish were so fresh that the smell was not overwhelming. There was bonita, tuna, shrimps, lobsters, squids, octopi, shark, turtles, frogs, trout, salmon, sea urchin, mackerel, eels, and hundreds of varieties of marine life he couldn't identify. Every color of the rainbow was represented, every bizarre beast imaginable on display in boxes of crushed ice. Some were dead, some were dying, and some looked like they were ready to take on all comers.

Men in high-topped boots lugged baskets of dripping marine life, hosed down empty containers, sliced open fish and held them up to prove freshness, and shouted to each other while cleaning fish. Anyone who thought the Japanese were always quiet would have been amazed at the scene. The noise level was bewildering.

Stark paused to get his bearings and feigned studying a box of fish. The vendor bustled over and launched a sales pitch in Japanese without really looking at Stark. Then he saw Stark was an Occidental.

"*Gaijin*," the vendor muttered, and began to turn away.

"Yes, but I'm opening a large seafood restaurant in your beautiful city and look forward to doing business," Stark responded in Japanese.

The vendor's attitude changed. It was nearing business day's end—the market began its day at four A.M.—and the fish remaining were rejects. The vendor tried to convince Stark that he would be the ideal supplier. Stark acted as if he knew what he was doing, sniffing fish, fingering texture, staring into the fishes' eyes. He made notes on his clipboard. The fishmonger kept up a constant sales patter in the background.

"Perhaps we will see," Stark said, a properly equivocal Japanese answer. "Someone had recommended Fuji Fish to me."

"Hmm."

"Do you know them?"

"If you have an agreement with them, I wouldn't try to steal your business." There was fear in the man's tone. He scuttled away from Stark, back to shoveling ice on the fish.

"Can you tell me where the Fuji Fish company is?"

The merchant pointed, not meeting Stark's eyes.

Stark continued in the indicated direction until he spotted the sign for Fuji Fish. They had a larger section than most of the dealers. They had apparently sold their wares already and closed for the day. Stark entered the large swinging metal door behind the stall area. There were a half-dozen floor bin refrigerators, three ice machines, a stack of wooden crates, and gear for metal strap wrapping. Nothing exceptional. He shivered. The room was kept cold.

He quickly searched the room, looking for something out of the ordinary. There were blood stains on the floor, but he presumed it belonged to fish and not humans. Though it would be a great place to dispose of a body, he thought.

There was a small desk with orders, bills of lading, inventory sheets, waybills, and stacked receipts. He thumbed through the papers. Several cartons with extra paid fees for special fragile handling had been shipped to an address on Kauai in Hawaii. Wasn't there a closer fish market for the Hawaiians? What sort of fish required that handling? He pocketed a scrap with the Kauai address on it.

The last place he checked was a garbage dumpster. Not a fun task in a place that sold fish. He longed for rubber gloves and a face mask. The stench made his stomach do flip-flops. Near the bottom of the bin he found several dozen small cartons from an electronincs shop in Akihabara. Most of the boxes had held capacitors—the component that stores a charge, builds it up, and releases it in a sudden spurt—although he uncovered ample indication of resistors, transistors, diodes, and miscellaneous hardware. There were several empty crates stamped PROPERTY OF U.S. GOVERNMENT—YOKOTA AIR FORCE BASE. Whatever they had held, it would have been well cushioned. He scribbled down the numbers stenciled on the side.

"Hey, what are you doing?"

A squat man twirling a pry bar faced him. The worker had a sallow complexion, as if he'd just gotten out of jail. A second man, holding a baling hook, was coming at him from another angle. He was missing a pinkie tip. Behind him stood a man who weighed at least three hundred pounds. His hair was up in a topknot, samurai-style. Only sumo wrestlers and former sumo wrestlers kept it that way.

The armed workers seemed surprised to have stumbled upon Stark. The wrestler watched with the faint hint of smile, like an adult amused by children quarreling.

"Come with us," Sallow Face said.

"I'm looking for Mr. Fuji," Stark responded. "I want to talk with him about garbage collection."

The sumo wrestler grunted.

"I'm from the government and I'm here to help you," Stark continued cheerfully. "It's a joint U.S.–Japanese project to dispose of waste in a safe and sanitary manner."

Sallow Face sneered and reached for Stark's lapel. Stark brushed his hand away. Sallow Face tried a couple of times and Stark repeated the movement. Frustrated, Sallow Face swung his pry bar. Stark stepped to one side at the last moment, deflecting the blow downward, seizing the man's wrist and twisted. The rusted pry bar clanged as it hit the floor.

"*Uchi komi dori,*" the sumo wrestler said, identifying Stark's move.

Stark nodded. "I'd like to leave without any trouble," Stark said to the wrestler.

The sumo man shook his head.

Pinkie Tip edged closer.

"I bet you didn't lose that"—Stark wiggled his little finger—"in an industrial accident."

Pinkie Tip cursed and swung his baling hook. Stark

ducked but the hook caught the tip of Stark's hard hat and pierced the visor. Stark lashed out with a raised knuckle punch to the man's stomach, then drove backward with his shoulder. Pinkie Tip crashed into Sallow Face and both fell over a carton. They jumped up, ready to renew their assault, but the sumo wrestler barked something and they froze.

The wrestler advanced slowly, arms stretched wide, legs plunking down like steel pillars with every step. Stark back-pedaled. The wrestler was between him and the door.

When the sumo wrestler charged, it was faster than Stark imagined someone that size could move. All that saved him from getting crushed against the wall was that he waited until the last moment before dodging. The sumo wrestler managed to get in one swipe, which knocked Stark over a few feet.

The wrestler closed in again, trying for a bear hug. Stark evaded and got in a full-strength elbow strike. There was a *whoomp* as Stark's elbow connected. But the fat over layers of muscle absorbed the blow with minimal effect. The wrestler hesitated, more annoyed than deterred.

The wrestler lunged, fully committed. Stark ducked under an incoming arm, got off a knife hand strike to the floating ribs, and did an *ukemi* forward roll. He was a few feet from the door. He slipped on the slimy concrete but made it out the door.

Racing down the aisle, Stark crashed into a man carrying a box of fish. The fish, still fluttering, went flying through the air, their silvery scales catching the light.

Fishmongers' shouts turned to cheers and the rowdy yells of boys watching a schoolyard fight.

Stark tried to leap over a stand, miscalculated, and crashed down into a box of ice and yellowtail. Pinkie Tip had been gaining steadily. He leapt. Stark rolled just before the baling hook buried itself where he had been. Stark slugged the man in the temple and he sprawled across the ice.

Stark was up and running, the ice that had fallen down his shirt adding to his adrenaline. He bashed and bumped into people and counters. The Japanese police still wanted him for questioning in the *shihan*'s death. His trespassing at the fish market would add to his popularity if police were called.

He made it to the huge parking lot. The demolition-derby–like traffic continued. Stark weaved in and out among the vehicles. He grabbed a passing truck. Hanging off the side, he got most of the way across the lot hidden from view. He jumped off the truck as it turned out of Tsukiji.

Stark walked at a normal pace, trying not to call too much attention to himself. The crowds on the sidewalk parted to let him pass. Then he saw a couple of children holding their noses and realized that his rooting through the fishy garbage had marked him. His own nose was desensitized.

Since he stood out so much in the street, he slipped into the first crowded business he saw. A pachinko parlor. More than two dozen men were at the vertical pinball machines, popping money in and firing ball bearings through peg obstacles. The air was thick with cigarette smoke, muting the fish smell. A radio played pop music through tinny loudspeakers. Occasionally an announcer in the parlor would cut into the broadcast to yell that someone had won. Prizes ranged from the usual teddy bear geegaws, to marital aids and small appliances.

The glass door was jerked open, and nearly off its hinges, by the sumo wrestler. Behind him was Sallow Face and Pinkie. The wrestler wasn't even breathing hard though the other two were gasping.

Stark dodged down an aisle but they had spotted him. As they raced toward him, Stark reached over the shoulder of a pachinko player, grabbed a fistful of ball bearings, and threw them to the floor. His three pursuers slipped as they hit the balls. The sumo wrestler fell with a massive crash; the other two landed on top of him.

The wrestler shoved the others off and got halfway up before Stark caught him on the jaw with a side snap kick. The wrestler fell back, stunned, pinning his two accomplices beneath him.

Stark took off out the door. He hailed a passing cab and hopped in before the trio reached the sidewalk.

# CHAPTER

## 24

Stark walked out of the Honolulu International Airport terminal to a bank of pay phones near a towering palm tree. Nearby, teenage girls in grass skirts draped leis over arriving tourists and posed for overpriced Polaroid shots with them. The ex–CIA man called Langley and using the parole "Buffy's Tuffy" was quickly put through to the director. Stark read off the address he'd gotten at Tsukiji. "I need the coordinates on that. And the registered owner. I plan a fly-by."

"Anything else?" Marshall asked.

Stark read him the number from the crates in Fuji Fish's garbage. "See if you can identify that. It's U.S. Air Force–issue. I would guess something sensitive."

"Such as electronic hardware?" Marshall asked in his patrician tones.

"Right. Or explosives."

Stark walked to another phone bank, waited a few minutes, then called Marshall back. The CIA director read him the coordinates for the address he'd been given.

"It's a five-hundred-acre estate on the north shore of Kauai," Marshall said. "The registered owner is a Hawaiian hoodlum with no clear means of support. A higher level computer check showed that it is believed to belong to Subu Soto. Are you on to something?''

"Maybe. I'll know better after my fly-by."

"Is this a secure phone?" Marshall asked.

"It's a pay phone chosen at random," Stark said. "Probably safe, but I'd be more worried about a pickup on your end."

"I'll take a chance. You were right. It was explosive."

"What sort?"

"That gets into areas which require a Q clearance. What you found relates to the project you were working on?"

"Yes."

"Shit," Marshall said. The word uttered with precise WASP diction was more dramatic than a string of obscenities.

A Q clearance meant nuclear secrets, and details about the explosives used for detonating a bomb were among the most classified information.

The problem had not been in making a nuclear weapon. That was easy—even college students had shown how it could be done. The problem was securing raw fissionable materials like plutonium 239 or uranium 235, arranging the explosives around it in a precise pattern, and preparing an adequate delivery system.

Scalish had succeeded in getting the weapons-quality plutonium. A senior technician at Nellis Air Force Base owed more than a hundred thousand dollars at one of Scalish's casinos. The mafioso had convinced the technician that he faced the imminent loss of his legs if he didn't pay off. All it cost the debtor was forty pounds of radioactive material swiped from the facility. That was a softball-size sphere, the largest amount that could be handled easily without worrying about a spontaneous explosion. More than nine thousand pounds of plutonium were MUF—material unaccounted for—worldwide by the mid 1980s, and forty more pounds made little difference.

The technician had smuggled it out in a lead-lined attaché case. He had then died in a car accident. There was no point in risking his betraying their plan.

The scientist hired to assemble the device worked at

Soto's Kauai estate. Soto's first action on returning to Hawaii had been to pressure the scientist to finish.

"It's impossible for me to complete this project any sooner," the former Los Alamos nuclear physicist said. When he had taught at MIT he was known as brilliant but obnoxious, the sort who had developed his mental but not social skills. He was used to verbally abusing anyone he didn't consider his equal, and he considered very few his equal.

"Why?" Subu Soto asked.

"Why? You ask why? Can you understand anything about making an atomic device? It's an art as much as a science. This is not just some simple gunpowder-with-a-fuse contraption. It involves extremely precise nuclear physics, metallurgy, electronics. Ask the government of India, whose first device was a dud. Even Ed Teller and the staff at Livermore had a fizzle. And that's working in a first-rate lab, which this place most certainly is not."

"We provided you with the components you requested. You have the training. You said you could do it."

"I'll explain this simply. Watch my lips," the scientist said. He had been working almost around the clock and was exceedingly short-tempered. "An atom bomb means bringing together two masses of subcritical fissile material and turning them supercritical. Picture someone holding erasers in either hand and clapping them together. If he swings those erasers together and they don't hit each other exactly, he winds up with chalk dust all over himself. Understand?"

"Yes."

"To get an atomic explosion, a plutonium 239 or uranium 235 ball about the size of a grapefruit is shaped around a walnut-size metal ball called an initiator. Around the grapefruit goes a beryllium sphere which acts as a reflector. High-explosive charges are placed symmetrically around the sphere. We call this the explosive lens. Are you still following me?"

Soto nodded, struggling to control his rage at the condescending tone.

"For Hiroshima they used a small amount of TNT to start the reaction," the scientist continued. "Today there are much more efficient and effective explosives. For this implosion technique, the blast is directed inward, making the unstable material supercritical and releasing neutrons from the initiator. That leads to a chain reaction and a nuclear blast.

"There are numerous variables. If the shape of the explosive is poor, it will blast the material apart without allowing it to go supercritical for the necessary chain reactions. If you have too much fissile material in one space, it can go critical on its own and you wind up with what we call a squib explosion. That's damaging for only a few hundred feet. Another possibility is radioactive contamination. You comprehend that, don't you? Like in your Godzilla movies."

Soto nodded, not trusting himself to speak.

"Also, you specifically asked for a dirty weapon, one that would spread fallout over a large area," the physicist said. "This requires special adjustments, fine tuning. This is not like building one of those VCRs you people do so well. This is extremely delicate work."

"How close to finished are you?" Soto asked through clenched teeth.

"Close enough."

"I will pay you a fifty-thousand-dollar bonus if you complete it today. I will subtract ten thousand dollars from that every day. So if you take more than five days, no bonus."

The scientist opened his mouth as if he were about to argue. Instead, he said, "I'd better get back to work."

Stark was envisioning a mushroom cloud as he reached the shed with the sign PLANES FOR RENT, LEASE, OR SALE—MAKE ME AN OFFER, I WANT TO GO SURFING. The belly of the gap-toothed plane rental proprietor poked out from underneath his yellow, orange, blue, and red Hawaiian shirt. He had an islander's laconic ease and seemed in no hurry to rent a plane. He waxed poetic about what a fine day it was for flying.

"Though it is always heaven here, except when it isn't," the proprietor said, chuckling. His belly jiggled.

Stark at last succeeded in guiding the man back to business. Stark was licensed to fly anything up to a DC-10, and after showing his FAA papers and his platinum American Express card, he picked out a Cessna 182RG, a four-seat propeller plane, white with a blue trim. Stark inspected the plane carefully before accepting it. He studied maps for several minutes, identifying landmarks that would guide him if the instruments failed.

The takeoff went smoothly and Stark was quickly above the island. He buzzed the high rises and beach at Waikiki, then circled the Diamond Head volcanic crater. He swung northwest following the spine of the Koolau Mountains. He passed through the dense white clouds trapped by the mountain range, bumped through turbulence, then over the surfers at Waimea Bay and the Kauai Channel. It was a picture-postcard paradise with verdant mountains, palm-lined beaches, and a turqoise ocean flecked with whitecaps.

Stark climbed to eight thousand feet to get a safe glide ratio. A standard precaution that meant if the engine died over the water, he could safely glide to Kauai.

In less than twenty minutes he was passing over Kauai, the "garden island," where Captain Cook had landed. Volcanic formations shaped by wind and water led to sheer cliffs, roaring waterfalls, hidden caves, and natural amphitheaters. In between the jagged rock formations was every shade of green imaginable.

He passed over a large patch of uniform green, perfectly square. Curious, he dropped two thousand feet and he saw it was camouflage netting. Kauai was a popular spot for growing marijuana. The hidden field below him looked like a few hundred acres of the stuff.

Then he was at Soto's property. Large chunks of the estate were covered with bamboo groves. A few acres were landscaped with an explosive rainbow of flowers. Several cars were parked in the long, curving driveway. There were six buildings—a main house, redwood paneled with lots of glass, which looked like a Malibu beach house, two matching guest houses, a three-car garage, and a kennel with long dog runs. Stark circled and came at it again from a few hundred feet lower.

The guest houses weren't really guest houses, and not storage sheds either. Squat, unadorned, they each had several vents and a chimney poking from the roof. The windows were boarded up.

Suddenly two men with rifles ran out from one of the structures and aimed at him.

He heard the thunk and felt the shudder even as he pushed in the knob for full throttle and pulled back on the control yoke. The plane climbed rapidly.

At ten thousand feet Stark began to smell fuel. Moments later the plane coughed. The fuel gauge went from three-quarters full to nearly empty.

He knew from the map that Bonham Air Force Base was the nearest landing strip. He doubted he could make it back to Lihue, the commercial airport on the other side of the island.

He glided five miles and dropped three thousand feet. The plane's coughs had grown weaker. The engine had given a final gasp, and then gone silent. The cockpit was eerily quiet, the only sound the air whistling through gaps in the plane's structure.

The radio crackled a warning from Bonham that he was approaching military airspace. Stark responded with a mayday call. Permission to land was granted.

He flew over Waimea Canyon, as awesome as the Grand Canyon but much greener. Ohia trees—with lichen-covered boughs and feathery red blossoms—silver oak, and eucalyptus trees lined the hillsides.

Then he skimmed over a sugarcane field. A few feet lower and he would crash. The plane's nose would dig into the ground, the fuselage would flip as the wings ripped off. A quick death.

Suddenly the sugarcane ended and he was over a landing field. He hit, bounced, hit again, bounced again. There was a burning smell. A few more bounces and screeches of gear, and he rolled to a halt.

Stark jumped and ran from the craft. Fire engines and military police in half tracks raced up. The cops surrounded him, guns drawn. He was handcuffed and taken into custody by Air Force security police.

"Do I get a phone call?" Stark asked.

"This is military justice, boy," the captain of the guards said. "First you answer our questions."

Stark persisted, and at last the base commander arrived.

"I need to make a secure call," Stark told the base commander.

"To where?"

"Langley. Virginia."

The base commander nodded and took Stark to a small room with two phones and walls that were specially insulated against electronic eavesdropping. Two military policeman stood outside as Stark shut the door. He threw a switch and a low hum signaled that a jamming device was activated. Stark picked up one of the phones that had a built-in scrambling device.

Again the password got him through. CIA Director Brandon Marshall came on.

"I just made an emergency landing on Bonham Air Force Base," Stark explained.

"Is this line safe?"

"At this end it is. Didn't it come through on your scrambled line?"

"So it did, so it did. It's hard to keep track with all these phones. About that explosive. It's an RDX derivative. State-of-the-art. It allows excellent shaping for the explosive blanket they wrap around the bomb. Very classified. There's been a major investigation at Yokota trying to find out where it went to."

"A garbage dumpster at Tsukiji Fish Market," Stark said. "At least that's where the carton was. I didn't see the contents."

"I'll notify the Air Force Criminal Investigations Division."

"Better not yet. The more people who know, the more jeopardy. There's leaks all over. Who knew about my getting a fake passport?"

Marshall cleared his throat. "Uh, inadvertently, the Hong Kong station was notified. The cable passed through several hands."

"Great," Stark said sarcastically. "If I request something else, can I be assured it won't be broadcast?"

"I'll handle it personally."

"I need a covert entry kit and an H and K assault weapon. Untraceable."

Marshall hesitated. "You realize that even though we will

deny knowing you, anything I send decreases our deniability."

"Are you refusing?"

"It will be sent. I just wanted to make the awkwardness of our position clear."

"If I get caught, I suspect I'll feel more than awkward."

Marshall cleared his throat. "Uhhm, I'm checking my directories. We've got an office at Barking Sands Naval Base right next door to Bonham. It'll be delivered there."

"I don't know whose tail you put salt on," the base commander said. "But I've been ordered to extend you full cooperation."

"I appreciate your hospitality."

"Heck, I don't want to be spending my winters back in Montana. Out here is God's country. That don't mean I like dealing with you spooky-spooks."

"I'll keep our dealings to a minimum. I need weather and ocean current information for the north shore of Kauai. If you have a map handy, I can show you where specifically. I'll also need a helicopter, silenced, to drop me offshore tonight. This information is on a strict need-to-know basis. I'd prefer you not delegate it to a subordinate."

"I'll take care of it personally."

"Just have the pilot available. Don't give him any idea where we'll be going."

"I know how to handle a covert op," the commander said testily.

"Great. I'm expecting a delivery at Barking Sands. When you get word about it, I'll fetch it myself."

"Understood."

"One last thing, do you have a gym or someplace I can work out for a few hours?"

The ex–Los Alamos physicist checked over the circuits. They appeared to be in order. What did Soto and his associates have planned? That was not the scientist's problem. He didn't invent the technology. Anyway, if he hadn't helped them, someone else would have.

He had oversold them on the atomic bomb. Like most laymen, they confused it with the far more devastating hydrogen bomb. The bomb that destroyed Hiroshima was the equivalent of twenty thousand tons of TNT. His was equal to about twice that. Even with his well-designed weapon, detonated under the best of circumstances, there would probably be no more than a million casualties.

A hydrogen bomb—now, there was a real challenge. The H-bomb used an A-bomb just to detonate it. Perhaps he could sell Soto on his services, building an H-bomb. Of course, it would require a better-equipped lab. And a great deal more money.

# CHAPTER
## 25

The Composite Signals Organization Station on the Chung Hom Kok peninsula on the south side of Hong Hong Island—not far from Repulse Bay—is one of the most important electronic intelligence (ELINT) centers in Asia. The British facility sweeps the Orient for electromagnetic patterns of interest. Radio messages from Soviet subs, Chinese tank maneuvers in the Gobi desert, telemetry from satellites, telephone calls from Vladivostock KGB offices to Moscow are collected, deciphered by high speed computers, and interpreted by skilled linguists. The information is relayed to GCHQ (Government Communications Headquarters) near Cheltenham in England. From there it is reevaluated and perhaps shared with its U.S. equivalent, the National Security Agency (NSA).

Six reinforced concrete guardhouses are evenly spaced around the forty-acre site. Cyclone fences topped with ribbon wire provide a sinewy, silvery link between them. Electronic sensors buried in the ground alert the security center to any intruder larger than a cat. Machine-gun-toting guards with German shepherds patrol the perimeter. But like most facilities, it is better prepared to detect a couple of covert intruders than to repulse a determined armed assault.

The three-story white buildings housing the millions of

pounds of high-tech snooping hardware are set far back from the roadway. The hundreds of antennae that bristle from the building and the grounds—ranging from stubby pieces of metal that look like bent coat hangers, to massive parabolic dishes as big as several houses—are checked three times a day by the ninety-man security force for sabotage. Security is so tight that it is rumored that the waiters hired for the canteen are deaf-mutes who cannot hear a stray secret that might escape someone's lips.

It was the middle of the night and still the facility hummed, because the middle of the night in Hong Kong meant seven P.M. in Moscow.

Ling stood on a hillside, watching the facility from a quarter mile away. He was thirty years old, painfully thin, and a cold-blooded killer. With knife, gun, or his kung-fu-trained hands, he had helped more than two dozen people into the next world.

On a snaking road below him, three Hong Kong punks revved up a Toyota pickup truck. They thought they were about to earn their way into the triad. None was older than sixteen. Pumped up on amphetamine and false promises, they believed they were immortal and destined for glory.

He heard the engine racing and saw the Toyota zoom down the road. On the front of the truck were rods with sharp edges to cut through wire. Inside the truck were two teens, clad in Mao jackets, armed with Chinese S1 7.62mm automatics. The gun was derived from the Russian Tokarev pistol, which was derived from the American Browning.

A third young man was seated in the bed of the pickup. Between his legs was a tripod-mounted 7.62mm machine gun, a Communist Chinese knockoff of the American M60.

Ling shouldered a LAW rocket launcher, aimed, and fired. The guardhouse on the far side of the compound exploded.

Moments later the three teenagers in the pickup crashed through a red and white wooden gate. As guards scrambled to stop them, the young men opened fire. There were shouts, screams, and the teens' excited whoops.

The pickup roared down the service road inside the compound, spewing death.

Ling lifted a hand-size radio transmitter.

The teenagers had strict orders. They were supposed to

reach the main building, park in front, and one was to race out and write "Death to Imperialists" on a front wall with a spray-paint can. A ridiculous assignment, but they believed that was their mission.

They had reached the building. One of the teens jumped out of the cab, ran to the building, and sprayed the slogan on the wall. A few technicians stupidly came outside to see what the fuss was about. The young man in the back of the pickup gunned them down.

Ling flipped a switch on the radio transmitter, then pressed a button. The Toyota truck blew up with the force of the fifty pounds of C-4 plastic explosive that had been hidden inside the body.

The blast was so powerful that even at the quarter-mile distance it staggered him. Ears ringing, he could barely hear the sirens going off and people yelling.

The main building was still standing, but its front half was rubble. A cross-section of the inside was exposed, like a body after a surgeon had made a rough cut. The truck was nothing but metal fragments. Smoldering pieces of flesh and clothing were scattered over the landscape.

Ling staggered to where he had hidden his motorcycle. On the way back to Hong Kong, where he would report his success to Sun Tzu, he stopped at a high cliff and tossed the radio transmitter and spent LAW rocket tube into the ocean.

Stark received the suitcase at Barking Sands and working through the Bonham base commander was able to get a wet suit in his size as well as mask, snorkel, and flippers.

The Bonham base commander had issued Stark a pass that allowed him to go just about anywhere. Stark carried the suitcase to a secure room and opened it. Inside was a black metal watertight case only a few inches smaller. He opened that, took out the H & K MP5, and worked the action. He loaded up three thirty-four-round clips and slapped one in. It was the same weapon used by Delta Force and the Secret Service, capable of 650 rounds per minute.

Stark set the weapon aside and reviewed the gear. There were aerosols which held Mace, a knockout spray, and a chilling agent for neutralizing alarm bells. There were rubber gloves to avoid leaving fingerprints, and heavy arm pads to neutralize a guard dog's bite. The kit also included a black cotton outfit—in his size, he noted—an insulated wire cutter, a bolt cutter, disposable plastic handcuffs, a titanium pry bar, deluxe lock-pick set, grappling hook with flare pistol launcher, K-bar knife, halogen flashlight, and Minox and Polaroid cameras. The tiny Minox was for documents. The Polaroid was to take an initial photo of the premises, which could be used later to put items back in place.

He tested everything and then checked his watch. The sun would set soon. He'd wait a few hours. He sat in a corner, facing the door, and meditated. At first he was too restless. Then one of the *shihan*'s favorite Zen sayings came and soothed him.

> Sitting quietly, doing nothing,
> Spring comes, and the grass grows by itself.

# CHAPTER
# 26

Subu Soto watched the sun set. The surf pounded the dark volcanic rocks at the foot of the cliff in front of him. Behind him was his magnificent garden with orchids, bougainvillea, and a spattering of bromeliads, ringed by groves of dozens of different kinds of trees and a forest of bamboo.

Soto had been in the garden, working on his prize-winning orchids, when the plane had buzzed the grounds earlier that day. Two of his men, drunk on sake, had run out and taken potshots at it. Fortunately, he believed, they hadn't hit it. The pilot was probably just looking for nude female sunbathers. The drunken shooters had been severely reprimanded and sent back to Japan on the next flight. Soto didn't want attention drawn to him because of idiots with bellies full of rice wine.

As he watched the sun set, he could be content. Even if police visited, the atomic bomb was gone from his property. Four of his men had left minutes earlier, escorting the completed weapon to Hong Kong, and then to Macao. Properly crated, it was about the size of a refrigerator.

The *yakuza* leader sat *seiza* style, on his heels. The stretch in his quadriceps felt good. He savored the moment, indifferent to the moaning of the bound and gagged man nearby.

Laid out before him was the samurai sword which had

been used to decapitate his brother, the sword that had been in his family since it was forged by a Norimune smith seven hundred years before. The soul of the samurai. Thirty inches of steel, with a ten-inch handle. He had coveted it since he was a child, and gone into a frustrated rage when he learned that it would be given to his older brother.

The sun touched the horizon line. Orange highlights glistened on the polished black sheath of the sword. Stealing it from the police property room had been a top priority. His underboss had arranged the theft, then hand-delivered the sword himself that afternoon.

The sun was half below the horizon as Soto rose from his seated position. He slipped the sword into his belt and exhaled. He approached the ex–Los Alamos scientist who was bound to a stake. The nuclear physicist's eyes widened and he emptied his bladder.

Soto bowed to the man.

"In olden days, samurai were allowed to practice on condemned criminals," Soto observed. "You, of course, are not a criminal. However, if I were to let you go, you might tell someone what work you had done. This way I get practice and our security is better." Soto smiled. "I also save the payment due you, but that is incidental. The primary reason is you were rude to me."

Soto drew the sword, holding it classically, right hand high on the hilt for control, left near the pommel for leverage.

The nuclear physicist whimpered through his gag. It disgusted Soto. The *yakuza* leader glanced at his watch. He had three hours before he had to fly to Honolulu to check up on his gun ranges and massage parlors. He decided to take his time with the scientist.

The nighttime sea was a shimmering obsidian mirror. Stark, in a Chinook helicopter hovering three hundred yards offshore, could see the lights of Soto's house glowing in the distance. The black chopper had a silenced engine which made it inaudible at two hundred yards. It had been modified for infiltration assignments, with minimal firepower and maximum handling and sensing hardware.

"Ready?" the Air Force chopper pilot asked.

Stark wore a black wet suit, face mask, flippers, and

snorkel. His face was blackened with grease. He looked down at the sea and thought about the sharks devouring the *yakuza* in Hong Kong harbor.

"Fire in the hole," he said, and pushed off.

Twenty feet free-fall, then he hit the water and sank another ten feet. The covert entry kit strapped to Stark's back threw him off, and he spun underwater, dazed. He forced down the panic and exhaled. He could feel the air bubbles roll across his face and flow toward the surface. He followed them up.

Stark blinked a small waterproof flashlight at the chopper. It took off. The water quieted as the whirlybird's wash disappeared.

Stark swam to shore as quickly and quietly as possible. His hands slicing through the water made bioluminescent plankton glow. He reached the wave-pounded rocks at the foot of the forty-foot-high cliff and was nearly bashed by a wave as he clambered ashore.

He dropped his flippers, mask, and snorkel into the ocean, then peeled off his wet suit.

Stark opened the kit and dressed in the black CIA *ninja* suit. His skin was damp, the night air was cool. Big waves hit the rock and sprayed him.

He removed the gun from the case and strapped it on his back. The assorted hardware in the kit attached to a black webbed belt, which Stark put around his waist. He pulled on padded arm guards.

Stark loaded the grappling hook into the modified flare pistol. He fired it up at the cliff edge. It fell back. He attempted four more times before it caught solidly enough for him to trust it.

He rappelled up the side of the cliff. At the top he knelt, gun ready, waiting for a noise. He thought of the Zenrin saying:

> Entering the forest, he moves not the grass,
> Entering the water, he makes not a ripple.

Well, his entrance into the water had hardly been ripple-free, but he could try his best on land.

His breathing slowed. He was in his primal mode, as close to the ideal state of *munen muso* as possible. No mind. Thought and action as one.

In a half crouch he doubled-timed across the grounds. There were no cars in the driveway and the lights in the house were out. The estate appeared deserted.

Stark felt the eyes on him. The attack was faster than anything human.

Two Rottweilers, four hundred pounds of muscle and fang. Silent except for their muffled panting and the sound of paws on grass.

Stark offered his padded arm to one beast. The force of its attack knocked him to the ground. When it clamped down on his arm, the pain was dizzying. He kicked out at the other one, trying to keep it from chomping down on his leg.

The first dog shook its massive head, twisting the arm. Stark stayed loose; resisting the Rottweiler's strength was pointless. In weakness there was strength.

With his free hand Stark got out the knockout spray. He held the spray can right on the dog's nose and squeezed. Five long seconds, and the dog was out cold.

Stark pushed it off him. Stark let the second Cerberus grab the arm, and repeated the treatment.

He scurried to one of the peculiar squat buildings. There were high-security locks on the door and an alarm bell mounted near the eaves. Stark sprayed the alarm with the freezing spray. It took him four minutes to crack the sophisticated locks.

The door swung open, revealing heavy wooden tables with stone tops and a wall of electronic testing gear including an oscilloscope and spectrometer. A lab of some sort.

He saw the lead shielding separating a smaller work area, and then the signs on lead-lined shelves warning RADIO-ACTIVE HAZARD. Stark took pictures with the Minox.

What was in the second building?

He closed the door and hurried across the grounds to the other squat structure, the one the riflemen had come out of. It had a simpler lock system. He popped the door with the titanium pry bar. There were fifty-five gallon drums, bunsen burners, and tables crowded with glassware and metal tubing.

Stark prowled the lab to confirm his suspicion—a drug lab. He spotted several of the chemical precursors of methamphetamine.

He smelled the cigarette smoke before he heard the lone guard.

The guard noticed the pry marks on the lab door seconds later. He drew his .45 automatic and rounded the corner. Stark launched himself. Unable to aim the gun, the guard swung the weapon, nearly catching Stark's temple.

"Put your hands in the air," the guard ordered. He was in his mid-twenties, with a wispy mustache, and a tremor in his hands as he aimed the weapon. The cigarette that had been dangling tough guy–style from his lips fell to the floor. "Didn't you hear me? Do it now!"

Stark obliged. The guard ordered him to unsling his gun and lower it to the floor.

"I'm a friend of Subu Soto," Stark said soothingly, leaning closer to the gunman. "He asked me to inspect security. You did quite well."

A flicker of indecision in the guard's eye. Stark took advantage of it to swivel at the hips, hands slapping the gun aside. The guard pulled the trigger. A bullet tore into a drum of n-methyl formide.

The sudden blast staggered both of them. The guard was nearer to the tank. His clothes caught fire. He ran in a circle, bashing into drums and glassware. Stark shoved him outside and to the ground.

Another drum caught fire with an even bigger blast.

Stark rolled the burning guard around on the grass, trying to extinguish the flames. The guard yowled, the horrid sound occasionally drowned out by a blast as the chemicals exploded.

No one came in response to the tumult. Soto and the others must have left. To leave the charred guard there would be a death sentence. Stark hoisted the *yakuza* on his shoulder and carried him off as the entire building behind them turned into a fireball.

Stark arranged for the burned guard to be medevaced to the burn ward at Honolulu General Hospital.

Stark waited in the ward for the guard to regain consciousness. Perhaps the *yakuza* could provide additional information, details about what radioactive material had been kept in the lab, how far along the project was, what was the goal. But the young man refused to say anything during his few moments of consciousness. Then he lapsed back into oblivion and a nurse shooed Stark from the room.

"I'll be back in a few hours," Stark said, though he wasn't optimistic.

There was the usual hospital clatter and smell, the paging announcer, the squeak of nurses' shoes on linoleum, the carts rolling down the halls. The white walls glowed, the chromed medical hardware gleamed. Doctors prowled the halls like lions over their turf.

He passed one doctor lecturing a nurse. She stood by docilely though her fingers twitched. Another doctor, younger, probably a resident, was bantering with a few nurses at the nurses' station.

Three quarters of the way down the long hall, Stark passed an Oriental doctor with a bad limp. His face was covered by a white gauze mask, his eyes as cold as Hokkaido in the winter.

There was something familiar about the eyes that haunted Stark as he continued down the hall. They reminded him of the *shihan*. The *shihan*'s eyes usually had a bemused twinkle. But when he executed a technique they were as deadly as if the maneuver were real.

The doctor was heading toward the *yakuza*'s room.

Stark turned and raced down the corridor. Nurses shouted "Wait!" "Stop." "You can't do that." Stark skidded to a stop just outside the *yakuza*'s room.

Inside, the "doctor" declared, "You betrayed me" to the barely conscious *yakuza*. The "doctor" had drawn a forty-inch sword from his supposed bad leg. The Norimune blade that had killed both the *shihan* and the physicist had been what made his leg appear stiff. He raised the blade above the *yakuza*.

The *yakuza* groaned, "Guh?"

"Hold it!" Stark yelled, unable to reach the bedside in time.

Subu Soto spun and shifted into a kendo on-guard position. With the gauze mask and surgical cap and gown, he looked like a *ninja*. "I didn't realize it was you," Soto said.

"The guard didn't betray you," Stark said. "I sabotaged your place. He tried his best to stop me. Nearly died in the process."

"No excuse for failure," Soto said, and brought the sword down. The blade bit into the injured *yakuza*'s carotid artery and blood spurted across the room.

Soto pulled the blade back immediately and charged. Stark grabbed a linen-supplies cart and shoved it at Soto. Soto's downward swing made him bump into the cart, cutting a thick stack of towels in half.

A nurse stepped into the room. "What's going—"

"Get back," Stark yelled.

Soto swung. Stark blocked, using a metal pole that held an IV bag, and the sword sliced through the plastic bag. The saline solution spewed around the room.

Soto backed Stark out of the room and down the hall with potentially deadly blows swishing within inches of Stark's head. Soto's long years of kendo training shaped his attack. The only thrust he considered was toward the throat, and most of his attacks were downward blows directed against the head and neck.

The *yakuza* chief was in good form. Each blow cut through the air in an unwavering straight line.

They passed another laundry cart. Stark tried to use it as a shield, but Soto's long sword easily reached over it. Stark tossed a laundry bag at Soto. He cleaved it in half.

Stark grabbed a bath towel and flicked it at Soto's face. The *yakuza* stepped back and slashed. Stark repeated the move and got the same response from Soto. The third time Stark stepped in, surprising Soto and preventing him from making use of the long blade. Soto smashed Stark's shoulder with the pommel of the sword, but Stark got in two elbow strikes to Soto's floating ribs.

As Soto lifted the sword above his head, Stark pushed him. Soto struggled to keep his balance and tried to bring the blade down. Stark sidestepped, simultaneously deflecting the weapon by slapping Soto's forearm.

Stark hit him in the throat with a knife-edge hand. The sword fell to the floor. He grabbed Soto's arms and twisted one over the other, *jujigatame,* throwing Soto and simultaneously breaking both his arms.

He stood over the fallen *yakuza,* in a combat stance, in case Soto was merely feigning unconsciousness.

A security guard who had been cowering in a stairwell peeped out of the door. He saw that Soto was down, drew his gun, and announced, "Nobody move."

Stark watched through a small, square window in the stainless steel door to the surgery theater. He admired the professionalism of the staff, who were doing their best to save Soto. Two doctors and four nurses worked as a briskly efficient team. They were a strangely anonymous organism, clad in blue-green surgical scrubs, with gauze masks and surgical caps.

Stark had been forced to use his CIA clout to keep from spending a night in jail. The local cops wanted to lock him up while they sorted out the circumstances behind the fire at Soto's estate, the murder of the burned *yakuza,* and the sword fight in the hall.

There had been dozens of phone calls between the Agency, local police, the State Department, the Japanese consulate, and the hospital administration. Stark had insisted on his right to remain silent. He was handcuffed, but the hospital staff created such a ruckus—he was seen as their savior—that he was released. But a big Samoan cop loomed over him.

Stark had fulfilled his obligation to the *shihan.* Subu Soto would be in prison enough years that any plans he had would fall apart. But Stark wondered about the evidence of a nuclear bomb. Should he just turn it over to the CIA? What if they bungled that? And sometimes it was in the Agency's interest to permit, or even encourage, evil. Dictators like Haiti's Papa Doc or Chile's Augusto Pinochet, as well as numerous Nazi scientists, could testify to that.

Stark saw the activity inside the theater stop after an hour and a half. The surgeon made a few notes on a piece of paper. The second doctor, the one who had been bantering with the nurses, came out after dropping his gown in a box and peeling off his gloves. Clearly exhausted, he faced Stark and shook his head. "We'll have to wait for the post mortem to be sure but it looks like you broke one of his ribs and then the fall drove it into his heart. Massive internal bleeding." The doctor sighed. "Can you tell me what this was all about?"

The Samoan cop edged closer, three hundred pounds in a juggernaut shuffle.

"I wish I knew, Doc, I wish I knew," Stark said.

# CHAPTER
## 27

Dao's legs were wrapped around Stark, her back against the wall. He thrust into her. She met each movement with a thrust of her own, perfect syncopated rhythm. They came within seconds of each other.

Her plum-colored nipples rose and fell with each breath as she lay back on the bed. "You are too much for me."

"It's you who's too much for me," Stark said. He entwined a finger in her pubic hair and played with the ringlets.

"I missed you so much," she said.

"I missed you too."

"I don't believe that."

"It's true," he said. He had thought of her numerous times. Just a quick mental picture of her was enough to set his loins a-throbbing.

"Tell me where you went, what you did. Don't insult me by saying you're working for a toy company."

He planted a kiss on her lips. "I thought Oriental women didn't question their men."

"You won't tell me?"

"Someday I will." He lay back and stretched.

Perhaps he could tell her a sanitized version. Why didn't he trust her? Just because he had met her at the spook party? There was something more. The undefinable sensitiv-

215

ity that develops between lovers. The way a kiss could signal a need for affection, the desire for sex, or the end of a relationship. He had come to know her body intimately, every muscle tensing, every blink of the eye. He had to trust his instincts. There was something she was holding back.

"A baht for your thoughts," she offered.

"I was wondering where we would eat tonight," he said.

"So romantic."

"You look good enough to eat," he said, taking a gentle bite of her shoulder. "But if that doesn't work, how about chicken in hot oil?"

"Oh. That reminds me. I bought you a present."

She hurried to her purse, retrieving a small gift-wrapped object.

Stark shook it. "Cologne?"

"I like your smell just the way it is."

"I guess that's a compliment," he said, and unwrapped the bottle. There was Chinese writing on the side.

"Let me guess, it's an aphrodisiac. You've been disappointed with my performance."

"No, silly. It's rubbing oil. For special massage. Roll over on your belly."

She ran her nails over his back, almost breaking the skin. Each nerve ending tingled. The oil smelled of camphor and mint. She rubbed it in slowly, deeply.

After a few minutes Stark felt incredibly sleepy, almost drugged.

"Endorphins," he mumbled.

Dao rolled him over. "Where were you?" she purred, rubbing the oil on his chest.

"Quick nap," he said, overcome by exhaustion.

"Soon. Tell me what happened."

"Sleep."

"Not yet. Tell me what happened."

"Machiavelli, Musashi, Sun Tzu. Criminals. Conspiracy. Causing trouble. Don't know what they want." Each slurred word was an effort to get out. She kept shaking him awake. He desperately wanted to sleep. She pinched and prodded each time he dozed off.

"Machiavelli was a gangster named Scalish," he murmured. "Killed. Musashi was a *yakuza* named Subu Soto. I killed in Hawaii. Didn't want to. Sun Tzu left."

"Who is he?" she asked.

"Don't know."

"Can you find out?"

"All dead ends. Gotta sleep," he said.

"What else?"

"Nothing." As part of CIA training he had been given a dose of sodium pentothal. The experience was similar to what he was feeling. He nipped the tip of his tongue. The pain brought him a few inches back from mental oblivion. It kept him from mentioning the evidence of a nuclear weapon.

"What are you going to do now?" she asked.

"Sleep."

"After that?"

"Nothing to do. Only Sun can't do anything."

"With only Sun Tzu left, nothing can be done?"

"Right."

"So you're going back to the U.S.?"

"Time with you."

"Yes. Spend time with me. We'll go to Tahiti."

"Tahiti."

"Somewhere nobody can find us. No more business, right?"

"Yes."

She got up.

"I'll see you later." She pecked him on the lips. By the time she stepped away from the bed, he was asleep.

He awoke, barely remembering what had happened. He stumbled to the bathroom and glanced in the mirror. His coordination was ever so slightly off, the mental cobwebs noticeable only because he knew his own capabilities. Drugged. Turning sideways, he could see Dao's deep nail-marks on his back.

How had she done it? The massage oil, with a DMSO-like skin penetrant? Perhaps she had been given an immunizing agent so she wouldn't be affected, or maybe her fingertips were coated with a sealant.

The drug in his system muted his anger and depressed him. How could she trick him? Whom was she working for?

He had nearly fallen for her. It made him feel vulnerable, and stupid. Betrayed.

Still groggy, he lay down for just a minute to think about his next move. His eyes refused to stay open.

The phone rang two hours later, waking him.

"Uhh," he grunted into it.

"Mr. Stark. This is Peter Wong."

"Who?"

"Peter Wong. The inspector handling the arson investigation."

"Oh, yes, sorry. I just woke up."

"Only mad dogs and Englishmen go out in the noonday sun," Wong said, but there was the hint of disapproval in his voice, as if Stark were the sort who moped around in bed all day. "Meet me in a half hour in the New Territories."

"Can you give me an idea what this is about?"

"Not over the phone." Wong gave him an address in Tsuen Wan.

"I'll be there."

Tsuen Wan is a rapidly expanding industrial town with 800,000 residents, and another 100,000 expected by 1993. Half of those who live there work in the area, at the light-industry factories that are springing up daily, or the Kwai Chung container port.

The address was a building under construction, a sprawling five-story structure located a short distance from the port. Stark could hear the whistles, horns, whining of machinery, and shouts of stevedores. There was wooden fence around the site, but the gate was unlocked. Piles of sand and lumber lay astrew on the hard-packed earth. A yellow bulldozer was parked off to one side. Instead of metal scaffolding, bamboo poles wrapped the structure. No one in sight.

"Mr. Stark?"

Wong stepped out from behind a piece of drywall. The lean cop seemed nervous.

"Inspector Wong. You've piqued my interest."

"Come with me, please," Wong said.

"Where are all the workers?" Stark asked as they walked toward the back of the project.

"The developer ran into money problems. They are putting together new financing. Through here." They walked carefully on the planks. The flooring was incomplete and a misstep could lead to an abrupt visit to the basement.

If Stark hadn't been fuzzy from the remnants of Dao's drug, he might have hesitated. Even as he stepped in front of Wong, his senses tingled.

But it was too late. The cop's blackjack caught him behind the ear, and Stark tumbled into darkness.

# CHAPTER
# 28

Stark awoke to the muted roar of an engine. He lay immobile in a tiny room, trying to identify where he was. The choppy movement and the small round window near his head made it clear.

He peered through the porthole. The colors were subdued. A gray sky over dark green water that in parts was reddish-brown from stirred-up mud. The walls along the shore were weathered gray stone. Hakka women—under their unique headgear which looked like coolie hats with a fringe trim—rowed skiffs with the slow-moving current. Hydrofoil ferries carrying hundreds between Hong Kong and Guangzhou stayed in the middle of the channel. Fishermen hoisted crab traps from the water. An occasional Chinese patrol boat passed by, uniformed young men looking serious on the bridge.

Stark tried the door and found it had been left open. He went up on deck. Wong stood near the front of the speed-boat, wearing casual clothes. His loose-fitting shirt flew backward in the wind. Another young man at the wheel piloted them at a steady course up the river.

"I regret that we had to bring you here so roughly," Wong said. "I trust I did not strike you too hard."

"Your concern is touching," Stark said sarcastically. "I would've accepted a gentler invitation."

"We could not be sure of that. The order to bring you left no room for refusal."

The wind whipped the words away from their mouths. They had to move closer to hear each other.

"We could not take a chance on your going to Hong Kong authorities," Wong continued. "My position is too fragile. Even the hint of scandal would ruin the plans."

"For what?"

"I will be police commissioner when Hong Kong returns to the rightful control of China."

"I see. Who do you work for? The *Diaochabu? Gonganbu?*" The first was the Bureau of Enquiry of the Communist Chinese Central Committee, which coordinated intelligence efforts. The second was the Ministry of Public Security, which handled police and counterespionage functions.

"The name of the agency is not important. We all work toward a common goal," Wong said. "Listen carefully. We will be joining a tour group. It is the easiest way to get you into the country. An individual traveler is under more suspicion. This way we do not have to advise anyone in passport control."

"If you're all working toward a common goal, why not get their cooperation?"

Wong frowned. "There are still revisionists and bourgeoisie among us. One of them told the kung fu instructor that you would be breaking into his studio. We regret that. The traitor has been taken care of."

"Why bother with me? Surely you have enough resources that you don't need a *gwai lo* like myself."

"Minister Li will explain."

Stark debated continuing questioning Wong or trying to escape. He decided the first would be fruitless and meeting the foreign minister would be the best way to learn more about what was going on.

He stood at the railing and enjoyed the view.

The guide pointed out the sites of Guangzhou:
"The large and stately white building you see in the

distance is the White Swan Hotel, the hotel where you will be staying tonight," the guide explained. "It is located on Shamian Island. The name in English means sand flat. That is what it was until the middle of the nineteenth century, when the Ching emperor allowed foreign traders to establish their businesses there. Foreigners were confined to the island for their trading. Later we will see the monument to the twenty-five martyrs killed by foreign troops."

"Something to look forward to," muttered a woman in a dress with big padded shoulders. In a louder voice she said, "When do we go shopping?"

"Later," the guide responded politely.

The buildings were mainly weathered two- and three-story structures that looked at least a hundred hard years old. But there was abundant labor-intensive construction. A pile driver was four men lifting and dropping a heavy weight. A bulldozer was six men behind a metal sheet. Muscle was cheaper than machine.

The tour bus jockeyed through busy streets, where vans, trucks, and hundreds of bicycles fought for space. Pedestrians had to throw themselves into the fray if they wanted to cross a street. Traffic lights were rare and often not heeded.

"Our first stop will be a Taoist temple," the guide said.

"I thought you people didn't allow religion," a thin man with a British accent piped up.

"In the past there had been excesses and lack of tolerance," the guide said. "Much as your countries went through. Now anyone is free to worship as they wish. It is mainly the old people, however, who go to the temples."

"Does that include Christianity?" a man with five thousand dollars in camera gear around his neck asked.

"Christianity, Muslim, Buddhism, Taoism."

"Can we go to the church?" asked a woman with a large crucifix wedged into her generous cleavage.

"Regrettably, no. We can pass by it, however. Too many tourists were disrupting services and the priests asked us to no longer bring groups. The Buddhist and Taoist temples are open. I think you will enjoy."

The temple, inside a one-acre walled compound, had more of an atmosphere of a country fair than a holy place. Throngs of people pitched coins at statues of various Taoist deities.

If the coin landed in certain cups, the wish would be fulfilled. There were amusement-park rides for children, picnic tables, food and souvenir stands. The Chinese had made the temple into a fun house. But Taoism had a sense of humor about itself.

"Come with me," Wong whispered as the group split up with instructions to meet at the main gate in twenty minutes.

Wong led Stark through the compound to an arched stone doorway. At a door a few paces farther in, two stern young men in the bright green uniforms of the Public Security Bureau stood guard.

Wong said something to the guards and they waved them through. Stark and Wong entered a virtually bare eight-by-ten-foot room. The foreign minister sat facing the doorway in a straight-back wooden chair with a folding table in front of him. He was reading papers. When he saw Stark he tucked the papers into a plain brown paper folder and stood.

"Mr. Stark, I am Wo Peng Li."

"It is an honor to meet you, Mr. Foreign Minister," Stark said in Mandarin.

"You speak the language?" Wong asked, surprised.

"Just a few words. I would prefer if we spoke in English," Stark said.

"That is prudent," Li said, switching to English. Aside from a slight singsong intonation to his words, Li's English was impeccable. He had previously been the Chinese representative to the United Nations and he was a skilled orator. "Chinese is best suited to negotiations. Your language is best suited to precision. That's why it has remained the international language of science."

"And aviation."

"True, Mr. Stark. I presume you are aware of the problems in Hong Kong?" Li asked. Without waiting for an answer, Li continued. "Nowadays a change in the breeze in Beijing means a typhoon in Hong Kong. Although we have assured the Hong Kong Chinese that little will change for fifty years, any unexpected action and the diaspora increases."

Stark listened to Li's speech about how smoothly the changeover would work, with "one country, two systems" until 2047. Li explained that with the billions the PRC had invested in Hong Kong, the Communists would be the biggest loser if Hong Kong were to have major troubles.

"Have you ever heard of Sun Tzu?" Li finally asked.

"He wrote the classic text on strategy, *The Art of War*. About twenty-five hundred years ago. I understand that Mao Tse-tung's copy was quite dog-eared."

"He went through several copies," Li said. "But the venerable Sun Tzu is not the one I am referring to. My country has been the victim of an extortion by criminals using the aliases Sun Tzu, Musashi, and Machiavelli."

"I don't see how this affects me."

"You have dispatched two of them. I doubt that it was coincidence. The deaths are unfortunate, akin to pulling off a tick and leaving the head to grow infected."

"Their deaths were the outcome of their own actions."

"That can be said of all of us," Li said. "Please, I'm not chastising you. I'm glad that your interests and ours run parallel. I am, however, curious as to how you arranged Mr. Scalish's precipitous fall from grace."

"Early on in my career we had to gain entry to a car with contraband in it. It took police officers six minutes to break in. I knew a car thief could've done it in as many seconds. Ever since, I've had the names of several dozen professional criminals in my files. Burglars, safecrackers, con men all can be helpful. Also, several of my key employees are ex-cons. They were indignant that Scalish tried to kidnap a woman I'm friendly with."

"Dr. Mirnov, I presume?"

Stark smiled.

"Getting back to the problem at hand," Li said. "We don't know who Sun Tzu is but just yesterday we received a message from an intermediary. He has given us an ultimatum. We have seventy-two hours to accede to his demands or he will take aggressive action."

"Does he say what action?"

"No."

"What actions have you taken? Aside from having Petey here hit me in the head and bring me here."

"I regret his excessive enthusiasm and trust that it doesn't adversely impact on our relationship," Li said. "Some of our best operatives have been investigating, trying to identify Sun Tzu. Our efforts have not been productive. Two of our agents were subsequently found dead. There has been betrayal. This hurts me greatly."

I don't imagine it was too much fun for the blown and burned agents, Stark thought.

"We were seeking someone with a fresh perspective," the foreign minister continued. "We have finally been able to assure the British that it was not a Communist group that bombed their signals intelligence building at Chung Hom Kok. The British prime minister initially withdrew their ambassador and threatened trade sanctions. We are still trying to undo the damage of that provocation. If one of our operatives were to be involved in any trouble, it would be very unfortunate timing. Of course we are still investigating, but there are certain limitations. These criminals are cunning. Your CIA was blamed for the factory arson. We were blamed for the subsequent riots. While the tiger and the dragon fight, the rat makes off with the food."

In the background was the noise of the happy crowd enjoying the Taoist temple and its attractions. A smell of incense wafted through the air.

"What is it that Sun Tzu wants?"

"Macao. He will infiltrate his accomplices into positions of power there. Our existing cadres are to work to support his people. We believe he will turn it into a criminal haven. Consider the possibilities."

"Drug transhipment. Passports for sale," Stark said, ticking off the criminal opportunities on his fingers. "Weapons smuggling. Extradition-free sanctuary."

"As well as gambling, whoring, pornography, and any other vice. It's a small country with a history of profiteering off human weakness."

"Speaking of vice, has a pornographic film featuring your premier surfaced?" Stark asked.

"It had surfaced in Shanghai and Hunan province. How did you know?"

"I stumbled upon the people involved in producing it."

"It is embarrassing. Your CIA tried a similar ploy with Sukarno in the 1950s, not realizing that the Indonesian people would be more charmed than upset by seeing their leader cavorting. Our premier is in his seventies, and if it merely showed his lookalike with a young woman, it would be regarded as a sign of health, and maybe an old man's foolishness. After all, even Chairman Mao had his dalliances. But this is filth.''

''If you can find out who is leaking it, you might get a lead on Sun Tzu. It's part of his harassment campaign.''

''I have put several agents on it.'' Li sighed. ''There are elements within my government who wish to give in. Hong Kong is too profitable to jeopardize. Macao, which becomes ours that same year, is little more than a nuisance. But all Chinese people should be under one nation.''

''I've heard manifest destiny refrains before. Excuse me if I'm not sympathetic,'' Stark said dryly.

''We would not be asking your assistance if the matter was not critical,'' Li said. ''They have threatened us with a nuclear device. We doubt that they have such technology, but cannot risk calling their bluff.''

''I don't think it is a bluff.''

''Why?''

Stark told Li what he had learned.

Li fired off a string of angry words in Chinese to Wong, who shook his head.

''Further proof, Mr. Stark, that we need you. With all of our agents, we were not aware of this development.''

''Why did you shanghai me here now? No pun intended.''

''We were afraid you were losing interest in the matter.''

Only Dao could have told them that. ''How long has Dao been working for you?'' Stark asked casually, as if it were a widely known fact and didn't matter to him.

''She doesn't work for us.''

Stark turned toward the door. ''Good day, Mr. Minister.''

Wong tensed. Li let Stark walk a few paces before reluctantly saying, ''For most of her adult life.''

''As an asset or an agent?''

Again he hesitated. Stark folded his arms across his chest.

''An agent,'' Li admitted.

''She's very good,'' Stark said in a monotone.

''I tell you so that it will help you to work better together. You should know that her assignment with you officially ended a while ago. She requested to stay.''

''I'm touched,'' Stark said sarcastically.

"Please do not let your feelings color your actions as far as Sun Tzu. We need your help. We will pay."

"He gave you seventy-two hours?" Stark asked.

"That's all." Li consulted an inexpensive Timex on his wrist. "Actually you haven't much more than forty-eight hours. Unfortunately time was wasted debating what should be done, and then arranging for this meeting."

"Have you decided what you'll do at the deadline?"

"We will meet his price."

# CHAPTER
## 29

"If there is any way I can be of assistance, please let me know," Wong offered during the ride back.

"Fine," Stark snapped. He had suspected Dao, but like a jealous husband who has his wife's adultery confirmed, he wished he'd been wrong.

"Do you have any ideas who Sun Tzu is?"

"Judging by his name, I would guess Sun Tzu is Chinese and a resident of Hong Kong or Macao," Stark said.

"That narrows it down to a few million. How can you be sure he's Chinese?"

"The other two players chose aliases consistent with their racial background," Stark said crisply. "I would guess Sun Tzu is quite vain. Choosing the name of a historical great is part of my impression. The other is the grandiose feel of the whole operation. I also believe he is high ranked in the triads."

"How do you know that?"

"His crime partners. If the head of General Motors were going into a joint automobile venture, it would be with a top exec from Ford, not a guy who works on the loading docks or who isn't even in the auto industry," Stark said. "This scam is just a giant variation on the protection racket, and

Machiavelli and Musashi would be partners only with a pro.''

"Why didn't you ask Minister Li for information about the triads? Our intelligence agents have much to offer.''

"I don't have absolute faith in his organization.''

"We are among the finest intelligence services in the world.''

"I'm sure you are. So's the CIA. But the more people involved, the more chances for screwups and sellouts.''

"What about me?''

"What about you?''

"You can trust me,'' Wong insisted.

"I always trust people who hit me over the head and kidnap me,'' Stark said.

"It was necessary. For the good of my country.''

"Does the fact that you expect to be made police commissioner have anything to do with your loyalty?''

After Wong dropped Stark off near the Star ferry terminal on Hong Kong Island, Stark went to the pay phone booths in the lobby of the grand Peninsula Hotel. He called Les Halliwell in New York and asked, "Is Pedro available?''

"He's been baby-sitting Sultana at the lodge,'' Halliwell said.

"She's probably safe now that Scalish is dead. Replace him with a couple of contract ops. How is she?''

"Let's put it this way, Pedro will be glad to come risk his life with you. It's easier than playing nursemaid to an enraged Russian.''

"I also need a surveillance team with assault capabilities, and a geiger counter.''

"What's going on?''

"It's a long story, Les, and this line isn't secure,'' Stark said. "What did you find out about those corporations?''

"Paydirt. I've got an address that they trace back to.''

"Let me guess, it's in Macao.''

"Son of a bitch. Do you ruin Christmas gifts too?''

"Let me have it.''

Halliwell read off an address on Avenida de Almeida Ribeiro. "That's a main drag. The Hotel Lisboa is at one end, the Senate and Municipal Building about midway, the floating casino at the other end. It's called the avenida do Infante D. Henrique on the southeast end. Most of the streets there go through more name changes than Liz Taylor had husbands."

"I'll find it. I'll check into the Lisboa under the name Paul McCarthy. Have Pedro ring my room and ask for himself. I'll meet him fifteen minutes after the call in the casino men's room on the lowest level."

"Got it. Are you okay? You sound like you got a bug up your butt."

"It falls into that long-story category, Les. I'll tell you when I get back."

Stark hung up and called Dao's business. She wasn't in, but her secretary gave him Dao's home number. He reached her there and she told him to hurry over.

After being inspected by the doorman, he rode the elevator to her twelfth-floor apartment. She gave him a lusty greeting, slipping her tongue deep into his mouth and pressing against him. She pulled back when he didn't respond. He stepped into the apartment and shut the door.

The room colors were white, black, and red. The white surfaces didn't have any hint of grime. The black stone tabletops were as shiny as mirrors. With its functional, modern style and professional decorator touches, the apartment lacked a lived-in look.

"What's the matter? Where have you been? I was worried," Dao said in a gush of words.

"I met with Foreign Minister Li. I gather he doesn't like to leave the mainland."

She stiffened ever so slightly. "Why did you go there?"

"Apparently your report got them excited."

"What are you talking about?"

"Forget the theatrics. He gave you up without any hesitation."

"I don't know what you're talking about."

"Did you think I wouldn't realize that your magic massage oil was drugged? What was it, a DMSO base with sodium pentothal?"

She folded her arms defensively across her chest and put on a petulant face. "I can't believe you're serious."

"Did they give you a file on me? All my likes and dislikes. It must've made your job easier."

"I don't understand what you're saying?"

"I'm going to Macao. Do you want to come?"

"Robert, what happened? Why are you so cold?"

"I need a translator. We can work together or we can part company. Make your decision. I leave in fifteen minutes."

"You really are a bastard."

"You're right. Go pack."

He walked to the balcony, which offered a spectacular view of the back side of Hong Kong Central's business district. He stared into space.

She went into the bedroom and came out with two minutes to spare. She had an overnight bag in one hand and a pistol in the other.

"Nice gun for a lady. An H and K .380 automatic. Good stopping power, nine shots, weighs little over a pound. Cute pearl handle grips you have on there."

She handed him the weapon. "If you hate me so much, kill me. Believe me, it was hell. Many times I wanted to tell you."

"I bet."

"What did I do so terrible? I worked for my country. And I fell in love."

"Put the gun away and kill the melodrama. Let's go," he said.

They rode by jetfoil to Macao, saying nothing during the less than one-hour ride. Stark had picked up a Macao guidebook at a newsstand, and was absorbed in his reading.

Hong Kong gave the impression that anything could be bought there, from knit shirts and electronic toys, to heroin and cheap hookers. Macao gave the feeling that the only growth industry was vice. It reminded Stark of a border town where sex, drugs, and violence could be bought for a nominal amount.

From the beggars at the boat terminal, to the cab driver, to the clerk in the hotel, there was a greedy wariness. It seemed they would have been quite pleased if he died and left his wallet on the floor.

They checked into a deluxe suite at the Hotel Lisboa. The

twelve-story hotel was an orange-and-white circular building with strange decorative rods protruding from the roof. To call it merely garish was a compliment. The bellhop tried to steer them to several tourist traps, and left only after pocketing his generous tip.

"Must you be so cold?" Dao asked as Stark unpacked. "Don't you care what happens here, what happens to us?"

"It's *ming*, right? Either I find Sun Tzu or I don't."

"You don't care about the Macanese people. About the Chinese people. About me."

"I care. I'm willing to overlook being used because a criminal with a nuclear weapon has to be stopped."

"Then why do you waste time unpacking? What are you going to do?"

"Would you like to visit the casino?"

She glared at him. "Are you crazy?"

"I have to check out a building, then more time with real estate records."

"I'll come with you."

He took her by the shoulders. "I don't want you relaying everything I gather back to Minister Li. I don't think he's plugged his leaks yet."

She raised her right hand, as if saying an oath. "I will not tell them anything you do not want me to. I will do whatever you say. Robert, can we ever go beyond what has come between us?"

He kissed her roughly. She began to respond and he pulled away.

"You still care about me, don't you?" she asked.

He shrugged. "Let's go."

Their first stop was a surprisingly new, relatively clean three-story building on the Avenida de Almeida Ribeiro. On the third floor, a smoked glass door had the name of its occupant scratched out. But it was the address Halliwell had tracked down as the base of the real estate syndicate.

The suite had the decor of a forties private eye's office. A ceiling fan struggling to move fetid air. Three plump secretaries sitting at small desks toying listlessly with papers. Each desk had five phones on it. The water cooler in the corner was empty. The coffee machine had brown stains all over it.

"I'm looking for the Wang Chung clothing distributor," Stark said.

The women gazed at him blankly.

Dao repeated in Cantonese what he had said.

"Not here," the oldest woman responded in English. She had harlequin glasses with rhinestones in the frame, the only touch of glamour in the shabby office.

"What is this place?" Stark asked in a friendly tone.

"Answering service," the woman said. As if to illustrate her words, a phone rang and one of the other women sluggishly answered it.

"I was thinking of hiring one myself. What's the procedure?"

The woman rose, went to the coffee machine, and filled her cracked cup.

"I am the office manager," the woman said imperiously. "Who do you want to know about?"

"Excuse me?" Stark asked.

"You are policeman. Even with this fancy lady on your arm, I can tell. You not local policeman, so you have no power. You tell me what you want, I tell you how much it cost."

"SMM Construction Limited," Stark said, recalling one of the names that Halliwell had turned up.

The office manager nodded. "Five hundred dollar. American."

Dao haggled with the woman, punctuating her remarks with emphatic hand-waving. The office manager seemed unimpressed. Back and forth a few times. The rapid-fire Cantonese conversation, with voices rising and falling to cover all nine tones, sounded like discordant music.

"Three hundred dollar, American," the woman finally agreed.

She took Stark's money to her battered wooden desk and locked it in a drawer. "I don't know," the office manager said.

Dao took a belligerent step forward. The other two women stood.

"The company you mentioned, along with several other clients, come for messages every few week," the office manager said. "A young man come to the door, take message, and leave. He pay in cash."

"What does he look like?" Stark asked.

"Typical. I could not recognize him in the street."

"You have no address for him?" Stark asked.

"No."

Stark nodded and turned to go. Dao fired a volley of angry words in Cantonese. The women sat in perfect synchronization. They remained unsmiling.

A minute later the office manager went to the window. She looked down, and saw Stark and Dao walk off. The office manager picked up the phone and dialed a local number.

Stark called the *Macao Times* and identified himself as a business consultant pondering commitments in Macao. He noted that he would be a major advertiser if he invested. He was able to get a luncheon appointment with the managing editor, the highest person available on such short notice.

Stark and Dao went to the real estate records office near the Leal Senado, the Loyal Senate. Decorated with Portuguese tile, wrought iron work, and historic stone carvings, the building was a throwback to the days when Portugal was a significant world power. There were high ceilings, polished teak wainscotting, marble floors, sweeping staircases, and oil paintings of former governors. The real estate records room was nowhere near as large or busy as in Hong Kong, but the two clerks on duty were as surly.

Dao grew fidgety as Stark reviewed records. He wouldn't tell her what names he was looking for. He suggested she take a walk around the Senate square, and she agreed.

"Did you find what you wanted?" she asked when they met an hour later.

"You cannot get it by thinking, you cannot seek it by not thinking," Stark said.

"What does that mean?"

"I'll explain later. We'd better hurry if we're going to meet Ng on time."

Managing editor Jesus Ng was waiting at the Cafe, a tentable restaurant on Rua da Praia do Bom Parto. It overlooked the Baia da Praia Grande, where tiny fishing boats that didn't look seaworthy plied their trade. The restaurant had white tableclothes, staff dressed in formal wear, and overly attentive waiters.

Stark used the cover name Paul McCarthy and introduced Dao, under a false name, as his translator. Ng eyed Dao and gave Stark an approving wink. Ng was a late-middle-aged man with thinning hair and a circular face. He wore an expensive blazer and sharply pressed chino pants.

Ng explained the unique Macanese cuisine, part Portuguese, part Chinese, and ordered for them. Dishes included African chicken in a thick brown sauce grilled with hot spices; *galinha a portugesa,* chicken with potatoes, onion, eggs, and saffron; and *minche,* minced meat with fried potatoes and onion.

For the first twenty minutes or so they discussed the food, the beauty of Macao, its long and fascinating history. Ng recommended a number of tourist attractions—various temples, the Guia Fortress, Sun Yat-sen's memorial home, and, of course, the ruins of São Paolo. The cathedral of Saint Paul, built in the first decade of the seventeenth century and burned down in a typhoon in 1835, was described by Ng as the greatest monument to Christianity in the east.

"Unfortunately all that remains is the facade, a sermon in stone of great beauty," Ng said. "There are also the stone steps leading up to it and a magnificent mosaic floor. You must see it."

Dao translated, growing impatient, barely touching her food. She kept looking at Stark, waiting for him to make his move.

"My country is quite compact," Ng said. "You can see most of it by pedicab, which I suggest most highly. Although we are a small nation, we have a great international importance. Strategic importance because of our location. You will note that our symbol is a cannon and a castle battlement."

"Yes. Your country has a fine history. And a promising future," Stark said. "At the real estate records office I noticed there's been quite a lot of activity beginning six months ago."

"I don't understand."

"Large clusters of property that had been in families for

generations were sold off," Stark said. "Usually for less than fair market value. Have you heard of anyone being threatened, forced to give up their land?"

"Never. I would know. We are like one family here."

"Would you know who has bought the land near the reservoir?"

"A group of businessmen."

"What are their names?"

"That is confidential."

"The warehouses on Rua do Almirante Sergio?"

Ng sighed. "What is your true occupation?"

From his wallet Stark took a business card identifying him as Paul McCarthy, senior investment analyst with a New York firm. Ng pocketed the card.

"Think of me as sort of a financial private investigator," Stark said. "I study balance sheets, check assessments, profit and loss, trends, find the bottom line."

Ng nodded.

"I have clients who are interested in Macao. They've heard rumors."

"What sort of rumors?"

"Oh, of big changes in the future."

"Can I trust you with a secret?" Ng asked.

"Of course."

Ng bent and whispered. "What they have heard is true. There are plans to build an airport here. An international airport. Great for business."

"Aren't the airport investors concerned, what with China due to take over in less than ten years?"

Ng regarded Stark as if he had committed a serious breach of table manners by bringing up a taboo subject.

"I shouldn't even have told you that," Ng said.

"Who are these investors?"

Ng was silent. He gnawed at a chicken bone, wiped the brown sauce from his lips delicately.

"I appreciate the information," Stark said. "I'll continue my inquiries. If I find anything that I think would be of interest to your paper, should I call you?"

"Mr. McCarthy, let me tell you a story," Ng said. "About three months ago a young man was hired by the paper. As many young men are, he was full of energy. He stumbled upon things that people didn't want in the newspaper. I spoke to him. He had seen *All the President's Men* and thought he would be famous if he got this story in the news. He tried selling it to a Hong Kong newspaper." Ng paused, picked up another bone, and gnawed. "His attempt was discovered. He was immediately fired. He subsequently threw himself into the river and drowned. They found his body by the Floating Casino."

"Were there any indications that he had help in throwing himself into the river?" Stark asked.

"You are missing the point," Ng said as he stood.

When Ng was gone, Dao turned to Stark and said, "Are we any closer to finding Sun Tzu?"

"Yes."

"What have you learned?"

Stark patted her thigh under the table. "What do you think would be good for dessert?"

Later that afternoon they had an appointment with the Macanese prosecutor. In the interim Stark took her to the Floating Casino, a garish barge outfitted with garish dragons and ornate red and green trim.

Inside was like a second-rate downtown Las Vegas casino, except for the sign that would light up in Chinese, Portuguese, and English if there were a typhoon approaching.

Although it was midday in midweek, the tables were packed. Hungry Tigers, the Chinese name for one-armed bandits, spun their reels and occasionally paid off. The noise was overwhelming, from crapshooters shouting words of encouragement to their dice, to fan-tan croupiers counting off the porcelain buttons, to the general huzzah of winners and losers. There were rusted spittoons every dozen feet, and spitters were hitting at least half their shots. Everyone seemed to be smoking, and with a barely eight-foot ceiling, the cloud burned eyes and throats like acid rain.

Stark played blackjack conservatively and retired ahead fifty American dollars after a half hour of play. Dao hovered at his side.

As he got up from the table and tipped the girl five dollars, he murmured, "Just as I expected."

Dao tugged at his arm and regarded him questioningly. He gave her a wink but no answers.

They took a pedicab, powered by the sinewy legs of an elderly toothless man, to the lush green Lou Lim Loc gardens. Dao was annoyed that Stark refused to barter with the old man and paid the inflated price.

The gardens, with twisting paths amid mock mountains and dense greenery, was modeled on a famous garden in Suchow, China. From certain perspectives it resembled a classic Chinese painting on a small scale. Stark took a few cryptic notes. Dao peeked but couldn't decipher anything.

They criss-crossed the 6.2 square mile peninsula, ending up at the temple of the fishermen's goddess, A-Ma. The peninsula was named after her. Over the years, Bay of A-Ma, or A-Ma-Go became Macao. The multilayered temple, notched into the side of Barra Hill, had numerous shrines to various deities. Worshipers burned joss sticks and left offerings at the stone shrines. The air was nearly as thick with incense as the casino had been with tobacco smoke.

Stark climbed to an upper level and gazed southeast toward the water.

"May I ask what you are doing?" Dao asked.

"Thinking."

She looked at her watch. "We have barely twenty-four hours before they must meet Sun Tzu's demand."

"Yup."

"Is that all you can say? Have you gone crazy?"

"What is sanity? Isn't it relative? Did I ever tell you about my instructor in Japan?" Stark recounted the *shihan*'s death to an impatient Dao, though she did appear shocked and sympathetic when he recounted the grisly end.

They sat in silence. She held his hand.

"Time for the prosecutor," Stark said.

They returned to the Leal Senado, to a large office with a ceiling fan beating overhead like a bat's wings. The prosecutor was a corpulent Portuguese man who sweated profusely and ogled Dao while answering Stark's questions. Or, more accurately, evading Stark's questions. The session ended again with a warning.

"We are a peaceful and happy community here," the prosecutor said. "Like a family. Just like a family, we become upset when outsiders come in and make trouble."

"Thank you for your time," Stark said as he stood.

"My pleasure," he said, still ogling Dao. He kissed her hand, leaving a wet spot.

"Pig," Dao muttered as soon as she and Stark were back in the street. "Will you tell me what's going on? I put up with that disgusting animal slobbering on me; I deserve at least that much."

"Sun Tzu hasn't been waiting for Chinese approval," Stark said. "The fix is already in. I'll bet half the people in power here have been bought off or scared silent."

"That seems true. But do you know where Sun Tzu is?"

"There is no place to seek the mind, it is like the footprints of the birds in the sky."

"What?"

"Nothing whatever is hidden. From of old, all is clear as daylight."

"What are you saying?"

"The Zenrin. Sometimes the best way to search is to stop searching. Then the obvious becomes more so."

"Gibberish. Why did we go to the gardens?"

"They were nice, weren't they?"

"You are cruel, you know that?" she said.

"It's getting dark. What say we finish off at the Guia Fortress," Stark said, ignoring her comment. "It was a fortress as well as a chapel, typical colonial dual purpose. More than three hundred and fifty years old. They have a picture in the tour book if you're interested."

Dao gave an exasperated grunt. "Are you here to sightsee or what?"

"It's the highest point in Macao. We should have a nice view of the sunset."

# CHAPTER
# 30

Pedro Quesada fretted during the long plane ride from the United States. At last he was getting in on the action, but they hadn't been able to assemble a full six-member team on such short notice. Halliwell-Stark had numerous contract agents in its Rolodex, but for this mission they had to fit specific requirements.

The operatives had to be combat veterans, skilled at surveillance, and either Oriental or able to pass as Oriental. One of the team was Chinese, a second Korean, the third Mexican, and the fourth Armenian. The Armenian had been with the Los Angeles Police Department bomb squad, but it wasn't exciting enough for him.

They waited at the baggage claim carousel at Kai Tak airport, eyes constantly moving but showing no recognition of each other. Although they were powerful men, they had to jerk hard to remove their baggage from the carousel. Each contained a weapon and a thousand rounds of ammo, a bulletproof vest, walkie-talkie, and long blade knife. Quesada had a second suitcase with special gear, including a geiger counter, night-scoped tranquilizer dart rifle, Stargazer binoculars, and four tape recorders.

They rode separate cabs to the Macao ferry terminal and

were lucky enough to catch a boat just leaving. The sun was setting as the boat pulled away from the slip.

Stark leaned against the battlements and watched as the sun went down. Dao studied him from a few feet away.

"I don't understand you," she said.

"We men are entitled to our mysteries."

"Are you deceiving Foreign Minister Li?"

"No. What would you have me do?"

"Certainly not watch the sun set."

"There'll never be that sunset again."

She harumphed. "Do you know how much time you have left?"

"I thought it was Occidentals who were obsessed with time. Save time. Make time. Keep time."

"There is a time for philosophy and a time for business."

"To every season, turn, turn, turn. Let's go back to the hotel and freshen up."

While she was in the bathroom, he wrote a note on a sheet of hotel paper and hid it in his pocket. He was sprawled on the bed when she came out.

"What are you doing?" she asked.

"I'm preparing to meditate."

He leaned against the headboard, half closed his eyes, and took several deep cleansing breaths. She brushed her hair and preened, watching him in the mirror.

The phone rang. He reached for it slowly.

"Hello, is Pedro Quesada there?" Pedro said, enough for Stark to recognize his voice.

"You must have the wrong room," Stark said. "No one here by that name." He hung up, waited a couple of minutes, and asked Dao, "Want to hit the casino?"

"What?"

"I feel lucky."

She shook her head but went with him. He ambled to a vacant seat at a blackjack table. She stood at his arm, resplendent in a silvery gown with sequins that shimmered when she moved.

Stark asked her to get him a Coke. She returned after five minutes with the drink. Two minutes later, reaching for his chips, he accidentally spilled it on her. He walked her to the elevator, apologizing the whole way.

"Damn. I left my chips on the table," he said as the elevator door opened. He gave her a gentle nudge in. "I'll be right up."

The door closed and he hurried back toward the table. All the chips had, of course, disappeared. He walked past the table and into the men's room. He passed Pedro the note. No one saw the exchange. Then he hurried up to the room, where a furious Dao awaited.

"What's happened to you?" she demanded.

"What do you mean?"

"You're a screwup."

"No. Sun Tzu is an hour away from the Graybar Hotel."

"What?"

"There's already a wiretap on his phone I arranged through police in Hong Kong. It's just a matter of bureaucratic b.s. before the cops mobilize. A joint U.S.–British–Hong Kong task force. Sun Tzu has no idea he's soon going to be a guest of the government."

"Really?"

"Trust me."

"I don't."

"Okay. You'll read about it in tomorrow's paper. Unless they sit on the story."

"Who is he?" Dao asked.

"Uh-uh. That's my secret."

"You know who he is?"

"Elementary, my dear Dao. How do we celebrate?"

"I'm too agitated."

He lay down. "Suit yourself. I'm gonna relax. Let the troops clean up the mess. The joys of being a boss."

"I must at least call the foreign minister. Let him know you have made progress."

"Sure." Stark picked up the phone.

"Not on a hotel phone," she said disapprovingly. "Are you sure you found Sun Tzu?"

Stark just grinned.

"I'm going out to make a call," she said.

He rolled over, face buried in the pillow, but kept one eye

half open. When she was out the door he got up. He would have to wait to be sure she had taken the bait.

Forty minutes later the phone rang. It was Pedro.

"Miguel is outside. He's driving a rented green Nissan. You'll know him 'cause he's so ugly."

Stark hurried outside. Miguel was waiting at the curb. He had a bushy eyebrow that stretched across his forehead and a wide scar that went from his ear to his nose. But he was softspoken and polite, and had the quiet confidence of a man who could handle himself.

"They followed her right to the house," Miguel said.

"Pedro have the geiger counter?" Stark asked.

"Yes. He hasn't been able to pinpoint anything."

"Describe the building," Stark said.

"It's a hundred-year-old villa set back on a half-acre lot with lots of shrubbery. Cyclone perimeter fencing topped with ribbon wire. The main gate is heavy stone stanchion with a motor-driven wrought iron gate.

"Mr. Quesada pretended to be an inspector of some sort, and gained entry to a similar-style structure in a half klik north. He prepared a rough drawing of what the interior of the target could look like.

"Externally there're six columns connected to arches on the front. Behind them is a terrace, then the windows to the house. Three stories. Brownstone. Appears to be alarms on the windows. Two guards patrolling the grounds. At least eight more inside."

"First-rate reporting."

"Thank you, sir. At this point, Mr. Quesada arranged for our men to be on all four sides." The young man spoke succinctly, in his best military-briefing manner. He was in his late twenties, and Stark wondered how long he'd been out of the service. "There're at least three entrances. A main door, a rear door, and a servants' entrance. I believe Mr. Quesada leans toward an assault on the servants' entrance. But I shouldn't speculate."

"At ease, soldier," Stark said with a smile.

"Actually, it was sailor, sir. I was a SEAL."

"Some of my best friends are pinnipeds."

"Sir?"

"Never mind. Has there been any activity since the lady arrived?"

"We observed them installing a machine-gun nest on the terrace."

"That's the down side of my little plan. We put them on alert status."

They parked a couple of blocks from the house and Miguel led him to Pedro Quesada. Stark's chief assistant had found a comfortable location on a hill overlooking the house. The observation post was on an undeveloped plot, overgrown with trees and foliage, with excellent concealment.

"I spotted four more hostiles," Pedro said. "That's a dozen. Automatic firepower. They look tough but not disciplined. Smoking, slouching, idle talking."

Stark nodded. "They're primed right now. Let's hang tight a couple hours. They'll see no cops arrive and discover there is no phone tap."

"And then they'll relax because they'll think you were bluffing."

"Right. I was hoping Dao would spook them into running elsewhere and we could grab them on the fly. But by now they would've made their move," Stark said.

"Should we contact the locals?"

"They're as honest as Chicago cops. Where are the others?"

"Kim's on the rooftop on the other side. Arbajanian is in a parked car. Lee rented a pedicab and is pretending to sleep it off in the street the way the drivers do."

They could hear people in the distance enjoying a party. The neighborhood was predominantly rambling homes with stone walls and tile roofs set on generous plots of land. Some of the houses were of grandiose design but run-down. The stone was cracked by the tropical moisture, tiles had been ripped off by typhoons, and the greenery grown until it threatened to swallow the buildings.

Time passed as slowly as in a dentist's office. The four contract agents checked in with Pedro every fifteen minutes. They reported changes in the house, like "left rear hall light turned on, bedroom light off."

Two hours later the only sign of activity came from the two guards posted on the balcony.

"What's your opinion?" Stark whispered to Pedro.

"We need more men, more firepower. I could telex Les."

"Not enough time. You bring the tape recorders?"

"Got 'em."

Stark checked his watch. It was three A.M. Most of the lights in the villa were out. "Signal the men and let's do it."

One of the guards on the terrace was dozing. The other, more alert, was puffing on a cigarette.

Pedro rested the tranquilizer dart rifle on Stark's shoulder.

"I don't even need the night scope," Pedro said. "The moron's cigarette makes a perfect bull's-eye."

"Proving once again smoking is bad for you."

The dozing guard stirred when he heard the *thwwwit,* but he didn't wake. The smoker felt the sting in his cheek and first thought it an insect. He pulled out the dart. He stared at it a fraction of a second, opened his mouth to shout, and slumped to the floor.

Pedro shot the second guard in the neck, assuring him a few more hours of sleep.

"High ground is gone," Stark said into the walkie-talkie. "Move out."

Stark, Quesada, and the team advanced from different directions. From Quesada's rough sketch of the other villa, they guessed which rooms would be dormitories for the guards and which would be the master bedroom.

Stark wondered whether Dao was in bed with Sun Tzu, literally as well as figuratively.

When the assault team was in position, Stark gave the signal to attack.

# CHAPTER
# 31

The guards awoke to the sounds of gunfire, shouted commands, and dozens of pounding feet. Groggy, disorganized, barefoot, wearing boxer shorts and T-shirts, they clumsily snatched up their weapons and ran out into the hall.

Blows from blackjacks and gun butts put them back to sleep. Stark, Pedro, and Lee had positioned themselves outside the bedroom door.

Stark and Lee bound the unconscious guards with disposable plastic handcuffs. Pedro collected the tape recorders, with the prerecorded battle sounds, which had convinced the sleepy guards they were under major attack.

Stark put his walkie-talkie to his lips.

"This is Hawk, do you copy, Falcon?"

"This is Falcon," Kim said. "We've got trouble."

Gunfire echoed down the long halls. Stark could tell it wasn't coming from the prerecorded battle tape.

Lights had been turned on throughout the villa. There were long corridors with gleaming black and white tile. Chandeliers hung from the high, vaulted ceilings. The ornate mahogany furniture boasted jade or mother-of-pearl inlay.

Most of the noise came from a large room at the end of the hall. Stark reached the threshold, which had ten-foot-

246

high partially open wooden doors. Crouching low, he peered around the corner of the doorframe. Inside was a formal dining room with a table that could seat sixteen comfortably. From the twenty-foot ceiling hung banners. Stark recognized the emblems on them as traditional triad symbols.

Gunfire had reduced the once-awsome dining area to chaos. Shards of broken glass and wood chips were everywhere. Two guards with automatic rifles were laying down heavy fire toward someone pinned in the corner.

There were four bodies visible. One was sprawled across the table like a drunken diner passed out. Another was slumped across three chairs. A third lay on the floor. Nearby was the fourth, Miguel.

The surviving guards were in a secure position, protected by a couple of pillars. Impossible for Stark, or whoever was pinned down, to get a clear shot at them.

Stark eyed the chandlier above the guards. He aimed at where it attached to the ceiling and fired. There was a spray of glass as his bullets hit. The fixture fell.

One guard was killed, the other managed to crawl out. Stark snapped a pair of the plastic cuffs on him.

"It's Hawk," Stark said to whoever was hiding in the corner. "I'm at the doorway."

"Arabajian," a voice responded, failing to use his prearranged raptor code name. "I've been hit."

The bomb expert's left hand was shot up. Another bullet had caught him in the right shin. Stark put a tourniquet around the hand and a pressure bandage around his leg. Arabajian was already pale from loss of blood.

"You stay here," Stark said.

"I ain't going anywhere," Arabajian said bitterly.

In the background one of the prerecorded battle tapes continued to play. There were loud commands in English, French, Spanish, Russian, Japanese, and Chinese, boots stomping, shots ricocheting. It sounded like an invasion by a U.N. peacekeeping force battalion.

In the next room Stark found Kim throwing up on a priceless Oriental carpet.

"I got two of them," Kim said between heaves. "Had to slit a throat." Kim pulled himself together, though he remained a decidedly unhealthy color.

"What happened?"

"A few of them were in an interior room playing poker. They were primed as it was. Came out shooting."

"Have you seen Dao? Or anyone who looks like a leader?"

"Negative."

Stark got on the walkie-talkie to Quesada. "Eagle, this is Hawk. Where are you?"

"Completing a search of the second floor. No more hostiles."

"The master bedroom?"

"Empty. But it looks like someone had been sleeping there. A smaller bedroom just off that also was occupied, but no one."

"Have you tried the geiger counter?"

"Yes. If they've got anything radioactive, it must be shielded."

"Roger. I'll meet you at the top of main stairway."

Stark turned to Kim, who was still bent double. "As soon as you can, go keep an eye on Arabajian."

Without waiting for an answer, Stark quickly but cautiously hurried down the long hall to the main stairway. The stairs were well-worn marble—with a polished brass banister—and curved gracefully from the main entrance hall to the second floor.

Lee stood guard at the top of the stairs while Stark and Pedro entered the master bedroom. There was a king-size canopied bed and lavish mahogany furnishings that dated back at least one hundred fifty years. The rumpled bed had clearly been slept in.

Stark and Pedro, moving as a team, entered the smaller adjacent bedroom. The furniture was less massive, with delicate scrollwork. There were pink curtains and a few makeup items before a vanity mirror. Stark went to the bed and sniffed. He recognized Dao's perfume.

"She couldn't have gotten by us," Stark said.

"It's a big house," Pedro responded as he swept the area with the geiger counter. The instrument gave a muted chirp, a normal amount of background radiation.

Stark held out his wrist. Quesada moved the wand near Stark's watch and the radium dial made it chirp louder.

"No, it's working," Quesada said.

"Let me have a look at that sketch you made of the other villa," Stark said. Pedro handed over a roughly drawn blueprint. "Look at this. There're two large rooms down the hall in the other place. Here there's just one more small bedroom."

They entered the third bedroom and tapped on the walls. There was a hollow sound near a five-foot-high armoire. Stark tried to open a drawer. The entire front was one solid piece.

As he pulled on the knob, the front opened. Behind the armoire was a passageway.

"Falcon, this is Hawk," Stark said into the walkie-talkie. "We're entering a trick door behind the dresser in the rear bedroom. Condor is at the top of the main stair. Rendezvous and keep premises secure. Do you copy?"

"Roger."

Stark turned to Pedro.

"Ready?"

"Maybe I should go first," Pedro suggested.

But Stark had already moved into the dark tunnel.

The first room he entered was small and dimly lit. This wasn't an inactive storage area—there was no musty smell, dust tumbleweeds, or cobwebs. On one side was a stack of gold bars the size of a desk. Gun racks held several different kinds of automatic weapons.

In a second room trunks and footlockers were piled to eye level. Stark didn't pause to examine them. Pedro swept the geiger counter over them and received no indication of radioactivity.

Then they were at a narrow stairway. It had once been the back stairs for the servants to use in returning to their quarters without troubling the masters.

Stark quietly padded up the stairs, but still they creaked. Stark was glad it was Pedro backing him up. In the narrow space, any shooting and Stark would most likely be the first one hit.

At the top of the stair was another long, dark corridor, barely as wide as Stark's shoulders. Stark, treading lightly, stepped on a floor panel and felt a slight give. He immediately shifted his weight to his rear foot as the panel dropped out. The trapdoor led to a chute, which plunged off into blackness.

Stark and Pedro hopped over the trap. They advanced down the hall toward a wooden door. Stark had moved a few feet when a steel door crashed down separating him from Pedro. Then steel bars slammed in front of him. He was trapped in a space not much larger than a phone booth.

The wooden door on the other side of the bars opened. He aimed.

There was no one in sight.

"Robert, throw down your gun or you will be killed."

Dao's voice.

With no real options Stark did as she commanded. Stark could hear Pedro on the other side of the steel door pounding it in frustration.

Dao stepped into view, aiming a pistol steadily at his midsection. "Hands above your head. Intertwine the fingers. I know how good you are." Her short terry-cloth robe left her bare from mid-thigh down.

"I'm just a babe in the woods," Stark said.

"Don't feel bad, Mr. Stark," a man's voice said from off to one side. "Even Samson could be undone by a woman."

The voice was vaguely familiar.

The bars slid up slowly.

The man stepped into view. It was the *Tai Lo* whom Stark had encountered at the party where he first met Dao.

"Please, Mr. Stark, step forward. I have a few questions for you."

# CHAPTER
## 32

The walls separating what had once been the servants' quarters had been knocked down. The room Stark stepped into was one large space, about eighteen by twenty feet. It was right under the roof, and there was a slant to the bare wood ceiling. A 500x telescope at one of the dormer windows pointed north. From the window anyone would have a clear view of the Communist Chinese border barely a kilometer away. Only a few faint lights glimmered in the night.

The room was furnished with a large desk and leather chair, oak file cabinets, and lawyer's bookcase. On the desk were a computer, a couple of phones, and a bank of black and white video monitors with index-card-size screens. One wall was dominated by a large painting of a misty Oriental mountain landscape. The only incongruous note was a washing machine sitting in the corner.

Sun Tzu stepped away from the video monitors he had been watching. Clad in a long maroon silk robe, he looked like a Chinese Hugh Hefner called away from a party. "Those tape recorders of yours were very clever, Mr. Stark. I fully thought we were being invaded when I ran up here."

"Is that the bomb?" Stark asked, indicating the washing machine.

Sun Tzu nodded. "Very difficult getting it up the stairs, as you might imagine. But the higher up, the greater the dispersal."

Stark's eyes took in the room, looking for a possible weapon, a way to get at Sun Tzu and Dao, who were about six feet from him.

Dao sensed his thoughts. "Sit down. On the floor. Cross your legs underneath you. Keep your fingers entwined."

"What do you intend to do with the bomb?" Stark asked as he did as she directed.

"A silly question," Dao said. "What does anyone ever do with bombs?"

"It was supposed to be the first of several, to be set up at the borders of Macao," Sun Tzu said. "In the event of an attack, they would be detonated."

"Nuclear suicide," Stark said. "How would the Macanese feel about that?"

"Don't you think your own president is plotting nuclear suicide when he considers war?" Dao piped up. "Isn't Mutual Assured Destruction homicide-suicide?"

"We have the weapon for the same reason as the other powers—security," the *Tai Lo* said. "Unlike the others, we have no need for missiles or elaborate delivery systems. If attacked, we would simply detonate the device. As close to the Chinese border as possible." The *Tai Lo* paced back and forth, his voice growing louder. "Communist China is our worst enemy and would be most injured. The bomb is a particularly dirty device with a great deal of fallout. The prevailing winds would assure that radioactive contamination destroys the Guangdong rice crop. All of China is dependent on that province's rice. There would be mass starvation, then revolution."

"You said the bomb was 'supposed to be the first'?" Stark asked when Sun Tzu's tirade ended.

"Unfortunately my Japanese associate killed the nuclear scientist. I can get someone else, but you created difficulties. This bomb will be detonated here. I can set the timer for up to one hour. The Chinese will see that I am a man of my word. They will regret their abusing this son of Han," Sun Tzu said, his voice surprisingly soft considering the subject matter. "I have politely answered your questions. You will answer mine."

"Then you will kill me?"

"It is necessary."

Dao said a few sentences in Cantonese. Sun Tzu responded. It was clear they were bargaining. Judging by Dao's crestfallen expression, she didn't get what she wanted.

"She wants to let you live," Sun Tzu said. "I cannot. If I allow my enemies to live, then more people will be willing to be my enemy."

There was a rapid thumping at the steel door. "Your associate is firing at the safety door," Sun Tzu said. "Unless he has a bazooka, it is a waste of ammunition."

"Why don't you open it, then, and let him in?"

"Very amusing," Sun Tzu said. "Now, how did you come to suspect Dao?"

"There were too many inconsistencies in her stories. At one point she told me she was an orphan. Later she talked about her extended family throughout Southeast Asia. When she spoke against the Communists to me, it seemed too sincere to be an act. Of course, she is a very good actress."

She gave him a look that mixed anger and sorrow.

"What clinched it was her druggy rubdown," Stark continued. "She suggested we go to Tahiti. Delaying me wasn't in the interest of the PRC. But it would have served your purposes nicely."

Dao listened, arms folded defensively across her chest.

"A large part of it was instinctive. Her personality just didn't add up. I can't really see her as a Communist."

Dao asked, "Why did you play that game with me, going to tourist attractions, meeting with the editor and the prosecutor?"

"The meetings and paper chase were legit. I needed to see how far the infiltration had gone here. The touristy stuff was to confuse you and give my team time to come over." Stark turned to the *Tai Lo*. "Why did you sic her on me?"

"She was to keep you busy and make sure you disposed of my greedy associates. Both Scalish and Soto had valuable contacts but overestimated their own value. By controlling you I kept the CIA from meddling as well."

"A strategy worthy of your namesake."

"Flattery will do you no good, Mr. Stark. You are working

253

for the Communists. They are the modern-day devils, and you have sold them your soul.''

"What happens now?" Stark asked. "You can't escape."

"I believe I can, though not with the bomb. Before we leave I will activate the device. If we are killed leaving, at least the Communist filth will also suffer. Good-bye." Their talk was all so civilized, as if they were chatting over a cup of tea.

"Wait. As a condemned man, don't I get a last wish?" Stark asked.

"What is it?"

"A kiss."

Dao regarded Stark, and then Sun Tzu.

"If she is willing," Sun Tzu said.

"No tricks?" she asked.

"You have my word," Stark said.

She handed the *Tai Lo* her gun and cautiously approached Stark. She leaned over, and they pressed their lips together. The usual electricity passed between them. Stark twisted slightly and she moved to compensate, putting her between Stark and Sun Tzu's gun.

Stark untwined his fingers as if he were going to embrace her. But his hands grabbed her shoulders, spinning her in front of him. One arm went across her throat.

"Put the gun down," Stark said to the *Tai Lo*.

"You lied!" Dao shrieked.

"I had my fingers crossed," Stark said boyishly.

"I thought you were an honorable man," Sun Tzu said.

"I make it a policy never to discuss ethics with crime bosses and potential mass murderers. Put the gun down."

The weapon in Sun Tzu's hand wavered.

"I'll kill your girlfriend here if you don't," Stark said, visibly increasing the pressure on her neck.

Sun Tzu smiled. "My girlfriend?"

"I'm his daughter," Dao said.

"That explains a little. No matter. Put the gun down."

Sun Tzu did.

Stark walked to where the weapon lay, still holding Dao before him, and picked it up. "Her gun too."

The *Tai Lo* smiled mirthlessly and produced Dao's small gun from his pocket. He set it down on the floor. Stark picked it up. He released Dao. She spit at him and marched to her father.

"You should have killed him," she said to the *Tai Lo*.

"If it's any consolation, I never would've really hurt you," Stark said to Dao.

"Liar."

The *Tai Lo* moved remarkably quickly for an old man. He grabbed a needle-sharp letter opener from his desk and cocked his arm back to throw it. Stark fired once. The slug caught him in the center of his chest. He fell back, gurgled blood, and died.

Dao fell to her knees by his side and buried her face on his neck. Stark looked around the room for the switch to lift the steel door.

He felt a sudden sharp pain in his thigh.

Dao had thrown the dagger. As he stumbled from the wound, she raced over to the bomb. She flicked one toggle switch and a red light went on. Her fingers were tight on a second switch.

"Dao, it's over."

"I will avenge him."

"Give it up. No more deaths."

"It is the Communists' fault. They ruined our lives. Ours had been a wealthy family. Everything was taken, our family humiliated."

"Both of you seemed to be living all right."

"You cannot understand. You are an American. You have no history. Our ancestors had lived in the same town for a thousand years." She blinked her eyes, trying not to cry. "My father would spend hours looking through the telescope, across the border." She rubbed her eyes. Tears smeared her black makeup, giving her a ghoulish appearance. "You tricked me," she said, her mood swinging from grief to rage. "Not many people have."

"Both of us let our emotions affect our judgment."

"I must do this. For him." She moved her wrist a fraction of an inch, preparing to throw the switch.

He fired three times in rapid succession. The shots hit her square in the chest, throwing the small body back away from the washer.

Stark found the switch for the door by Sun Tzu's desk.

He opened the door. Pedro ran in. Stark pointed to the "washing machine," and Quesada raced to it. He had a stethoscope around his neck and a tool kit in his hand. He knelt and listened.

"Nothing."

He carefully opened the machine. The guts of the washer had been removed and replaced with what looked like a large metallic medicine ball. There were panels of circuit boards mounted along the inner walls of the washer. Pedro moved the bell of the stethoscope—it was coated with Teflon to reduce friction—over the ball.

Stark bent over Dao.

"It hurts," she said.

"I'm sorry."

"Sad," she said, and died.

Pedro cautiously opened the cabinet. "Son of a bitch. Look at this." He held up two wires that had become separated on the main circuit board. The bomb was a dud.

Stark looked down at Dao's body. It hadn't been necessary to kill her.


Stark's final business in Hong Kong involved Miller, the CIA station chief who had first introduced Stark to Dao.

Stark visited him the day after the Macao shootout.

"You had to kill her?" Miller asked.

Stark nodded. "You were lovers?"

"All too briefly," Miller said softly.

"Was it you who tipped the Japanese that I was coming in on a fake passport?"

After a long silence Miller nodded. "I wanted them to throw you in jail. You stole her from me. I wanted you to fail."

Stark got up to leave. As he opened the door—a prearranged signal—two CIA security men from the counterintelligence staff of the Operations Division entered and took Miller into custody.

# *Epilogue*

Three months after the incident in Macao, and still the image of Dao haunted him. Stark had killed before, but never anyone he had been intimate with. Nightmares of sex and death interrupted most nights' sleep.

At the pistol range Stark's marksman-level shooting suffered. He had a tendency to flinch just enough to take shots out of the kill zone.

The entire antiterrorist business had lost its appeal. He could make speeches, do analysis of security breaches, shuffle paperwork, but his heart wasn't in it. Les urged him to take a vacation.

"Talk to a few cops somewhere exotic," Halliwell said. "Terrorism in Tahiti. Virgin Island violence. It'll all be tax deductible."

Halliwell was in a great mood, since the Macao case had turned out to be good for business. Foreign Minister Li had arranged for Macanese officials suspected of loyalty to Sun Tzu to be purged. There had been a couple of questionable suicides and numerous resignations. The Chinese had offered Stark a Heroic People's medal, their highest civilian honor. He had declined. It would be injudicious to accept a medal from a Communist power since his business meant working with capitalists and American government officials.

# SEIZE THE DRAGON

Spurning it had required fancy diplomatic footwork. Les Halliwell had deftly parlayed the PRC's gratitude into a contract that would pay off in millions. Halliwell-Stark would handle security consulting for overseas Chinese businesses. Making money was acceptable with any trading partner.

Pedro tried to resuscitate Stark's relationship with Dr. Mirnov. He kept Stark apprised of her situation, and pushed for him to give her a call. Sultana Mirnov had quit her job at the private lab and gone back into research at a university. She had chosen her usual solution to emotional hard times and spent more than sixteen hours a day in the lab. Stark couldn't bring himself to call her.

Pedro knocked at the door to Stark's office, breaking into his memories. Stark was sitting at his desk, staring out the window at the lights of another New York night.

"Still mooning for that Oriental chick?" Quesada asked.

"Maybe."

"How can you?"

"I have a recurring dream about her. Her face on a lotus flower plant. I run over it with a motorboat."

"She was bad news."

"In Oriental mythology the lotus grows out of the mud into a beautiful flower."

"Gimme a break. She was a liar and a whore and she betrayed you."

Stark fixed Pedro with a glare that made Pedro wince. "I'm sorry," Pedro said.

"Her being an agent confirmed my initial suspicions, so in a way it felt good. I was constantly waiting for the shoe to drop, to see why she wanted me. She was just too beautiful to fall for me like that."

"You never had any trouble with women that I've seen," Quesada said.

"All the women I've met that have been *that* beautiful have been manipulative. They're hardened at an early age, so used to men coming on to them that they don't know how to operate without a scheme and a scam."

"What about Sultana?"

"She's pretty, but not in that class."

"No, I meant what about giving her a call?"

"Maybe soon. I've got to work out what happened with Dao. I feel like a rat who saw a tempting bit of cheese in a trap. I knew it was a trap, but I had to grab the cheese."

"Poetic," Quesada said.

Stark ignored his jibe. "If you have any sort of desire, it makes you vulnerable. If you have, you want to keep. If you don't have, you want."

"Yeah. Life sucks."

"And that's on the good days."

Pedro nodded, and took out a letter. "This came for you. Bunny thought it had something to do with Dao and didn't know whether to give it to you."

"I'm a big boy," Stark said testily. "I don't need people censoring my mail."

"She did it only because she cares about you," Pedro said. "We all do. You've been really out of it ever since you got back." Pedro handed him the letter and headed out.

"Pedro!"

He turned. "Yeah?"

"Thanks."

"Ahhhh," Pedro said with a gesture of dismissal. "The next time you want cheese, I'll pick you up some Jarlsberg. Don't go for the Limburger." He walked out, leaving Stark with the letter.

Stark toyed with it for a while. It was from Fumiko. In neat *romanji* script, written for her by a friend. *The Hawaiian police have returned the sword to the Japanese police, who have at last returned it to me. I humbly request that if it not be too much trouble, you come and retrieve it.*

Why hadn't she offered to ship it? Obviously she wanted Stark to visit the dojo.

Three hours later he was on an ANA flight to Tokyo.

"I am so glad you could come," Fumiko said as she poured him hot green tea. "There is something besides the sword which the *shihan* wanted to give you."

She got up. "Please wait here," she said. Her feet made a shuffling noise on the tatami. She came back with a long narrow wooden box. The *okuden,* the most secret teachings of the school. She lay the box down in front of him.

"He wanted you to have this if you accepted the task and succeeded."

Stark bowed deeply. The *shihan*'s blind wife could tell what he was doing from the rustle of his clothing.

"It is I who should bow to you," she said. "My responsibilities to my late husband are now complete." She sensed the turmoil in Stark but felt it improper to comment on it. "I will leave you to read."

Alone, he held the box in his hand like a scholar offered a Gutenberg Bible, a musician entrusted with a Stradivarius.

The secrets of the system, passed down for generations. He would be the first person who was not a member of the Soto clan to read the ancient words.

He slid open the top of the box and took out the yellowing scroll inside. There was a purple ribbon binding it. His pulse pounded.

What would it say? What could it tell him? What secrets had the ancient masters passed on?

His fingers picked clumsily at the knot. Finally the ribbon gave way. The scroll unrolled like something alive. It was not paper, maybe vellum, almost as thick as animal skin.

Would the secrets be practical techniques or philosophical commentary? Would his non-Japanese mind be able to grasp the nuances?

He expected to see *kanji*, Chinese characters, covering the paper. But all that was written, with bold brush strokes in the middle of the scroll, were the words:

There are no secrets.

Fumiko, in the next room, heard his laughter shaking the rice-paper walls. She knew her late husband had chosen well.